For Charlie, without whom life would be dull.

And I would like to thank…

Annie, Jackie, Helen, Charlie, Tom, Robin, Rich, Roz,

Mary, Terri, Meurig, Paul, Fay, Celia,

and Tall Richard.

You all know what you did … I couldn't have done it without you.

4

The Legend of the Torrimaya Axe

First published in United Kingdom 2018
Copyright © C J Phillips 2018
The right of C J Phillips to be identified as the Author of the Work
has been asserted by C J Phillips in accordance with the Copyright,
Designs and Patents Act 1988.

All characters in this publication are fictitious.

ISBN 978-0-244-99914-8

C J Phillips, PO Box 5348, Warminster, BA12 2BX

The Legend Of
The Torrimaya Axe

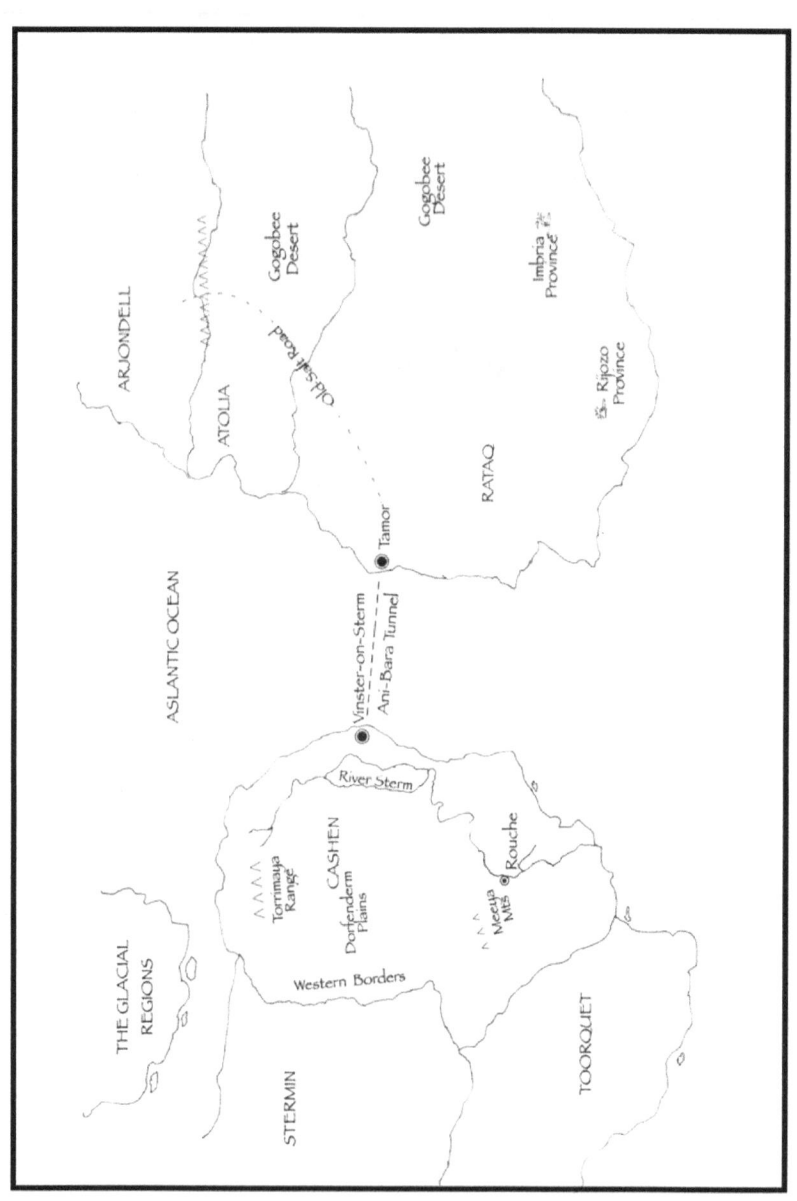

ON THE PLANET ERIS
In Vinster-on-Sterm - capital city of Cashen.

It is a belief universally acknowledged that a business-fairy in possession of an immense fortune must want to increase his profit margins. The best laid plans, however...

Of Mice and Fairies, by Austin Burnstyne

* * *

It was extremely rare to find a dwarf in the axe-making night class for beginners. Norman Shale, therefore, stood out as the only dwarvish student in the foundry. It was his first lesson. Sadly, practical tasks were not the young dwarf's forté.

'No! No! No!' the tutor bawled. 'How can you expect to get any momentum when you're holding the hammer like an arthritic pixie!'

This admonishment came from a leathery-skinned dwarf, with mean-looking eyes and a scar on his left cheek.

'But it was getting heavy,' said Norman, looking at the hammer despondently.

The tutor gave Norman a clip 'round the ear.

'Of course it's heavy!' the tutor bellowed. 'And this thing looks more like a doorstop than an axe! Call yourself a dwarf?!' he hollered, before stomping off to the other end of the room - to chastise an arthritic pixie who'd accidentally kicked over a bucket of water.

Ten years ago, in his home village of Svart, Norman had been expelled from axe-making classes. His father (Svart's most senior forgemaster) had broken his favourite hammer with rage on hearing the news. Had Norman's mother been alive she may have been able to smooth things over. Instead it was made abundantly clear, not only by his father but also by his six older siblings, that the dishonour Norman had brought to the family was unforgivable. Everyone in Svart knew that a dwarf wasn't a real dwarf unless he could make his own axe.

Only Norman's gran, Granny Stumble, had had any faith in her youngest grandson.

'Don't you pay no mind to them lot,' she'd said. 'Any ol' grunt can make an axe but none of 'em taught 'emselves to read ancient Cashenian did they? No they didn't! You mark my words our Norm', I've a feelin' in me waters yer set fer bigger things'n axe-making, and me waters 'ave been right more'n once!'

Granny's 'waters' may or may not have predicted Norman's next step but the night Norman ran away his gran hadn't seemed surprised. When Norman woke his gran to say goodbye she'd rummaged under her mattress, handed him ten florins, and told her youngest grandson to come back for a visit once in a while, preferably before she popped her clogs.

Norman looked down at the workbench and hoped that the heat from the furnaces hid the flush on his face. What possessed him, he thought? Here he was, at Assay University, the country's most prestigious academic establishment, trying to make an axe knowing full well that this attempt would be as fruitless as all the others.

Earlier that day, however, Norman had been consumed by an inexplicable and yet overwhelming desire to make his own axe. So powerful had been the urge that Norman had left work and, with only a hazy recollection of his walk to the foundry, found himself standing outside the doors. Potential consequences of such a foolhardy action only dawned on Norman after he'd walked over the threshold - by which time everyone had seen him and he was too embarrassed to leave.

'That's enough for this week!' the tutor shouted, over the roar of the furnace and the sound of hammering.

There was much banging and clanging as everyone started to pack up. Norman sighed and picked up the lump of metal from the workbench. It vaguely resembled an axe-head, he thought, if he squinted, turned it to one side, and ignored the knobbly edge that should have been the blade.

Norman put the misshapen object into his satchel and tried to think of anyone he knew who might need a doorstop.

* * *

Professor Bauxite was an elderly dwarf who was head of the Archaeology and Artefacts department, also at Assay University. He had no idea who Norman was.

In the fading light of the summer evening, Professor Bauxite walked towards the University's main entrance and thought about the flagon of Triple Axe ale and the bread and cheese that he knew would be waiting for him on the kitchen table, courtesy of his neighbour and cleaning dwarf, Mrs Poto.

The Professor's thoughts then drifted to an earlier conundrum, that of finding a journal which contained his notes on a recent dig in the Glacial Regions. He knew he'd seen it somewhere in his office. During his search, earlier that day, he'd found several leather sandals, a pewter flagon with *I Dig Archaeology* engraved on the side, and a piece of stale cheese that had grown so hard he momentarily mistook it for a rock specimen. The journal, however, remained elusive, which was hardly surprising given that his office was barely visible under piles of books, parchments and other impedimenta.

On the plus-side, the Professor had found a letter from the bursar that confirmed funding to employ a full-time assistant. As dusk fell, Professor Bauxite ambled along the winding path and contemplated potential candidates.

He remained blissfully unaware of Norman's existence...until a strange cry rent the air.

'AAAARGH!'

The Professor stopped in his tracks.

'Who's there?' he called out.

'Oomph!'

Something heavy clanged to the floor. Footsteps ran off

into the distance. From somewhere further along the path came a quiet groan. Professor Bauxite took a deep breath and trotted, as fast as his rotundness would allow, until he rounded a curve and saw someone lying motionless on the path.

'Are you alright?' The Professor stopped, and leaned over a prostrate dwarf. 'Are you hurt at all?' he asked, after his first question elicited no response.

From the direction of the main gate a light bobbed up and down and came towards the Professor.

'Woss going on 'ere then?' wheezed a dwarf, holding a lamp in one hand and an axe in the other.

'Oh, it's you, Professor. Ev'ryfin' alright?'

'It would seem not, Mr Borgenberry. We may have malefactors on campus.'

'Eh?'

'Thieves, Mr Borgenberry. Ne'er do wells of the criminal variety.'

'Didn't see no one come by the gate,' replied the security dwarf.

'Mmrf,' mumbled the recumbent dwarf, as he slowly rolled over.

A hat lay on the ground near the dwarf's head. The Professor recognised the item as this year's must-have accessory, as worn by many of the new students - a floppy hat with a tassel, generally worn at a rakish angle with the tassel dangling to one side. Lying next to the dwarf the Professor saw a well-worn leather satchel, out of which several less recognisable objects had fallen.

'Come on. Let's get you up,' the Professor said.

The security dwarf and the Professor bent down to help the dwarf to his feet.

'That's it. Easy does it lad,' Mr Borgenberry said.

'You look familiar. Do I know you?' the Professor asked the now upright dwarf.

'Let's be lookin' at ya,' said Mr Borgenberry, as he held up his lamp to offer a little more light.

'Dr Tellurium!' the Professor said, as, for the first time, he saw the young dwarf's face.

'Norman Shale,' said Norman, as he rubbed the back of his head.

'Norman Shale?' the puzzled Professor repeated.

'My name's Norman Shale, sir,' replied Norman.

'Oh. I'm so sorry. In this light you look just like Dr Tellurium. Uncanny in fact. Is he a relative of yours?'

'No, sir.'

'D'ya see anyone?' asked Mr Borgenberry, with a frown.

'I was rearranging my hat when they jumped out of the bushes,' said Norman.

'Who jumped out of the bushes?' asked the Professor, looking at the shrubbery beside them.

'I don't know but I think there were two of them,' replied Norman.

'Did they take anything?' the Professor asked, facing the young dwarf once again.

'They tried to take me, sir,' said Norman.

'Take you? Take you where?' asked the Professor.

'I've no idea. They just tried to pick me up and carry me off,' Norman replied.

Mr Borgenberry, who'd heard many outrageous excuses from drunken students trying to get away with some misdemeanour or other, was less convinced.

'You sure?' he asked.

From the moment he could walk, until he'd left home, Norman had been tripped up, trapped and jumped on by one or all of his six brothers at any given moment. Escapology was his only practical skill. He definitely knew when someone was trying to pick him up and carry him off.

'Yes, sir, I'm sure,' replied Norman.

'How strange,' the Professor said. 'And are you a student here?'

'I was, um, trying out a night class,' Norman mumbled,

'but I work for Dr Clastic during the day. I'm one of his lab-assistants,' he said, in a slightly less embarrassed voice.

'Ah yes, Clastic. Geochemistry I believe. Had real potential as I recall,' the Professor mused.

Norman crouched down to retrieve the stray items that had fallen out of his satchel.

'Why didn't I just go home?' Norman whispered to himself.

'What was that?' asked the the Professor.

'Oh, nothing, sir. Sorry,' said Norman.

'Here, let me help you,' the Professor said, as he bent over and reached for an object.

'No, no, I'm fine, really,' said Norman, desperately searching for the axe-head in the dim light.

'Is this yours?' The Professor picked up the axe-head. 'What is it?'

Norman stood up and held out his hand. The Professor handed over the misshapen lump. Norman looked at it then at Professor Bauxite.

'Um, it's a work in progress,' he said, and then put the shameful object into his satchel. 'May I go home now?'

'Certainly. Mr Borgenberry, are we expecting any trade-folk at this time of the evening?'

'Meat wagon's due up from the kitchen block any minute,' replied Mr Borgenberry.

'Then perhaps we could ask the driver to see that young Norman here makes it home safely.'

'Please sir, I can walk. It's no trouble,' Norman said.

'Nonsense, you've had a nasty shock. I might even hop on myself. Saves waiting for the horse-bus. Where do you live?'

'Thank you,' mumbled Norman, who did not want the lift but was nothing if not a polite dwarf. 'I live on Forge Lane.'

'I don't think I know Forge Lane but I'm sure we'll find it. Mr Borgenberry, I shall need a courier. Can one be arranged?'

'There's one at the main gate, Professor,' replied Mr Borgenberry.

'Jolly good. Oh, and my name is Professor Bauxite,' said the Professor, smiling at Norman.

'Nice to meet you, sir,' said Norman.

'Ev'ryone ready?' asked Mr Borgenberry.

'Lead on, McBluff!' the Professor said, cheerily.

Mr Borgenberry raised his lamp and led the way. As all three walked along the path the sun dropped off the side of the planet and a bright, full moon sharpened the shadows on the ground.

Norman considered the assault. He'd been mugged before. The attempted robberies were often embarrassing affairs as he never had anything worth stealing but, until this evening, no one had ever tried to pick him up and forcibly take him somewhere else. Norman had a headache. He wanted a cup of mushroom tea, not a bumpy ride on a smelly meat wagon with an ancient Professor.

After only a short walk, the three dwarves arrived at the University's main entrance. Next to one of the gates was a security hut and it was from here that Mr Borgenberry monitored the comings and goings of the staff, trade carts and, of course, the students.

Inside the hut was a young pixie wearing the distinctive white colour of a night courier. That pixies make the best couriers is a well-known fact all over Eris. Pixies were known to have low-grade magical abilities, but the expenditure of said magic rarely out-weighed the side-effects. This is why they used their other, more useful, asset - speed, an attribute that made them ideal messengers. Needless to say, every criminal gang on the planet had its own get-away pixie

Professor Bauxite wrote a message, folded the note, and handed it to the pixie along with half a florin. The pixie thanked the Professor, left the hut and raced off towards the city. Shortly afterwards the meat wagon arrived and Professor Bauxite asked the driver if he had room for two small passengers. The troll looked down at the portly dwarf and shrugged his shoulders.

'You'll have to sit at the back,' he replied.

The Professor and Norman seated themselves on the back step. The cart lurched forward, went through the University's gates, and onto the main road towards the city.

'So tell me Norman, was your evening class in... art?' asked the Professor.

'I was at the axe-making class,' Norman said, looking down at his feet.

'Axe-making? Oh? Have things changed? Don't they do that kind of thing at school for young dwarves anymore? Used to be compulsory in my day.'

Not wishing to get into the whole, *What do you mean you can't make an axe?* discussion, Norman quickly changed the subject.

'If you don't mind me asking, sir, you mentioned Dr Tellurium earlier and I know he's famous because Dr Clastic talks about him all the time but what exactly is he famous *for*?'

'Ah, yes, your doppelgänger. His speciality is geochemistry, although he's recently been dabbling in theoretical thaumurtological armaments,' the Professor said.

'Thaumurtological armaments? Is that even possible? I thought that ever since the Wand Wars no magic could be infused into any weapon larger than a small slingshot?' asked Norman.

'This is of course quite true but Dr Tellurium has proposed a new theory, which he hopes will finally overcome this long-standing magical mystery,' said the Professor.

'What kind of theory?' asked Norman.

Norman's and the Professor's legs swayed in time to the motion of the cart and, as the wagon rumbled along the dirt road towards Vinster-on-Sterm, Professor Bauxite explained that Dr Tellurium had written a doctoral thesis entitled, *Legend or Potential Reality? The Science Behind the Torrimaya Axe*, as published in the well-respected journal *Science of the Times*.

'Thaumurtological historians have long speculated that the ancient fairy chieftain, Halvar the Just, created a magical fail-safe preventing the fusion of magic into, as you said, any weapon larger than a slingshot. Dr Tellurium suggests, however, due to recent advancements in techno-magic, that it might be possible to create a weapon of equal force to that of the Torrimaya Axe simply by formulating an override-spell,' said the Professor.

'A weapon of equal force to *The* Torrimaya Axe? As in the most destructive magical weapon ever invented? The one that put an end to the Wand Wars and killed hundreds of folk in the process? *That* Torrimaya Axe?!'

Norman turned his head and stared at the Professor, astonished at the possibility of such a thing.

'Is there another Torrimaya Axe?' the Professor said, not unkindly.

The wagon jolted as a wheel rolled over a rock.

'No, but, I mean, well, an over-ride spell? That would need tons of magic and I thought that kind of high-level spell-casting could kill a fairy? And what about the Bi-Continental Convention banning, in over twenty nations, *including* Cashen, the use of magic to kill, torture or capture?!' said Norman. 'Not to mention the fact that it's illegal to use high-level magic of any kind in Cashen,' he added.

The horse and cart lumbered past the Pixies of Mercy orphanage, a gloomy, two-storied building drenched in shadow except for the flickering lamp above the main entrance.

'Ah, yes…' started the Professor.

'I mean,' interrupted Norman, 'the King's forces have a

hard enough time dealing with the black-market use of high-level magic. The last thing we need is some kind of magical weapon of mass destruction.'

Norman took a deep breath. The Professor smiled into his bushy, grey beard and thought he saw a little of his young self in Norman - a bold, keen dwarf with an enquiring mind.

'Unfortunately life is not always black and white. There are many who would argue that simply *having* a weapon capable of causing untold damage might in fact prevent nations from going to war.'

Norman looked up at the clear, night sky and thought about this for a moment.

'But if one country has a magical weapon of mass destruction then won't other countries want to develop their own, similar weapons?'

The dirt road became cobbled and the horses' shoes clopped rhythmically on the stones.

'Dr Tellurium's theory has certainly opened a new hive of bees and while I'm all in favour of exploring things that we don't fully understand, I suspect that you might be right. There are always some things that are probably best left well alone,' the Professor said.

'But Dr Tellurium's theory's been published, which means that someone, somewhere, is bound to try to build *some* kind of super-weapon,' Norman said.

Before the Professor could respond, the cart driver shouted from the front.

'This is the closest I can get to Forge Lane!' shouted the troll, as he stopped the wagon.

Norman recognised the dank odour of The Murks, the least salubrious of Vinster-on-Sterm's residential quarters, where accommodation and, occasionally, life were cheap.

'It seems this is your stop,' said the Professor. 'It's been a pleasure talking to you, Norman. Should you wish to discuss Dr Tellurium's theory further do stop by my office. It's 27B Barchan Tunnel East.'

'Thank you, Professor,' said Norman, as he hopped off the wagon.

Norman jogged to the front of the cart to thank the driver.

'Take care, Norman,' the Professor said, as the cart trundled towards the city.

There were no street lamps in The Murks but the light of the moon provided ample light for Norman to navigate his way through the alleyways. Norman trundled down Hoggington Lane, across to Kettle Street and slipped through Squeeze Alley, all the while he mulled over the conversation he'd had with Professor Bauxite. As he rounded the corner of Forge Lane he decided that, despite the Professor's argument, no one could possibly think that building some kind of super-weapon would be a good idea. In fact, it would be utter madness, he thought. Although, he concluded, scientists did have a habit of wanting to prove their own theories.

He was almost home, and had stepped out to cross the lane, when something crashed into him at high speed. Norman fell and hit his head - again.

'Ow,' he groaned.

A pixie tumbled, roly-polyed to a stop, jumped up and stormed over to Norman.

'Why don't you look where you're going!'

Norman picked up his satchel, stood up and brushed himself down.

'Sorry. I didn't see you,' Norman said, as he looked at the pixie standing in front of him.

Her round, dark, face had a slight sheen in the moonlight. She had black hair, which was tied back in a plait, and she was wearing black clothes, black boots, and was carrying a black courier bag. She didn't seem appropriately dressed for a night courier, thought Norman.

'It's idiots like you that make my job dangerous! Why don't you look before you randomly walk out into the middle of a lane!'

Norman wasn't oblivious to the pixie's anger, he just didn't respond to it. All his life someone, somewhere, had been angry with Norman for something he had done or said and he had subsequently developed the knack of being able to switch off to most tirades. Norman believed that, more often than not, deflection was the key to anger deflation.

'Is black the best colour to be wearing on a night shift?' he asked.

As soon the words left his mouth Norman knew his usual tactic was about to fail.

'Watch where you're going in future,' the pixie said, in a quiet, yet distinctly menacing, tone.

'Sorry,' said Norman, as he looked down at his boots.

When he looked up the courier had gone. Stealth was another useful pixie attribute.

Norman winced, rubbed the back of his head and walked across the lane towards home. As he put the key in his front door a cloth hood was yanked over his head.

'Ouch! Not agai.. Mmmf!'

What seemed like several pairs of hands grabbed Norman.

'Get heez feets!' said a deep, heavily accented male voice.

This order was greeted with, 'He kick!'

As Norman tried to recall his favourite slip and twist manoeuvre his assailants' grip seemed to loosen and they started to shout out in apparent confusion.

'Aeei-ya!'

'Ow-eesh!'

It seemed that Norman's foreign attackers had become the attacked. The perpetrators let go of Norman and ran off into the Murks.

The hood was lifted from his head.

'Good job I was wearing black. They didn't see me coming!' declared the pixie courier.

SECRETS AND SUBTERFUGE
Of the military kind.

Professor Bauxite had travelled with the meat wagon as far as Halvar Piazza in the city centre and from there he'd taken a cab to the residence of General Sir Hamish Macjooste.

Fairies were, on average, two or three feet taller than many of Eris' other inhabitants and, in the most well-mannered homes, allowances were always made for this difference in height. Professor Bauxite was not, however, sitting in the available, beautifully-crafted, small chair. He was, instead, pacing the room waiting to be seen.

The General (who preferred to use his military, rather than his aristocratic, title), was at the helm of King Egbert IV's armed forces. Firm but fair, General Macjooste was the King's right-hand fairy and worked hard to sustain military accord with Cashen's neighbours. Equally, many parts of the country were policed by the King's soldiers and the shenanigans of the ethnically diverse population often required as much, if not more, of the General's attention than a full-scale conflict.

The white, gilt-framed, double doors of the anteroom opened and the handsome General, still dressed in military garb, gestured for his visitor to follow him into the hallway.

'Professor Bauxite. Please, come through to my study,' he said, in the soft, northern lilt of the Highlands of Cashen.

'Apologies for the lateness of my visit, General, but I came as quickly as I could,' the Professor said. 'I'm afraid we may have a problem.'

'Your message was a wee bit alarming, if only for its complete lack of information. How may I help?'

'Something untoward has occurred and I'm a little concerned, not because of the incident per se but because of what has come to light,' said Professor Bauxite.

The General gestured for the Professor to be seated and

then sat opposite his dwarf guest. General Macjooste listened and furrowed his brow when he learned how a young dwarf named Norman Shale had been attacked on the University's grounds. When the Professor then revealed that Norman bore an uncanny resemblance to Dr Simon Tellurium, the General steepled his fingers and raised both of his eyebrows. The Professor concluded by saying that it was all probably nothing to worry about but, given the current status of the project, he thought it best to let the General know.

'You were right to tell me, Professor. I wonder why we've no' heard of this Norman Shale before?' the General asked.

'Why would we? All I know is that he's a lab-assistant for one of the faculty … and apparently he's learning how to make an axe…' the Professor looked up at the portrait of Lady Macjooste on the wall behind the General, and considered this fact for a moment. 'Seems a nice enough dwarf though,' he eventually said, drawing his gaze from the painting and smiling at the General.

'I see,' said the General. 'And this Mr Shale said someone actually tried to carry him away, is that right?'

'Oh, yes. Said he was sure of it,' the Professor replied.

'So you think whoever tried to take Mr Shale, was really after Dr Tellurium?' the General reiterated.

'I believe this is a possibility, yes,' said the Professor.

The General nodded and stood up.

'So do I.' He walked towards the study door. 'Professor, I'll have to inform the King. I can have my driver drop you off in Queensbridge if you'd like?'

'Very kind of you General.'

'I'll send for the carriage,' the General said, 'and I'd better let my wife know.'

General Macjooste left the Professor, who promptly stood up and walked towards a bookcase near the door. He barely had time to scan the spines when the General's wife entered the room. Lady Maria Macjooste was an elegant fairy, with flowing silver hair and delicate features. She was wearing an air-blue, silk gown which whispered as she moved across the room.

'Professor Bauxite. How lovely to see you again,' said Lady Macjooste, with a smile.

'Lady Macjooste, always a pleasure.' The Professor bowed his head. 'How is your genealogical search progressing?'

'Terribly slowly, I'm afraid,' she said. 'Has my husband abandoned you?'

'No, no, but I'm afraid my visit has prompted him to make a late night excursion.'

'Oh dear, so late? No doubt it will be something to do with that wretched project. It keeps him awake at night, you know.'

'I'm sure he's been very busy. So much to do.'

'And do you approve of this project, Professor?'

'I am but a lowly consultant of ancient artefacts. I neither approve nor disapprove of any decision made by His Highness.'

'How diplomatic of you. No wonder you and Hamish get on so well,' said Lady Macjooste.

The General entered the library.

'Ah, there you are,' he said, as he strode across the room while buttoning his cape.

'Professor Bauxite tells me you have to go,' said Lady Macjooste.

'I should'nae be long, dinnae wait up though,' the General said, as he kissed his wife on the cheek. 'Are you ready Professor?'

The General gestured for Professor Bauxite to lead the way.

'Goodbye Professor Bauxite. I do hope we shall see you again soon, and perhaps we can continue the discussion we were having at the royal garden party about your dig in the Glacial Regions.'

'I look forward to it, Lady Macjooste,' said the

Professor, with a smile and a small bow.

Lady Macjooste returned the smile and the Professor and the General departed.

* * *

King Egbert IV of Cashen was enjoying a glass of Hejoun brandy and reading *Military Fairies Through the Ages: Cashen's Finest Leaders*, when General Macjooste was announced and shown into the palace's library.

'Your Highness,' said the General, as he bowed.

'Ah, Hamish.' The King did not move from his chair but did close his book. 'At any other time of the day I would be delighted to see you, at past ten in the evening, however, I am assuming you come bearing some kind of news that will put paid to my quiet indulgence. Do have a seat.'

'Apologies, Your Highness, but I've worrying news,' said the General, as he sat opposite the King.

'Skirmishes on the western border among the trolls? Another spate of buccaneering in the Ani-Bara tunnel? I do hope not. Pirates pilfered an entire cargo of King Razarro's brandy last month. He was not best pleased.'

'No, Your Highness, it's neither the trolls, nor the tunnel pirates. It's to do with Project Green Pastures.'

The King uncrossed his legs, leaned forward and placed the book on the marble-topped coffee table in front of him.

'Ah.' The King frowned.

Project Green Pastures was the codename given to the development of a military programme based on Dr Tellurium's doctoral thesis. The project had been operational for almost two years and was a joint fairy-dwarf undertaking. Dr Tellurium was the senior geochemist, Dr Philomena Foxglove was the fairy thaumurtologist who managed it, and Professor Bauxite was the project's ancient history consultant.

A specialised team of Cashen's most senior scientists and engineers had been collaborating on the construction of a weapon that, in theory, had the potential to cause mass destruction. At the moment, however, it was nothing more than a very expensive hollow metal ball because the override-spell, that was supposed to turn the object into something more devastating than a gigantic slingshot pellet, had thus far eluded every fairy on the team.

As if one potential super-weapon wasn't enough, General Macjooste's intelligence agents had recently discovered that the Rataquian monarch, King Razarro, had his own team of scientists working on a project very similar to that of Green Pastures.

Neither King Egbert nor King Razzaro had openly admitted that such projects existed. Consequently, the resulting arms race had been keeping scientists, as well as the two nations' intelligence services, extremely busy as both countries tried to advance their respective programmes.

General Macjooste relayed Professor Bauxite's encounter to the King.

'…And so, Professor Bauxite thinks this dwarf, Norman Shale, might have been mistaken for Dr Tellurium, and I'm inclined to agree, Your Highness,' the General concluded.

'Of course this begs the question who else, apart from the Rataquians, knows about Project Green Pastures?' said the King.

'Aye, and how could anyone know that Dr Tellurium is working on the project?' added the General.

'Quite,' said the King. 'I take it Dr Tellurium is safe?'

'Aye, Your Highness, I've sent an agent to keep an eye on him and, as a precautionary measure, I've raised the project's security status to amber alert. I'm away now to put a squadron on standby,' the General said.

The King stood up, as did the General. The King put his hands behind his back, under his pearlescent, blue wings and looked down at the floor as they walked towards the door.

'Was it Hamletta who said, *A mote is to trouble the mind's eye?*'

'Indeed, Your Highness. But let us hope that this small thing will not escalate further.'

'Hmm.' The King furrowed his brow as he looked up at the General. 'I shall expect a further report in the morning.'

'Of course, Your Highness,' said the General, as he bowed and left the room.

'And thus bad begins…' whispered King Egbert.

VINSTER-ON-STERM AFTER DARK
The night before the morning after.

Norman had lived in his two-roomed hovel on Forge Lane for the past five years. The accommodation was far superior to his previous residence (a rented room in Mrs Stabbins' rat-infested, overcrowded boarding house). Norman was extremely grateful that, for only eight florins a month, he had two rooms to himself and that the front door could be locked, from both sides.

The young dwarf had never entertained a member of the opposite sex before. Now he came to think of it, he'd never had *anyone* visit him before. It had all happened so quickly. Before Norman had had time to pick up his satchel the pixie-courier had introduced herself as Talula Ewesage, invited herself into Norman's house, and had then insisted on making him a cup of tea.

The pixie was now washing a teapot, a mug, and a teaspoon while she waited for the kettle to boil. Norman sat on the only chair at his table and was feeling slightly bemused by the evening's events.

'Who were those dwarves?' Talula asked, as she poured boiling water into the teapot.

'So they *were* dwarves,' said Norman.

'And they reeked of cologne. Only dwarves I know with that kind of cash 'round here are the Lenders. Do you owe them money?'

'I don't owe money to anyone. I live within my means,' Norman said, earnestly.

'Good for you,' Talula said, as she glanced at the shabby, sparsely furnished abode.

'And I could've got away from them you know,' Norman said, with a hint of dented pride in his voice.

'I'm sure you could.' Talula handed Norman a cup of tea. 'Here.'

'Thanks. You didn't have to do all this,' said Norman, taking the cup and placing it on the table.

'True, but I did and you'll live to walk out in front of another unsuspecting courier.'

With her flawless skin and pretty round eyes, Norman was reminded of a portrait of the notorious warrior fairy, Queen Esther the Gory, which was on display in the Vinster City Gallery. Talula may have been shorter than the queen, and probably far less violent but, Norman thought, the young pixie was definitely more beautiful.

Talula folded her arms and looked at Norman, who then realised he was being rude and had been staring at her. He blushed and looked down at his tea.

'What if they come back?' Norman wondered - out loud.

'*I'm* not staying here to protect you!'

'No! I mean...I was just thinking...' Norman's embarrassment notched itself up a level.

'Are you a student?' Talula asked, glossing over Norman's awkwardness.

'I'm a lab-assistant.'

'Up at the University?'

'Yep,' replied Norman, who then took a sip of tea.

'Are you working on some kind of secret project?' Talula asked

Norman's instant response was to laugh at this suggestion. Unfortunately he was mid-swallow. Norman choked on his tea, snot exploded out of his nose, and his mortification was complete.

Talula looked discreetly at her fingernails and tried not to laugh. Norman stood up and searched for a rag to sort out the mess.

'How 'bout I buy you an ale?' said Talula, as nonchalantly as possible.

The first unwritten rule for staying alive, among the lower echelon of Vinster-on-Sterm's society, was never, ever, under any circumstances, step into someone else's fight. Talula was fully aware of this potentially life-saving guideline but, for a reason she was currently unable to fathom, Norman had been different. On her way back from delivering a message, Talula had felt uncontrollably compelled to assist the dwarf when she saw him being attacked. She'd battled with herself for a good few seconds before being shoved by her conscience into interfering and rescuing the dwarf who had walked out in front of her. After the snot incident, however, Talula just felt sorry for the unworldly-looking dwarf, and so she had issued the invitation.

'I've got work in the morning. I should probably go to bed,' said Norman.

'What?! What kind of dwarf refuses a free drink?!' replied Talula, incredulously.

Aware that his dwarfhood was already under question, Norman capitulated.

'Just one then and I'll return the favour when I get paid.'

* * *

Iffies was near the city centre and was one of a handful of drinking establishments that served drinks with small axes in them. It was owned by a dwarf known simply as Axe, who had been the lead axe-thrower in the City team five years in a row. Fights at the inn were rare and no one ever left without paying - possibly due to the collection of sharp, and easily accessible, axes hanging on the wall behind the bar.

Talula rented the attic room at Iffies and, in exchange for unregistered courier favours for the staff, she received discounted food and drink.

'I'm just saying,' Talula said, over the guffaws and shouting of the crowd, 'you look like that dwarf over there with the fancy hat.'

'What? I look nothing like him,' Norman said.

Unlike most dwarves Norman rarely drank alcohol. After only half a flagon of Triple Axe ale, Norman's woes and headache were gradually dissolving and he was experiencing a warm, glow. In fact, Norman was feeling so comfortable that he'd drifted into a mild trance and was currently staring over Talula's shoulder.

Talula followed Norman's gaze and turned to see an old dwarf sitting at a table near the empty fireplace. A grey and white skinny dog, of indeterminate breed, was sleeping by the dwarf's feet.

Talula looked from the dwarf to Norman.

'That's Arthur. You don't look anything like him.'

'That's what *I* thought,' said Norman.

'And the dwarf with the fancy red hat at the bar?' Talula folded her arms, and looked at Norman across the table.

Norman blinked and turned his head to look for the dwarf in question.

'Oh, him. I do look a bit like him don't I?' said Norman, with the merest suggestion of a slur.

'Do you know him?' Talula asked.

'That must be the famed Dr Tellurriminium,' Norman took a deep breath, and slowly articulated the doctor's name, 'Dr Teh-ll-ur-ee-um.'

Talula shook her head took a sip of her own ale.

'So who is he?' she continued.

'He's famous.'

'So you've said but, I've never seen him in here before or smelled him for that matter. What is it with you dwarves and perfume?'

Norman ignored the insult and while he told Talula about Dr Tellurium's science-behind-the-axe theory, Talula observed Norman's lookalike as he held court at the bar with several star-struck student dwarves.

Talula could see that the celebrity geochemist had nearly finished a Furnace Dipper. Unlike most alcoholic beverages this potent cocktail affected the imbiber from the feet upwards. The drink was popular with pre-wedding parties where the still conscious, albeit 'legless', groom would inevitably be carried home by friends.

Dr Tellurium, like Norman, was taller than the average

dwarf by at least an inch. Unlike Norman, however, Dr Tellurium was dressed in designer clothes. Atop his blonde, curly locks, was a sumptuous, red velvet hat, with a gold-coloured tassel hanging to one side. On his feet was a pair of soft, leather boots - a sign that Tellurium was not only rich enough to afford such a luxury but that he was also a dwarf who rarely walked long distances.

Talula turned to face Norman whose uncontrollable mop of frizzy hair poked out from under a cheap dark blue hat, the tassel of which had already started to fray. Norman's short, shaggy beard did not resemble Tellurium's neatly trimmed facial hair but, Talula thought, if Norman put on a few pounds, and had a *complete* makeover, it would have been difficult to tell the two dwarves apart - especially in the dark.

Talula looked towards the bar and, while Norman continued to drone on about the Torrimaya Axe and theories she didn't understand, she noticed that Dr Tellurium was making familiar, *No, I really must be going*, gestures.

'…And I reckon, thanks to him, someone's going to try and make another, hu-rp… 'scuse me …'

'Another what?'

'Not for me thanks,' said Norman.

Talula sighed.

'No, you said someone's making another something. What was it?'

'Oh, sorry. Another Torrimaya Axe-type, weapon, thing-umy-bob,' said Norman, as he took another sip of ale.

'You think that dwarf over *there*, is making another version of the Torrimaya Axe?!'

'Well, I don't know if it's *him* 'sactly but you know what scientists are like. Never happy 'til they prove a theory, so I'm sure *someone'll* try to build some kind of mad, bad, super-weapon, thing-umy-bob, thanks to Tellurininium. Tellinurinium.' Norman sighed and said,

'Him at the bar.'

Norman put his elbows on the table and placed his chin in his hands. He stared at nothing in particular and fell into a comfortable numbness.

Talula sat in silence and closely examined her ale, then, with a very straight face, she slowly raised her head and looked straight into Norman's eyes.

'You know what this means don't you,' she said.

'Hmm,' Norman said, still in a trance.

'Well?' said Talula.

'Well, what?' said Norman, refocussing his eyes to look at Talula.

'You? Attempted kidnap? Weapon? Dr Tellurium lookalike?' Talula paused. 'Hello?'

Norman's eyes widened as the implication sank in.

'Oh!'

'There it is,' Talula whispered, sarcastically.

'You mean...?'

'No offence but, why would anyone want to kidnap you?'

'Um... They wouldn't? Should we tell Dr Temul... Him at the bar, to be careful on his way home?'

'Ya think?' said Talula, facetiously.

Norman and Talula looked towards the bar simultaneously. Dr Tellurium had gone.

Norman and Talula abandoned their drinks and left the inn. There was no sign of the celebrity geochemist among the late-night crowds.

'We need to find him,' Talula said, as she looked frantically up and down the street.

'But he could be anywhere,' said Norman, as he too searched for any sign of his lookalike.

'We should do something,' Talula said.

'Like what?' Norman asked, marginally perplexed by Talula's insistent tone.

'I don't know. Maybe we should report it.'

Talula scanned the street from left to right. It seemed

that every dwarf she spotted was wearing a similar hat to that of Tellurium's, although few of them looked as expensive.

'Report what? That Dr Tellurium's left the building?' Norman said, surprised at his, apparently instant, sobriety.

Talula turned to face Norman.

'If this Tellurium is as important as you say he is, and given that he looks like you, granted in a less shambolic, scrawny, kind of way, you who have been jumped on, not once but twice in one night, then maybe, just *maybe*, something dodgy is going on.' Talula paused. 'This has wrong written all over it,' she said. 'I just think we should tell someone.'

'You know, I'm not sure there's much to tell. Scientist goes for a drink, scientist goes home. Most people wouldn't think that's particularly odd for a Tuesday night.'

Norman glanced across the road to Pixie Piccolo's Kebabs and, *phft*... Talula was gone. Norman blinked... *phft*... and there she was again.

'Look,' she said holding an expensive-looking, red velvet hat with a gold-coloured tassel. 'I found it on that street corner.' Talula pointed in the direction of the corner.

Norman looked down the street, then at the hat, and then up at Talula.

'That looks just like the one Dr Tellurium was wearing,' he finally said.

Talula put a hand on her hip.

'You're not the sharpest axe in the tree stump are you?' she said. 'Of course it's his hat! We should definitely tell someone he's been kidnapped.'

Norman held up his hands.

'Whoa! Hold on a minute. A *hat* hardly constitutes concrete evidence of a *kidnapping*.'

Talula watched a group of City supporters, wearing the distinctive yellow and blue striped jerkins, go into the kebab shop.

'No,' said Talula, 'but it's not completely beyond the

realms of possibility, given tonight's events.'

'Maybe a *bit* beyond the realms', Norman mumbled, unconvinced by Talula's theory.

'What?' said Talula.

'Who would you tell?' he replied, not wishing to upset Talula further.

Talula looked at the hat in her hand and then at Norman.

'I don't know,' she said.

'Look, why don't we just assume that *someone* lost their hat and that *I* was assaulted for normal criminal reasons,' said Norman.

Talula shook her head, sighed and looked at Norman.

'I've got a feeling in my bones about this,' she said. 'Something's not right.'

'I'm sure it's nothing to worry about. I've been mugged before and Dr Tellurium probably jumped in a cab and is on his way home as we speak.'

The grey and white skinny dog, of indeterminate breed, trotted out of Iffies and came over to Talula. The dog sniffed the hat and Talula looked down.

'Hello, Doyle. Where's Arthur?' Talula said, looking around to see if Arthur, who she assumed was Doyle's owner, was nearby.

''Ere Miss.' The old dwarf was leaning against the inn wall, smoking a roll-up. 'Doyle's just takin' 'imself off to do 'is business,' said Arthur.

'Nice,' said Talula. 'Go on then. Go do what you have to do.'

The dog looked at Talula, cocked his head and then, with his nose to the ground, headed off into the crowd.

'I'm sure Dr Tellurium will be fine,' said Norman.

'You might be right,' Talula turned to face Norman. 'But I doubt it. You don't look like a dwarf who often gets things right.'

'Thanks,' said Norman, only marginally offended at the quip.

'Anyway, I've done enough poking into other folks' business for one night,' said Talula.

The city's clocks began to strike the hour. It was eleven o'clock. Norman looked at Talula and smiled.

'Thanks for the drink. I know where to find you so it's my round next time,' he said. 'And thanks for, you know, earlier.'

'Here, you might as well have this,' said Talula, holding out the hat.

Norman stared at the accessory and then looked at Talula.

'Um.'

'Take it or I'll throw it in the bin.'

'You can't do that! Perfectly good hat that. I'll look after it,' said Norman, taking the hat.

'See you 'round,' Talula said, as she went back inside and left Norman standing outside Iffies.

Norman stood, awkwardly, holding the hat, not quite sure what to do with it.

'Bit strange, that one,' said Arthur.

'No she's not.' Norman scrunched up the hat and tried to put it in his trouser pocket. 'She helped me out earlier.' The hat left an unsightly bulge, so he took it out again.

'Suit yourself.'

Arthur threw his roll-up on the ground and walked off down the street.

* * *

Doyle had indeed gone off to do his business but it was not the sort of business one might normally expect of a dog. Agent Doyle was following Dr Tellurium or, more precisely, he was pursuing the aroma of three separate, expensive, colognes all of which were emitting something akin to nose-high breadcrumb trails. He had smelled the colognes on three different dwarves at Iffies, two of whom had strong Rataquian accents. From the hat Talula had been holding in her hand outside Iffies, Doyle confirmed that the third scent belonged to Dr Tellurium, whom he had been sent to watch.

'Hmmm...' Doyle whispered to himself as he ducked down an alley. 'Musk from the Dellabella bat scrotum. Very expensive. And just a whiff of lime, orange blossom and...' Doyle sniffed again, 'is that Neffian vanilla?' His pace quickened to a run. 'Cinnamon. Mountain lily, no wait, *desert orchid* from the Rataquian province of Imbria. I'm guessing we have Monte Nano, Galiardo and Vistoso. Very nice. Continental colognes for dwarves about town.'

Doyle was a well-known agent in the King's secret service, not least because he was one of only a handful of hounds who had, by royal decree, been spelled with the power of speech. Agent Doyle's unique knowledge of perfumes and colognes had enabled General Macjooste to foil many crimes in recent years. Indeed, Doyle's monograph - entitled *Enhanced Olfactory Senses in Crime Detection: with Specific Reference to Perfumes and Colognes* - had since become a standard training manual for all canine agents. When he wasn't on duty, Agent Doyle could often be found loitering outside one of the city's many perfumeries.

The scent of the River Sterm's sludge grew stronger and Doyle followed the path towards the river port.

'No boats. Please don't get on a boat.' Doyle raced down the riverbank and came to a sudden stop. 'You had to get on a boat didn't you,' he whined.

Doyle had made it to the Vinster-on-Sterm river port in time to see two burly dwarves on a barge folding up a rope. From the river's edge the skinny dog identified the dwarves as the owners of the Monte Nano and Galiardo scents. The canine agent inhaled the night air once more and detected the faint aroma of the scent Dr Tellurium had been wearing, the Vistoso. Doyle couldn't *see* the celebrity geochemist but was absolutely certain that Dr Tellurium was somewhere on that barge. There was no horse on the tow path and yet the boat pulled away quickly.

'Powered by magic,' said Doyle. 'LUSU we have a problem.'

FENDER ONION SOUP
Perilous in more ways than one.

Assay University was built beneath a mountain called Mount Mukai, which loomed over the city of Vinster-on-Sterm. All that could be seen of the University above ground was a grey stone wall surrounding the grounds, a sports field, perfectly manicured gardens, and several domed entrances. Beneath the mountain, however, was a sprawling campus, constructed with cross-vaulted arches, that sported ornamental scrolly bits, atop columns that held unfathomable amounts of weight.

Four months ago, after an incident involving a platter of cream cakes and the resident cat, Norman had lost his job as a kitchen porter at the Royal Vinster Hotel. When he applied for the post of a junior lab-assistant, at Assay University's geochemistry department, he hadn't expected to get an interview, never mind the job. He was, therefore, ecstatic, and more than a little shocked, when the post was offered to him - not least because he had no lab-related work experience whatsoever.

During the interview Norman hadn't mentioned the fact that he couldn't make an axe. He did, however, explain that he'd learned a great deal about the composition of metals while working in his father's foundry. Norman had hitherto assumed that it was this knowledge that had landed him the job. After last night's revelation, however, it briefly occurred to Norman that he had been hired solely because of his resemblance to Dr Tellurium, the celebrity geochemist with whom everyone in the scientific community, including his boss Dr Clastic, wanted to be seen.

Norman was a willing enough employee and his ability to recall every last document and item in the laboratory had occasionally proven useful. Unfortunately, Norman's clumsiness meant that Dr Clastic often had cause to yell at Norman who was rather prone to dropping, cracking or bending the lab's apparatus. In fact, as Dr Clastic was forever reminding Norman, because of these frequent breakages the department budget had taken a severe hammering in the short time Norman had been in the University's employ.

As luck would have it, over the past week there had been no accidents. Not one piece of equipment had been dropped, cracked or bent and Norman was feeling quite pleased with himself, even slightly optimistic. He felt he was finally starting to get the hang of things and hoped that Dr Clastic had noticed. If things continued to go well, Norman thought, he might even get a pay rise.

This morning Dr Clastic had arrived before Norman and was preparing the relevant apparatus to continue his work on a soup favoured by Cashen's troll population.

The delicacy was made from Fender onions, which were grown in the heart of the Dorfenderm plains, a province on the western border of Cashen. No other race on the planet could safely digest the corrosive substance. Even a troll's cast-iron digestive tract responded to the soup with violent, noxious flatulence, which (naturally) made Fender onion soup popular among immature, adolescent, male trolls.

The acidity of the soup was so strong that it could clean several layers of ground-in dirt on metal in a matter of seconds. The extreme chemical reaction, however, meant that the liquid didn't just clean the metal but ate through it completely. For the past several months, Dr Clastic had been attempting to create a formula with a less extreme response and more of a real-world application.

'Norman, pass me that beaker of Fender soup... *carefully*,' said Dr Clastic, as he prepared to light a bunsen burner.

As instructed, and with great care, Norman picked up the beaker in front of him. It was dangerously overfull, so much so that a meniscus was visible above the rim. Norman focussed all his attention on the receptacle and slowly passed it to the Professor.

Midway during this painfully slow process, Dr Clastic sneezed. In response to this unexpected noise, Norman's hand trembled slightly and a small drop of the liquid spilled onto his thumb.

'Aaargh!' Norman dropped the beaker. 'Ow! Ow! Ow!' he said, holding out his hand while dashing to the tap to wash off the substance.

Dr Clastic stared, horrified, at the pool on the workbench. The liquid hissed and fizzed as it started to eat its way through the metal surface of the workbench.

Norman turned off the tap and wiped his, unharmed, thumb on his lab coat.

Hissssssssssss, fizzzzzzzzzzzzz, psssssssst.

Norman looked up and froze with fear as he realised what was making the sound. He slowly turned around and watched as Dr Clastic's expression morphed from pale, dumbfounded disbelief to puce-coloured rage. Dr Clastic looked from the workbench to Norman. Norman tensed in anticipation of a tirade from his employer.

'I'm...' Norman began.

'Out,' said the enraged Dr Clastic, in an uncharacteristically calm tone. He pointed to the door. 'Out and do not come back.'

'Sorry...' said Norman.

'No.' The dwarf raised a hand. 'Do not apologise. Do not talk to me. Get your things and leave. I never, *ever*, want to see you again.'

With that Dr Clastic lowered his hand and shouted for his senior assistant, who had just walked through the door.

'Fingal! Order a new workbench from supplies! And clean up this mess!'

Fingal hurriedly put on his lab-coat and went straight to the sink to retrieve the acid-proof gloves and a clay bucket.

Norman took off his lab-coat, retrieved his jacket and satchel from the coat stand, and closed the door softly behind him. He stood in the empty corridor for a few moments not knowing quite what to do or where to go. He looked to his left and then to his right. It didn't matter which direction he chose, neither would lead him to a new job. Norman sloped through the labyrinth of tunnels in a state of shock. It wasn't until he smelled the familiar aroma of freshly baked bread that he became aware of his proximity to the canteen, which, he thought, seemed as good a place as any to gather his thoughts.

* * *

Norman sighed as he put his satchel and a cup of dandelion coffee on one of the tables. He barely noticed the students as they grabbed their hot beverages and rushed off to morning lectures. The despondent Norman sat by himself and checked his thumb. Apart from a small red dot on the tip, the digit remained intact. Norman stared, blankly, at the far wall of the canteen. He replayed the incident in his head, several times, and berated himself for having lost yet another job due to his ineptitude.

Norman's misery was interrupted by a friendly voice from behind.

'Is that young Norman Shale?'

Norman turned his head and saw Professor Bauxite. As Norman stood up to greet the elderly dwarf, he knocked the table and spilled his drink.

'Balderdash!' said Norman. 'Oh, I'm so sorry Professor Bauxite.'

'Accidents happen,' said the Professor, glancing at the puddle of coffee, before looking up and smiling at Norman. 'I dropped by Dr Clastic's lab to see how you were and he informed me that you'd left.'

What the Professor omitted from this statement was the fact that he knew Norman had been fired, not least because of the tirade of abuse that had come from Dr Clastic who used words such as 'imbecile', 'oaf' and, worst of all, 'son-of-a-troll.'

'Um, yes,' said Norman, staring at the puddle on the table.

'I'm glad I found you here.' The Professor looked once more at the pool of liquid. 'Hmm. Coffee. Just the ticket. I shall get us both a cup. And perhaps we might move to another table. I shall inform the staff of the spillage,' said the Professor, before he waddled off.

* * *

'And how are you after your little contretemps last night?' asked the Professor, returning with two steaming cups of coffee. 'Are you feeling better this morning?'

'Thank you. I'm fine,' said Norman, trying to disguise his glum mood.

'Are you quite sure?' the Professor enquired.

Norman was quiet for a moment.

'I'm a bit tired, and there was … um … an incident in Dr Clastic's lab,' said Norman glancing at his thumb. 'That's why I, erm, left.'

The Professor leaned back in his chair and folded his arms.

'Of course, experimental science can often be messier than the humanities,' he said. 'Mind you, I've done my fair share of tramping about in mud or sand and occasionally ice. I spent much of my youth digging up ancient axes and rotten sandals. If I had a florin for every sandal I've found on my travels I could have retired years ago,' the Professor said.

'Have you been to other countries then?' asked Norman, grateful for the distraction.

'Oh, goodness yes. You don't think the University would continue to pay me if I hadn't occasionally left my office in search of some legendary artefact like the Spoon of Sllek, or the Shield of Pormorphya do you?'

'You found the Shield of Pormorphya?' asked Norman, instantly fascinated.

'You've heard of it then?' the Professor asked.

'The shield is evidence of the first defensive equipment made by dwarves, possibly over three hundred thousand years ago. Its discovery suggests that both warfare and weapon-making were practised far earlier than the estimated two hundred thousand years, as proposed, six hundred years ago, by Dr Finkelclast.'

The Professor looked at Norman.

'I see you've been to the history museum recently,' said the Professor, scooping a spoon of coconut blossom sugar from the bowl on the table.

'Not lately, but I used to go when I first moved here.'

The Professor put the sugar into the cup and stirred his coffee.

'And how long ago was that?'

'About ten years now,' Norman said.

The Professor raised an eyebrow.

'Tell me, do you remember when the shield was discovered?'

Without hesitation, Norman replied, 'A hundred and three years ago, sir.'

Before the Professor was able to make any further comment on Norman's aptitude for remembering historical facts and figures, a pixie came over to the table and handed the Professor a note, one that he promptly read.

'I'm so sorry, I have to cut our conversation short but perhaps you could come by my office this afternoon? I'd like to continue our little chat.'

'Really?' said Norman.

The Professor smiled.

'27B Barchan Tunnel East. I look forward to seeing you later.'

Professor Bauxite stood up, picked up his coffee, and looked at Norman.

'27B Barchan Tunnel East,' repeated Norman.

'Excellent,' said the Professor. 'I shall see you this afternoon then.'

Norman watched the Professor as he left the canteen. Alone once more, Norman looked at his coffee, then at his thumb, and gave a low moan of despair.

KNOWLEDGE IS POWER
Except when it isn't because only half the facts are available.

To the west of Vinster was Trifolium Palace, a rambling, grey, rather unattractive, building which had been built by King Jorge I, a warrior fairy with little use for architectural aesthetics. King Jorge's primary goal had been to protect himself from all threats to his sovereignty, which resulted in a palace with stone walls that were several feet thick and spell-protected against magical attacks.

The current monarch, King Egbert IV, was sitting at his desk in the Lily Room. The walls and soft-furnishings were in varying shades of white, cream and beige. When Queen Petra had redecorated the King's office, some years ago, she had told her husband that the neutral tones would help reduce his stress levels. King Egbert had responded to this notion by stating that not being King would eradicate his stress altogether.

The sun streamed through the open doors and in the middle of the King's private garden water trickled from a fountain that was constructed in the shape of a wand, one end of which was stuck in a rock. The wand was made entirely of crystal. The water feature had been sculpted by Tamiun Urst, a post-post-post Illuminary artist of whom the Queen was a great fan. King Egbert was not enamoured of this particular work of art but was profoundly thankful that it was not one of Urst's more experimental pieces, such as the string of pickled badger snouts currently on display at the Vinster City Gallery.

At that moment, however, King Egbert was oblivious to the view and was reviewing some of the household's accounts with his private secretary - an immaculately-groomed fairy named Alfonse. Traditionally the accounts were left to the Queen but she was currently out of the country visiting her youngest sister, the expectant Queen Alexandra of Stermin. As no one knew exactly when

Queen Petra would return, the onerous task of signing off certain invoices had fallen to King Egbert.

'Tell me, Alfonse, how is it possible to spend so much on products for a lady's toilette? What is this *Sheen and Gloss Hair Honey*?'

'I believe it to be a cleaning solution for one's hair, Your Highness. It is a favourite with the young ladies,' said his secretary.

'Is that so?' said the King. 'Twenty florins seems an excessive amount to spend on hair soap.'

'Indeed, Your Highness,' replied Alfonse.

The King sighed and signed the invoices in front of him.

'Sometimes, just sometimes, Alfonse, I wonder if I would prefer a shorter life-expectancy than the average two hundred and fifty years I am due. Granted, one might achieve much in that time, and thirty-one or so years of adolescence seems to fly by when one is young but, when one *has* young time seems eternal.'

'But the princesses *do* have very shiny hair, Your Highness,' said Alfonse.

'Oh, well that's alright then,' said the king, acerbically. 'The city's merchants are complaining about cheap imported goods coming through the Ani-Bara tunnel, many of which have been produced with the aid of techno-magic, a development that is *already* starting to cause problems but, all is right with the world because my daughters have *shiny hair!*'

'The General is due for his nine o'clock meeting, Your Highness. Shall I send him in upon his arrival?' asked Alfonse.

'I wonder if Hamish has this kind of trouble with his daughters?' the King queried, ignoring his secretary's attempt to change the subject.

'I believe the Macjooste household also uses the aforementioned hair soap,' Alfonse replied.

The King stared incredulously at the fairy but before he

could comment further there was a knock at the door.

'Come,' said the King.

The office doors opened and the General was announced.

'Good morning, Your Highness,' said the General, as he entered.

'You look dreadful, Hamish. Have you had any sleep?' the King asked.

'Some, Your Highness,' the General lied, as he bowed to the King.

Alfonse collected the pile of invoices from the King's desk, bowed, and left the room.

'I do hope you have better news this morning,' said the King.

'Unfortunately no, Your Highness,' replied the General.

'Oh?'

'Dr Tellurium has been kidnapped.'

The King stood up, put his hands behind his back and tucked them under his wings which fluttered slightly in the process.

'The gods of every race seem to be conspiring against us. How did this happen? More importantly do we know who has taken our best geochemist or where they have taken him?' asked the King, as he began to pace in front of the window.

'We're no' sure who's behind the kidnapping, Your Highness, but Agent Doyle tracked two Rataquian dwarves and Dr Tellurium to the river port where an illegally magic-powered barge departed in a southerly direction.'

'I see,' said the King, coming to a halt and looking up at the General. 'And were we able to track this barge?'

'Aye, Your Highness. Flight Lieutenant Wand followed it down the Sterm.'

'Wand?' queried the King.

'James Wand. Double one seven squadron. LUSU Red Wings,' replied the General.

'Name rings a bell,' said the King. 'And where's Tellurium now?'

'Last known location was the outskirts of Rouche,' the General replied.

'Rouche? Home of the Rouchefort vineyards in the Beaux region? That Rouche?'

'Aye, Your Highness,' said the General, with a nod of confirmation.

'Good fairy, Algernon Rouchefort. Former LUSU agent. My father always spoke very highly of him. Do continue,' said the king, as he carried on pacing in front of the window.

'Wand caught a glimpse of the party as they disembarked but lost them on a road leading into the mountains,' the General said.

'Lost them? They can't have just vanished,' said the King, with a frown.

'Actually, that's precisely what happened. The barge arrived, six individuals disembarked and immediately boarded an enclosed carriage. The carriage made for the foothills and then vanished.'

'I see,' The King paused. 'An invisibility-transportation spell?' he asked.

'Almost certainly,' the General replied.

'Six individuals? I thought you said there were three?'

'Wand reported seeing four female fairies and two trolls, disembarking from the barge,' the General said.

'Did he see the colour of their wings? Do we know the nationality of these fairies?'

'They were all wearing cloaks but he said they looked drained.'

'No wonder. I'm surprised they were still standing after using such high-level magic. Perhaps we should send a squadron,' said the King.

'With such a blatant use of illegal magic, we cannae be sure who we're dealing with. I'd suggest keeping a low profile, at least until we know who's behind the kidnapping.'

The King nodded.

'Yes, right. Well then, have Wand contact Rouchefort. He'll know what's going on in that part of the world.'

'Yes, Your Highness,' replied the General.

The King stood by the open window, looked out at the fountain, and silently digested the information. After a moment or two he inhaled deeply and then turned to face General Macjooste.

'And Agent Doyle is sure these dwarves were Rataquian?' the King asked.

'Best nose in LUSU, Your Highness,' replied the General. 'Can identify ten types of water, when blindfolded, with a cold. Although, on this occasion, he said he definitely heard the accents.'

King Egbert raised an eyebrow.

'Are we absolutely certain that King Razarro was not responsible?' asked the King.

'Intelligence reports that the Rataquian government is no' responsible on this particular occasion. It would be unfortunate if this proved to be untrue but I'd be reluctant to point my wand at the Rataquians just yet, Your Highness,' said the General.

'Might it therefore be possible that Dr Tellurium's abduction was designed to have us *believe* that King Razarro was responsible for the crime?' asked the King.

Before the General could respond there was a knock on the door and a very worried-looking Alfonse entered.

'My most sincere apologies for the intrusion, Your Highness, but an urgent message has come from the Rataquian ambassador,' Alfonse said, handing a message to the King.

King Egbert read the note, sighed and handed it to General Macjooste.

'It says Cashenian soldiers have kidnapped a senior Rataquian fairy thaumurtologist,' said the King. 'Have we kidnapped any Rataquian thaumurtologists recently,

Hamish?'

'Most certainly not, Your Highness,' replied the General.

'Then, is it just me or is there a pattern starting to form here?' The King addressed his private secretary. 'Alfonse, please extend an immediate invitation to the Rataquian ambassador, shall we say for eleven o'clock this morning? And, Hamish, I think you should join us.'

'Of course, Your Highness. I hope to have more news by then,' the General said.

Alfonse nodded, bowed, and left.

'I fear someone is trying to upset the proverbial cabbage cart, Hamish. I do hope we can find out who is behind this before things become unnecessarily messy.'

ACQUAINTANCES
Friends in the making.

The encounter in the canteen with Professor Bauxite had temporarily lifted Norman's mood but, as he trudged through the University grounds towards the main gates, he was once again faced with the reality of his situation. He had been doing so well, had had no accidents in the lab for a whole week and then suddenly everything had gone frog-shaped.

The axe-making evening class had, obviously, been a huge mistake, the two assaults the night before had been somewhat disconcerting, and the debacle in the lab was decidedly catastrophic. The combination of these events, however, paled into insignificance when compared to the more gruelling task Norman now faced of having to find a new job.

Norman went past the security hut and started walking towards the city. Trade carts rattled past packs of students, and pixies raced along the courier lanes. Norman was only vaguely aware of his surroundings, focussing instead on the ground while contemplating the prospect of traipsing around the city to look for work.

Norman started to make a mental list of the places where he might or, more depressingly, might not, expect to find employment. It was a long list and he had already ruled out several possibilities.

'Eateries are out,' he mumbled. 'In fact nothing with crockery.'

'How's your head this morning?' said a familiar female voice.

Norman stopped and looked up. Standing on the steps to his left, at the door of the Pixies of Mercy Orphanage, was Talula.

'What are you doing here?' Norman asked.

Talula came down the steps and looked Norman in the eye.

'Never mind what I'm doing here, why are you looking

so miserable?' she replied.

'Oh, it's nothing,' Norman said, in a tone that indicated 'nothing' was in fact something he'd rather not talk about.

'Okay.' Talula paused. 'Then why aren't you at work?' she asked, clearly unwilling to let the matter drop.

Norman struggled to answer this question. He looked at Talula, then up at the sign above the orphanage's main entrance.

'Um…'

'You've been sacked haven't you?' Talula guessed.

Norman answered with a nod.

A cart pulled up in front of the orphanage and the driver started to unload boxes of fruit and vegetables.

'Ain't you got jobs to go to?' a large troll said, as he lifted several boxes at once from the cart.

'I know what you need,' Talula said, as she glared at the troll.

'A job that involves parchment? It's the only thing I've never broken,' Norman said, then added, 'Oh, actually, that's not strictly true…'

'Oh stop feeling sorry for yourself,' interrupted Talula. 'Follow me.'

'I should really start looking for another job. My rent's due soon,' Norman said, as Talula started off down the road.

'Later. It won't take long. Promise.'

The mid-morning sun shone from a cloudless sky. Norman, who was more accustomed to the coolness of the University's subterranean rooms during the hot summer days, was beginning to feel uncomfortably warm.

'Do you have to walk so quickly?' Norman asked, as Talula skipped ahead of him.

'Do you have to walk so slowly? I could have been there and back three times by now,' she said, over her shoulder.

Talula and Norman went past a row of cottages where dwarf, goblin and pixie toddlers played in the small front gardens while their mothers gossiped as they hung out lines and lines of washing.

As they approached the temple run by the fairy Nuns of Serenity, Talula slowed and said, 'We can always get a cup of tea here afterwards.'

The Nuns of Serenity were a gentle order originally from the Serenity Mountains of Toorquet. The nuns prayed a lot, constantly burned incense, and told anyone who would listen that the gift of life was magical enough without having to use spells. The temple was largely attended by the city's homeless who knew that there would be free tea and cakes after the lunchtime service.

Past the temple there was a long, high, stone wall, behind which was the city's oldest cemetery. Honeysuckle trailed down the sides of the stones and its sweet scent was a welcome relief from the smell of the dusty, dung-splattered road.

'Where are we going?' asked Norman, who was becoming increasingly hot.

'This way,' Talula said.

Hidden behind a tangle of honeysuckle and ivy was a wooden door. It was warped and faded with age. Talula lifted the latch, pushed it inward with her shoulder and made enough of a gap so that they could both squeeze through.

Behind the door was the graveyard. Here avenues of trees lined the cobblestone paths, either side of which were row upon row of graves. Birds swooped from branch to branch and a pair of pigeons was wing-slapping each other noisily somewhere above Norman's head.

'Ever been here before?' Talula asked.

The shade from the trees was a relief from the heat. Talula slowed her pace to look at some of the headstones.

'Never really considered a cemetery to be a recreational destination before,' Norman said.

'I like it here. It's peaceful.' Talula said, as she led Norman from the main path onto a narrow dirt track through a clump of trees.

'Why were you at the orphanage?' Norman asked.

'Who said I was at the orphanage?' said Talula, evasively.

'Oh, I just assumed…'

'I find it best never to assume anything,' said Talula.

'Funny that, my gran used to say the same thing, except she said I could *always* assume I'd never take over the family business,' said Norman.

'Which is?' asked Talula.

'A foundry,' replied Norman.

'Makes sense. I had you pegged as one of those bookey kind of dwarves. You're hands are too soft.'

Norman looked at his hands.

'Soft?'

'Soft as fluff on a dandelion clock. Here we are,' Talula announced.

The pair arrived at a clearing, in front of which was a river.

'Is that the River Sterm?' asked Norman.

'Yep,' Talula replied.

'It looks clean,' said Norman, who had only ever been to the docks where the mouth of the river ran into the sea, as did much of the city's effluent.

Talula sat down and took off her boots and socks. She rolled up her leggings and tip-toed into the water.

'How did you find this place?' Norman asked.

'I used to come here when I was little.'

'Were you born in Vinster then?'

'I guess,' Talula said, as she swished towards a nettle-free patch on the bank.

'You guess?' Norman sat down, and took off his boots and socks in order to join Talula.

'If you must know, I grew up in the orphanage. The nuns were good to us so I volunteer on Wednesday mornings.'

Talula sat on a soft, mossy ledge and let her feet dangle

in the water.

'Oh. What was it like growing up in an orphanage?' asked Norman, as he sploshed his way over and sat next to Talula.

Talula gave a resigned sigh.

'It was cold in the winter, hot in the summer and crowded all year round,' she said.

'Right,' said Norman.

'Why did you get sacked?' she asked.

Norman looked up at the tow-path across the river and considered the best response.

'I'm more of a bookey kind of dwarf,' he finally said.

Talula smiled.

'And I'm more of a get-up-and-go kind of pixie,' she said.

'So you became a courier.'

'I'm a trainee with Vinster Parcel Services but I'm applying for a full licence so I can set up my own business. I've got my test with the AVC in a couple of weeks' time.'

Vinster-on-Sterm's couriers, it was said, were the best in the world. There was some debate as to whether or not this was true but certainly Vinster was the only city on the planet with the Know-How exam. To attain a full courier licence, trainees were required by law (as laid out by the Association of Vinster-on-Sterm Couriers - AVC) to take the rigorous Know-How course and test. To pass the test, trainees were expected to learn the myriad streets, alleys, cul-de-sacs, bridges, squares and statues above ground as well as every bunker, cave, sewer and subterranean canal (often inhabited by those of a more criminal persuasion) below the city,

'You're lucky. I wish I knew what I wanted to do,' Norman said.

Talula swished her feet.

'Luck's got nothing to do with it. I've worked really hard and...' Talula froze.

'What?'

'Ssh.' Talula put her finger to her lips. 'Quick, grab your things,' she whispered.

Talula and Norman jumped up onto the bank, grabbed their belongings, and quickly hid behind a tree, just in time to see a barge drift by. It wasn't being towed by a horse. A troll, dressed entirely in black, was standing on the deck smoking a roll-up.

'Thump,' came a female voice, from inside the barge.

'Yeah?' replied the troll.

A green-winged fairy, wearing a black dress, came out from below deck.

'Inside,' she said. 'It's time.'

The troll and the fairy both went below deck and then the barge was gone. Not just gone as in gently down the stream but, vanished as in, disappeared into thin air.

Norman and Talula waited until the ripples from the wake had dissipated into the natural flow of the river before coming out from behind the tree. They looked at the river, then at each other. The barge was, most definitely, no longer in the vicinity.

LUSU
And diplomatic biscuits.

Situated to the west of the city, near but not actually inside the palace grounds, were the Cashen Military Headquarters. There were seven floors in total, all of which were situated beneath the barracks and stables. The underground complex housed spell-protected offices and departments for military personnel and administrative staff.

In the basement of the complex was the top secret intelligence service, the Licensed to Use Spells Unit, otherwise known as LUSU. Overseen by General Macjooste, LUSU agents bent the King's laws, magical or otherwise, in the name of keeping the peace. A well-funded research and development laboratory invented and developed a host of gizmos and gadgets, all of which were designed to protect agents as well as monitor the affairs of criminals, potential troublemakers and, naturally, other nations.

LUSU's main observation room was currently swarming with fairies, pixies, imps, elves, goblins and dwarves, all of whom were rushing from one desk to another as information, regarding any number of cases or missions, was retrieved, logged and disseminated to the relevant team leader.

Leading off the observation room were several other rooms, one of which was the Remote Tracking room. It was here that trained fairies were, usually, able to establish the whereabouts of individuals or objects on LUSU's most wanted list.

Twenty trackers were currently sitting at their desks and in front of each fairy was a crystal bowl filled with clear water that had been infused with a vision-charm. The twenty fairies stared into the perfectly still surfaces and made notes of the images they saw.

General Macjooste walked into the room. All of the fairies stood up and saluted.

'As you were. Have we an update on Dr Tellurium?' the General asked the Captain, a female fairy holding a clipboard.

The uniformed fairy trackers sat down and resumed their tasks.

'Nothing new since Flight Lieutenant Wand's last report, sir. He's waiting at the jetty near Rouche to see if anything appears. As yet he's seen no one. But...'

The other trackers looked up. The General noticed this uniform movement but maintained eye contact with the Captain.

'But?'

'One of our trackers picked up the signal of a magically propelled barge on the river near the cemetery but then it vanished. We think the occupants may have used a double-casting,' the team leader said.

'How many fairies does it take to magically transport a barge?' the General asked, realising too late that this sounded like the beginning of a hackneyed fairy joke.

'Off the top of my head I'd say four, minimum. Possibly more,' the team leader replied, with a straight face.

'Aye, I'd say the same,' the General nodded. 'And, did anyone send a canine agent to the cemetery?' he asked.

'Yes, sir. I'm afraid there was no sign or scent of anything by the time he arrived.'

The General looked at the trackers and then at the Captain.

'Someone must be paying handsomely for this high-level magic,' said the General.

The majority of Eris's fairy population never took advantage of their magical abilities, not only because it was illegal in many countries but also because using too much magic caused a dramatic drain on an individual's life-force. Over-use of magic led to premature death in all but the rarest of cases.

The General inhaled deeply and reached for his pocket

watch. It was almost ten thirty.

'Contact Wand and tell him to stay put,' he said. I've a feeling this second barge will end up in Rouche as well.' He looked around the room and added, 'Keep me posted.'

The Captain saluted and the General left the fairies to their work.

* * *

King Egbert, General Macjooste and the Rataquian ambassador, Lord Ronaldo Esodo, were in the King's office, sitting around a marble-topped coffee table. In front of the three fairies was a selection of hot and cold beverages. A plate of Tico-Tico biscuits, freshly baked and still warm, was in the middle of the table.

Tico-Ticos were one of Chef François Cappo's signature pastries and were immensely popular with palace visitors. At last month's royal garden party, King Egbert had quietly observed Lord Esodo polish off an entire platter of these light, almond sweet-treats and had deduced that these were an irresistible favourite of the Ambassador. The King, fully aware of the diplomatic value of food, had therefore asked Chef Cappo to whip up a large batch of the delicacies in preparation for the meeting.

The King offered refreshments to the Ambassador and the General, both of whom accepted a cup of dandelion coffee from Alfonse. The King chose fruit nectar and as he took a sip he observed Lord Esodo eyeing the tasty delights. The General politely declined when Alfonse offered the plate but the Ambassador took one of the biscuits and placed it on a plate, next to his coffee.

King Egbert opened the meeting with a general enquiry as to the well-being of King Razarro, to which the Ambassador responded by saying that his king was looking forward to holidaying at the royal oasis in Imbria although, the Ambassador added, only if this worrying situation could soon be resolved.

'It grieves me to talk on such a matter, Your Highness

but, King Razarro he is most concerned that our best thaumurtologist he is missing.' The Ambassador paused. 'And it is great worry that witnesses say Dr Vincenzo he is taken by two Cashenian trolls in military uniform.'

King Egbert crossed his legs.

'I too was most distressed to hear of Dr Vincenzo's abduction and this is indeed a very serious matter but, Ambassador, please be assured that Cashen is not responsible for Dr Vincenzo's abduction,' said the King, in response to the Ambassador's comment.

The Ambassador shrugged as he raised both hands.

'I, of course, want to believe you but, King Razarro he is most worried, Your Highness.'

King Egbert nodded his head.

'As am I, Ambassador, as am I, not least because we too have experienced a similar incident.' The King paused and watched as Lord Esodo shifted, a fraction of an inch, in his chair. 'You will not be aware,' he continued, 'but, Dr Tellurium, our most eminent geochemist, has also been kidnapped. Rather worryingly, witnesses say two Rataquian dwarves were responsible for the deed.'

Lord Esodo said nothing. He slowly reached for the biscuit on his plate and popped it in his mouth. While he ate the biscuit he scooped and stirred two spoons of coconut blossom sugar into his coffee. The Rataquian Ambassador completely avoided eye contact with the King. This gesture suggested to King Egbert that the Rataquian Secret Service and, therefore, Lord Esodo, in fact knew all about Dr Tellurium's abduction

'I am very sorry to hear this, Your Highness,' said the Ambassador, as he leaned back in his chair, cup and saucer in hand.

The sophisticated intelligence networks operated by both Rataq and Cashen were extremely well-informed. Due to the very nature of espionage, however, King Egbert and Lord Esodo were hampered in their discussion, mainly because no one was supposed to know that the other side knew anything.

The King picked up the plate of biscuits and offered it to the Ambassador for a second time.

'Please, do have another,' the King said, with a smile. 'I find they're even nicer when they're still warm.'

Lord Esodo hesitated for a moment then leaned forward and accepted another of the tasty morsels. The King took a biscuit for himself and replaced the plate directly in front of the Ambassador.

'Thank you, Your Highness,' Lord Esodo said, glancing at the biscuit in his hand, before looking at the king. 'I will, of course, send word to King Razarro telling him of abduction of your scientist, but, I am most very certain that Rataq is not responsible for such outrageous act.'

Observing the look of sincerity on Lord Esodo's face, King Egbert nodded in response to the Ambassador's statement. Lord Esodo put the small biscuit in his mouth.

'I am in no way suggesting that your country is responsible for the kidnapping of Dr Tellurium but, you do see how this looks don't you, Ambassador?' said the King.

'Some might say that abduction of Rataquian citizen by two uniformed Cashenian soldiers is act of hostility and His Majesties, King Razarro, he say that until Dr Vincenzo is found we must to consider this a threat to Rataq security.'

Lord Esodo glanced at the plate again and, after what appeared to be some kind of inner battle, he took another Tico-Tico.

'Yes, Ambassador. However, it could also be argued that Cashen is very much in the same position. Until the whereabouts of Dr Tellurium is discovered we too can only interpret the abduction of our most senior geochemist by Rataquian dwarves as a hostile act and, I assume you will agree, this could equally be construed as a threat to Cashen's security.'

The room fell silent for a moment as the diplomatic

see-sawing came to a temporary halt.

The King took this opportunity to ring for Alfonse and asked him to refill the empty coffee cups. After doing so, Alfonse picked up the plate and offered the Tico-Ticos to the King and his guests. The King took one and watched while Lord Esodo valiantly tried to refuse.

'Petra constantly warns me about my waistline but who could possibly resist these?' the King said, with a smile.

'Constanza, she says I eat too much,' Lord Esodo said, patting his podgy stomach before succumbing to temptation once again.

The General, abstemious in his habits, was again about to refuse when he caught the King's eye. The General instantly recognised that he was being called upon to join the conversation and accepted a biscuit.

'No one makes Tico-Ticos like the palace chef, do you no' agree Lord Esodo?' the General said.

'Si,' Lord Esodo said, who by now had consumed several and was looking far more relaxed. 'It is much shame we discuss unpleasantness when our nations have been friends for so long but, something must to be done.'

While the Ambassador leaned forward and helped himself to yet another biscuit, the King nodded.

'Hmm...' The King looked deep in thought. 'As you rightly say, Ambassador, we do not want to jeopordise our special relationship but it seems we have hit an impasse,' he said.

'If I may, Your Highness, Lord Esodo, I would like to propose a theory,' the General said.

'Please do,' said the King, 'I'm sure the Ambassador is more than willing to hear your thoughts on the matter,' said the King, who received a nod of confirmation from Lord Esodo.

'Well, there are similarities in both abductions, especially because both incidents happened within a similar time frame. If we assume that Rataq did'nae order the kidnap of Dr Tellurium and accept that we were no' responsible for Dr Vincenzo's disappearance, then is it no' possible that an outside force is deliberately trying to set our two nations against each other?'

The King looked at Lord Esodo, who held the King's enquiring gaze.

'What do you make of this suggestion, Ambassador?' asked the King.

Lord Esodo took a sip of his dandelion coffee, placed the cup on the coffee table in front of him, and glanced once more at the temptation on the plate before looking directly at the King, who returned the Ambassador's look with a reassuring smile.

'I will propose to King Razarro,' the Ambassador finally said, with a nod of acceptance.

* * *

Lord Esodo had made a considerable dent into the plate of Tico-Ticos by the time the meeting had drawn to a natural close, a sign, the King hoped, that the first round of diplomacy had gone well. King Egbert finally rose from his chair, with the General and Lord Esodo quickly following suit, and rang for Alfonse.

'Your Highness,' Lord Esodo said, 'if as you say, outside force is responsible, how will you to handle?'

The King smiled at the Ambassador.

'Ronaldo, please trust that we will do absolutely everything in our power to discover who is responsible for these reprehensible acts. General Macjooste takes the business of national security very seriously, isn't that so, General?'

'Aye, Your Highness,' the General said, with a grave countenance.

'And we will provide you with updates as and when we have more news,' the King added.

The door opened and Alfonse walked in carrying the Ambassador's beautifully tailored, orange and red, hand-embroidered silk cloak.

'Let us hope, Your Highness, this situation to resolve

quickly then,' said Lord Esodo, draping the cloak over his arm.

'And should you discover anything, please feel you can contact me at any time. I am always at your disposal.' The King smiled.

'Many thank yous, Your Highness.' Lord Esodo, bowed low and smiled at the King. 'Goodbye, General.'

General Macjooste nodded his farewell and the Ambassador left.

'He'll no' tell us a thing,' the General said, when the door was closed.

'No, and of course we will tell him very little. Nonetheless, I shall have Alfonse send a box of Tico-Tico's to the Ambassador's residence. We are, for the moment, still friends, a situation we must do everything in our power to maintain.'

THEORY AND SPECULATION
A pixie's power of persuasion.

'We have to tell someone,' Talula said, as she marched in front of Norman towards the wooden gate.

'But who? We had this problem last night, remember?' Norman said, as he tried to keep up with the fast-paced pixie.

'It needs to be someone who'll take us seriously,' Talula turned around and walked backwards so that she could look at Norman, 'or who'll take me seriously, at least,' she said, and then turned to face forwards again.

'And you were doing so well with the whole making me feel better thing,' Norman mumbled, before saying, 'What about Professor Bauxite?'

'Is he the one who told you about the Torrimaya Axe, weapon-thing-umy-bob?'

'He didn't exactly say there was a weapon,' Norman said, wishing he hadn't said anything to Talula. 'He just said that Dr Tellurium's theory had set the scientific community to *wondering* if a super-weapon could be made.'

'Yes, yes, but this Tellurium is *probably* involved in some kind of super-weapon project, right?' Talula said, skating around Norman's response while at the same time yanking open the aged door. 'Can this Professor Bauxite be trusted?' she asked.

'I think so,' Norman replied. 'He seems like a nice dwarf and I'm sure he'd know who to talk to about the barge. I was going to see him later anyway.'

'Then we'll tell him,' said Talula, as she squeezed through the gap. 'I mean, we all know fairies use a bit of magic now and then but a disappearing barge is hardly the same as a flick of the wrist to get rid of the dirty dishes when unexpected guests come 'round. I haven't seen a vanishing-spell like that since...' Talula waited for Norman to join her. 'Actually, I don't think I've ever seen a vanishing-spell that spectacular before.'

While the two walked towards the University, Norman struggled to convince Talula that what he had said about the weapon, after an ale, was his opinion and not a matter of fact. Talula, meanwhile, argued that he should have more faith in his own opinions. It was obvious, she insisted, that someone had tried to nab Norman having mistaken him for Dr Tellurium, which meant something must be going on in the weapon-making department.

'No offence but, I really can't see why anyone would want to kidnap you. Dr Tellurium, on the other hand, is far more likely to have information someone might actually want, wouldn't you say?' suggested Talula.

The discussion between Norman and Talula became very animated as they hurried to Assay's campus. By the time the pair found 27B Barchan Tunnel East Talula was convinced that the previous night's events and the recent vanishing barge scenario, were probably connected, although, as yet, she wasn't sure how.

'We probably shouldn't say all this to the Professor,' Norman whispered, as they stood outside the Professor's office door.

'Why not?'

Norman took off his hat.

'Because we don't actually have any evidence to back up your theory!' he whispered, loudly.

'Just knock on the door,' Talula said, impatiently.

Norman knocked on the door.

'Enter,' came a muffled voice from the other side.

Talula followed Norman into the office. There was no sign of the Professor but immediately to their left was a wheelbarrow loaded with several pairs of old boots. On the floor nearby, was an open canvas bag out of which spewed trowels, hammers and hand brushes. Three spades, two pick-axes and a mallet were leaning against the wall behind the door.

'Hello?' said Norman.

'Come in,' came Professor Bauxite's muffled voice

from somewhere behind a large, wooden desk.

Norman and Talula looked in the direction of the desk, on top of which were pillars of books and stacks of precariously balanced parchments. From behind these piles, Professor Bauxite emerged.

'Ah, young Norman. Good to see you again,' said the Professor, as he looked over his spectacles at a clock on the wall above the door. 'You're early, and you've brought a friend I see,' he said with a smile. 'Do come in.'

'This is Talula Ewesage, sir. Talula, this is Professor Bauxite,' said Norman.

'Miss Ewesage, a pleasure to meet you.'

'Nice to meet you, sir,' said Talula.

'Come in, come in,' said the Professor, gesturing for his visitors to come out of the doorway.

'Thank you,' said Norman.

Talula and Norman gingerly made their way through the chaos, trying to avoid the obstacles on the floor.

'I haven't had a chance to tidy up in here lately,' the Professor said, as he guided them past the desk. 'Come this way. I have a small sitting room where we'll be able to sit and have a cup of tea.'

The Professor opened a door behind which stood an ancient leather sofa and an equally battered-looking, leather chair. There were several opened books scattered on the floor as well on the furniture.

'This is cosy,' said Talula.

'I'm afraid it needs a once-over but please, do have a seat.' The Professor went to a pot-bellied stove, on top of which was a kettle. 'Mushroom tea?' he asked, kettle in hand.

Norman and Talula carefully removed several books from the sofa and placed them on the floor before sitting down.

'Tea would be lovely, thank you,' said Norman, who was parched. 'Oh, and I have Dr Tellurium's hat.' Norman retrieved the item from his satchel. 'Maybe you could give it to him when you see him.'

The Professor turned to face Norman and Talula.

'Dr Tellurium's hat?'

'That's sort of why we're here,' Norman said.

The Professor stared, uncomprehendingly.

'You're here to give me Dr Tellurium's hat?'

'Not exactly,' Talula said, giving Norman a sideways look. 'We came because a barge vanished before our eyes and we didn't know who to report this use of high-level magic to.'

The Professor looked at Norman, then at Talula.

'A vanishing barge? Are you sure?' the Professor asked, with a frown.

The Professor's response momentarily silenced Norman and Talula. It was one thing talking about the matter to each other but quite another discussing the event with a complete stranger. The unlicensed use of high-level magic for nefarious purposes was a serious offence... and woe betide anyone caught informing the authorities.

'We didn't know who else to tell,' said Norman, nervously.

'And we think there may be a connection to what happened to Norman last night,' added Talula.

Norman turned to face his recently acquired pixie friend. Talula looked at Norman.

Norman's facial expression said, *What are you doing?!*

Talula's face replied, *What? I'm only saying!*

The Professor, who was still holding the kettle, watched this silent exchange and finally said, 'I see. Perhaps you could expand a little on these events?'

Norman and Talula, although mainly Talula, proceeded to tell the Professor everything that had happened subsequent to Norman's first assault on the campus grounds.

When Norman said that they had both heard foreign accents during the second assault, outside his home, the Professor shook his head and tutted. Talula then told the

Professor that she had found Dr Tellurium's hat in the street outside Iffies and that she suspected Dr Tellurium may have been taken somewhere against his will.

'I'm pretty sure the whole attempted kidnap, foreign dwarf, disappearing barge thing are all connected to Dr Tellurium, because, let's be honest, who'd want to take Norman? And a disappearing barge probably needs a ton of magic,' Talula stopped talking and looked at the floor, 'Oh,' she said, 'and if you were going to kidnap someone important, you'd want to get them as far away from the King's forces as possible,' she looked at the Professor, then at Norman. 'And I bet that's how all of this is connected. Someone's kidnapped Dr Tellurium and taken him out of the city on a barge!' Talula said, triumphantly.

'This is most certainly an unusual sequence of events. However, we must be careful not to jump to conclusions,' the Professor said, as he placed the kettle back on the pot-bellied stove.

Talula looked slightly deflated by the Professor's comment.

'We haven't done anything wrong, have we?' Norman asked.

'Wrong? Most definitely not. You were both absolutely right to come to me with this. I am a personal acquaintance of General Macjooste and I'm sure he can find some time to look into this matter. Even, Miss Ewesage, if it's to rule out your more serious kidnapping hypothesis.'

The Professor left the pair and went into his office.

'General Macjooste?' whispered Talula. 'He's top of the military tree.'

'I told you he'd know what to do,' Norman whispered.

'Talula, might I ask if you are, perchance, a courier when you are not helping Norman here to overcome his unfortunate ordeals?' the Professor called out, from the other room.

Talula turned to Norman and shrugged her shoulders.

'Yes, sir, I'm a courier.'

'Excellent,' the Professor said. 'I wonder if I might trouble you for your services? I could of course call for another pixie if you would prefer.'

'No,' Talula said. 'I'll deliver a message for you. Where do you want me to go?'

The Professor came into the sitting room, folding a piece of parchment. He handed Talula the document.

'This is for General Macjooste at Military Headquarters. The sooner he talks to you both the better, and Norman, I wonder if, in the interests of your personal safety, it might be best for you to stay here with me for a while, hmm? At least until we can speak to the General.' The Professor rummaged in his waistcoat pocket and took out half a florin.

'I'm not actually on duty,' Talula said.

'Nonsense,' the Professor said, as he held out his hand. 'I always pay someone for their services. Whether you declare it or not is entirely up to you.'

The elderly dwarf winked at Talula and gave her the money

THICKENING OF THE PLOT
Still more questions than answers.

General Macjooste had left Trifolium Palace and returned to military headquarters. The General's office, unlike Professor Bauxite's, was neat and orderly. A wall-to-ceiling bookcase lined one wall where volumes of military and legal books filled the shelves. Titles ranged from tomes such as *The Bi-continental Convention of Civil Rights: A Soldier's Legal Responsibility During Wartime*, to small pamphlets, including *How to Clean Your Wand*. On the wall above the General's desk was a glass-fronted display case, inside of which was the Wand of Office, a replica of the weapon that had been used by the great Cashenian military leader, Victor Von Wandhoven. Beneath the glass, on a brass plaque, was the inscription, *Subdue The Enemy Without Using Magic And You Have Won*.'

General Macjooste was reviewing the latest intelligence communiqués from Rataq when there was a tap on the door.

'Come,' he said.

'Captain Meejum for you, sir,' said the General's assistant, a female elf named Captain Florina.

'Meejum?' The General looked up from the reports.

'Remote tracking, sir. She said she saw you earlier,' said Captain Florina.

'Send her in,' said the General.

Captain Meejum saluted to the General.

'I'm Flight Lieutenant Wand's contact in the field, sir, and I have a report,' said Captain Meejum.

'Has the barge appeared in Rouche?' asked the General.

'Yes, sir. The Flight Lieutenant reported four female fairies and two trolls leaving the barge. The two trolls were carrying a rolled-up rug, which, Wand said, may have been concealing the Rataquian thaumurtologist, Dr Vincenzo.'

'I see.' The General frowned. 'Presumably a carriage was waiting for them.'

'Yes, sir, and this time Wand was able to follow them.'

'Did the carriage no' disappear again?' the General asked.

'It did, sir. An invisibility-transportation spell. I took the liberty of asking R&D to send a new piece of equipment that allows Wand to tune into thaumurtological wavelengths.'

'Is that the whizzy thing with the magically infused aluminium core?' asked the General, who had always been a fan of the LUSU boffins' gadgets.

'Yes, sir. It's called an MPS,' Captain Meejum said.

'MPS?'

'Magical Positioning System. It can detect and follow magic within a five mile radius,' Meejum said.

'I'm no' going to ask how it got there so quickly.'

'I...' started Meejum.

'Please dinnae tell me. I'll read it in the report later. Where's Wand now?' the General asked.

'He followed the carriage from the jetty to a security-spelled entrance in what we now know to be Mount Dou,' said Meejum.

'Is he still there?' asked the General.

'Awaiting your orders, sir,' Meejum replied.

As Captain Meejum concluded her report there was another knock on the door.

'Come,' said the General.

'Sorry, sir,' said Captain Florina. 'There's a message here from a local courier who's waiting for a reply.'

Captain Florina handed the message to the General who quickly scanned the message.

'Can you escort her from the main gate, Captain.'

'Yes, sir,' said Florina as she left the room.

'What shall I tell the Flight Lieutenant, sir?' asked Captain Meejum.

'Tell him to take a room at the Grape and Goblet

hostelry in Rouche. He needs to contact Colonel Algernon Rouchefort and ask for a meeting. We need to find out who owns that mountain, and if anyone knows what's going on inside it'll be Rouchefort,' the General said. 'And tell Wand that the Colonel can be trusted,' he added.

Captain Meejum saluted, did an about-face and left. The General stood up, unbuttoned his jacket and hung it on the back of his chair. He stretched his wings, rubbed his aching neck and noticed that Captain Florina had left a vial of wake-up formula, WUF for short, on the desk. The General drank the contents of the vial and considered the potential consequences of a Rataquian scientist being held captive, by an unknown force, in a Cashenian mountain. The situation was fast developing into a political nightmare. As the formula began to take effect the General felt a surge of energy course through his body.

'Right,' he sighed, 'As if Rataquian involvement isn't bad enough we now have civilians in the mix. Just what I need.'

The General put on his jacket and waited for the pixie-courier.

DOORS
The closing of one and the opening of another.

In Professor Bauxite's small sitting room, the Professor took advantage of Talula's absence to ask Norman if he had plans for his future now that he was no longer in Dr Clastic's employ. Norman said that his immediate task was to find another job.

'Did you enjoy working here at the University?' the Professor asked.

'Yes, sir, and I learned a lot about cleaning metal. Dr Clastic said he wanted to produce something that didn't involve any elbow grease, and I reckon when he reduces the acid content in the Fender onion soup he'll be onto a winner. He talked about a dip and shine product, which my gran would love,' Norman said.

The Professor smiled at the earnest young dwarf sitting opposite him.

'Indeed, Dr Clastic is a valued member of our faculty.'

The Professor stood up and disappeared into his office. He rummaged around for a few moments, then returned to the sitting room and handed Norman a parchment.

'What's this?' asked Norman.

'This,' said the Professor, as he looked over his spectacles at Norman, 'is a short piece I wrote on the dig where we found the Shield of Pormorphya.'

'You want me to read it?' Norman asked, surprised at the Professor's request.

'If you wouldn't mind. It won't take you long. I shall give you a moment or two.'

The Professor left Norman and went in search of the bursar's letter in order to establish exactly how much money was available to hire an assistant.

A few minutes later Norman was standing in the doorway between the office and the sitting room.

'I've finished, sir,' said Norman.

'My word, that was quick,' the Professor said, who could only be heard and not seen from behind the mountains of paperwork on his desk. 'Would you mind if I asked you a few questions about the text? You expressed an interest in the Shield of Pormorphya in the canteen earlier and I thought you might like to talk about the dig.'

The Professor appeared from behind the piles, holding the letter.

'Okay,' Norman said, as he followed the Professor back into the sitting room.

'Wonderful,' the Professor said, as he and Norman sat in their respective seats. 'It was a very delicate operation, as I recall. Can you remember which tool was used to clean the soil covering the shield?' the Professor asked.

'A hand brush, with bristles made from the long-haired cat from the Serenity Mountains,' Norman said, without hesitation.

The Professor nodded and looked up at a painting of Mount Mukai above Norman's head.

'And while we had expected the weather to be cold, we hadn't anticipated the volume of rain that fell on the last day. Luckily we rescued the shield before it was ruined. Can you tell me how many inches of rain we recorded that day?' the Professor asked.

'Four,' said Norman, slightly bemused. 'Would you like me to read the parchment to you?'

'No need,' the Professor smiled. 'Just tell me what else you remember of the text,' he said.

Without looking at the parchment, Norman described what he had read. In fact he recited the entire text, verbatim.

'It must have been incredible seeing the shield for the first time,' concluded Norman.

'Indeed it was,' responded the Professor. 'But tell me, am I right in thinking you remembered every word of the text?'

Norman looked down at his knees.

'Yes,' he mumbled. 'The words just seem to stick in my head.' Norman looked up. 'Is that strange?'

'Strange? Goodness me, no. You have a rare and unique talent.' The Professor stood up. 'I don't suppose you happened to notice a notebook with several sketches of mountains somewhere in the depths of my office did you?' The Professor looked expectantly at Norman.

'I saw an open notebook under your desk. It had a diagram of what looked like a boat stuck up a hill, if that's any help?' replied Norman.

'That's the very one!' the Professor said, as he scuttled out of the room, traversed his office and got down on his hands and knees to retrieve the notebook.

The Professor then said something, which Norman understood as, 'I flounder'f myoudmee persistent ina-ob.'

Norman stood up, went to the doorway and watched as the Professor backed out from under the desk.

'Sorry, what was that?' Norman asked, as the Professor hauled himself up with the help of the desk.

'I asked if you would be interested in a job working as my assistant,' the Professor said.

'You want me, to work for you?' Norman asked, in disbelief.

'I can only offer you forty florins a week,' the Professor said, as he wiped away crumbs from the pages of the book.

Norman's head started to spin. Forty florins a week. A hundred and sixty florins a month. Norman wanted to sit down. His legs were growing weak with the thought of having so much money.

'I'd offer you more,' said the Professor, who was now studying the recovered notebook, 'but my budget won't allow it I'm afraid.'

'No!' Norman said, perhaps a little too sharply.

The Professor looked up with a slightly puzzled expression.

'Are you alright?'

'I'm sorry. I just mean, no, thank you, forty florins is ... is...' he wanted to say, more than enough, a small fortune, more money than anyone had ever paid him and more than he probably deserved. Finally he managed to say, 'Forty florins is very generous, thank you.'

A surge of relief and happiness welled up inside Norman, only to be immediately replaced by a wave of despair as Norman realised he wouldn't, after all, be offered the job once the Professor knew the truth. Norman took a deep breath.

'Are you sure you're alright?' the Professor repeated.

'There's something you ought to know,' Norman said. 'I didn't leave Dr Clastic's office willingly,' Norman paused. 'He fired me.'

The Professor nodded his head and said, 'Dr Clastic's loss is certainly my gain.' As an afterthought, and with a smile that was barely noticeable under the bushiness of the his beard, he added, 'Perhaps we should make it a rule not to have liquids near any documents or books.'

The Professor looked down at his notebook and asked Norman to close the door so that they could talk some more.

ROUCHE
Rouche of the Rouchefort vineyards, in the Beaux region...that Rouche.

Mount Dou was one of a small cluster of mountains that were part of a range in southern Cashen known as the Meeya Mounts. A mile or so from the foothills lay the fertile plains of the Beaux province. Here, hot summers and mild winters created the ideal environment for grape growing and many of the country's finest wines were produced in this region.

The River Sterm snaked through Beaux, past many towns and villages including the town of Rouche. Named after its original settlers, Rouche was home to the famous Rouchefort family, who were the proprietors of the famous Rouchefort vineyards. In the fields immediately surrounding the town, a pink grape called the Rouche Rose was grown. For many years there had been whisperings that the Rouche Rose vines were imbued with a touch of magic as the wine produced from this unique grape, a delicate, crisp rosé, was known to generate in the imbiber a feeling somewhat akin to the first flush of youth and young love. The Rouscheforts publicly denied any use of magic in their wine production but, despite this repudiation, the rumours persisted, thereby adding a touch of mystery and romance to the distinctive, and somewhat expensive, Rouchefort Rosé.

The Rouscheforts had been living in the region for so long, and were so successful, that the grape growing family had acquired, either through marriage or through straightforward purchase, much of the Beaux region.

Flight Lieutenant James Wand had of course heard of the Rouchefort family, and their wine, but this was his first mission in the area. On his way from Mount Dou to Rouche, James had flown past seemingly never-ending rows of vines, some of which were still visible from the window in the room he had taken at the Grape and Goblet hostelry.

In accordance with General Macjooste's order, James had contacted Colonel Algernon Rouchefort, who was the current head of the wine-making dynasty and a former LUSU agent.

Rather than use the Grape and Goblet's wax seal on his message to the Colonel, James had used the standard LUSU issue seal: a small, brass stamp on which the insignia of two wings and a wand were etched. LUSU agents were expected to carry these innocuous-looking pieces of equipment on all solo missions, not just because the insignia acted as a means of identification but also because the unobtrusive object doubled as a vial which contained a soupçon of potent liquid tranquilliser. It was, on occasion, deemed more politic to immobilise an opponent with a blow dart dipped in sleeping formula than to kill him or her.

James had barely made himself presentable when the Colonel's carriage arrived outside the hostelry, along with a message inviting the Flight Lieutenant to a late lunch at Rouchefort Villa. As James buttoned his jacket his head started to go fuzzy. It was an incoming message from Captain Meejum. James sat on the floor, crossed his legs and closed his eyes.

LUSU's long-distance telepathic communication system was very specialised and required considerable concentration from both the sender and receiver. It had taken many years to develop the system. Only the most intelligent and lateral-thinking agents had been considered suitable for training. The Thought Communication System or, as it was inevitably shortened to, TCS, had proved to be a most useful tool, for both the agent in the field and for General Macjooste.

'Wand receiving,' he thought-said.

'LUSU Base, receiving you Wand. Have you made contact with Colonel Rouchefort?' thought-asked Captain Meejum.

'I'm on my way to lunch with him now. I'll contact you

as soon as I get back to my room,' thought-replied James.

'Can't wait that long. We need to know who owns that mountain. Let me know as soon as you have a name,' Meejum thought-answered.

'Understood. Have to go. There's a carriage waiting for me.'

'Do you need an extra pair of wings?' asked Meejum.

'Let's see what Rouchefort has to say first. Signing off now. Will contact you as soon as I know who owns the mountain,' thought-said James.

'Understood. Over and out.'

James took a moment to compose himself, then went downstairs to the open-top, horse-drawn buggy that was waiting to take him to the villa.

As the carriage set off along the cobbled street, James observed that Rouche seemed an affluent town. Most of the shops were now closed for lunch. Outside the barbers several elderly dwarves were sitting around a table playing cards while a moustachioed dwarf, in a white smock, stood in the doorway. James smiled and nodded at the dwarf. The barber said something inaudible to the card-playing dwarves who looked up and watched as James drove by.

At the end of the street the driver turned into a tree-lined avenue that ran alongside the river. The canopy from the trees protected James from the glare of the afternoon sun allowing him to take in his surroundings. To his left was the river Sterm on which was a horse-drawn barge, resplendent in the Rouchefort navy-blue and fuchsia livery, slowly making its way northwards towards Vinster-on-Sterm. On the right-hand side of the buggy was a high, white, stone wall. As the buggy drove on, James looked through several sets of wrought iron gates and noted large villas, complete with picturesque courtyards and swathes of foliage.

The buggy approached the last villa on the right where the wall was draped in jasmine. The driver slowed the horse then expertly turned and drove through the gates into a large, circular courtyard, complete with a working fountain, the centrepiece of which was a bunch of stone grapes. James barely had time to take in any detail before the carriage came to a halt in front of a set of terracotta, tiled steps where a liveried fairy was waiting to escort James to Colonel Rouchefort's study.

'Flight Lieutenant Wand,' said Colonel Rouchefort, with a smile as he rose from behind his desk.

'Colonel Rouchefort,' said James, as he walked across the room. 'Thank you for seeing me at such short notice. I do hope I haven't kept you waiting.'

The two shook hands and the Colonel gestured for James to be seated.

'Youngest daughter, eldest son and his family are here today, so we'd planned to eat slightly later. Please, have a seat. I recognised the seal on your message. It's been an age since I've seen the General. Good fairy, Macjooste. Always liked him. He and my eldest, Max, were at the Academy together.'

'Oh? I had no idea,' said James, who hoped that the conversation wouldn't turn into a series of nostalgic anecdotes involving Rouchefort's son and General Macjooste.

'Anyway,' said the Colonel, 'I'm not sure what could possibly bring you to Rouche. The most exciting thing to happen here recently was an incident involving my granddaughter's slingshot and my wife's favourite vase. The dust has almost settled but it was hardly a matter for LUSU.'

James smiled and asked, 'How many grandchildren do you have?'

'Four sons, three daughters and twelve grandchildren, one of whom is our newest addition, my youngest daughter's first child,' the Colonel beamed.

James shifted in his chair, not sure whether to be impressed or intimidated by the size of the Colonel's family.

'Do they all live in Rouche?' James asked.

'More or less. Max and his family live on the estate not far from here,' the Colonel said. 'But I'm sure the complexities and machinations of my squadron are of no interest to you. How can I be of assistance?'

'Do you know who, if anyone, owns Mount Dou?' asked James.

'Is that all?' asked the Colonel, mildly perplexed. 'It's that Blasting fellow. What's he done?'

'Theodore Blasting? Of Blasting Weapons?' asked James.

'That's the one,' replied the Colonel.

'Forgive me, Colonel, but I have to report this information to HQ immediately. Would you mind...'

'Quickest way is by imp-relay. We have our own team set up,' interrupted the Colonel.

'Actually, LUSU uses TCS now, I just need...'

'TCS?' interrupted Rouchefort, again.

'Telepathic Communication System,' said James.

'Is that what they're calling it?' The Colonel said. 'The Trips use it all the time. Useful little trick.'

'The Trips?' said James.

'The triplets. Max's wife, Celeste, produced three identical girls. They're a fearsome trio if you get on the wrong side of them. They can sulk for weeks. The silence is maddening but they can be enormously helpful in the vineyards,' said the Colonel.

'You mean they're telepathic?' asked James, incredulously.

James may not have known much about children but everyone knew that fairy triplets were incredibly rare. It was said of triplets that their magical force was extremely potent, in addition to which they were the only fairies who did not lose any life-force when their magic was used as a trio. In his twenty-five years with LUSU, James had never encountered triplets.

'Yes and they're better at keeping secrets than most agents,' the Colonel said, as he stood up. 'I shall give you a moment then we can have lunch and you can meet some of the troops. Perhaps afterwards, you can tell me what that Blasting's been up to.'

James nodded and thanked the Colonel as he left the study. Before settling down to make contact with Meejum, the thought occurred to James that there was far more to the Rouchefort's than winemaking and domestic minutiae.

TO THE HEART OF THE MATTER
And the mountain.

Two and a half years ago, a frisson of excitement had rippled through Rouche when the fairy bachelor and weapons' manufacturing tycoon, Theodore Blasting (of Blasting Weapons, by Royal Appointment to King Egbert IV), had bought Mount Dou. A rich bachelor of any description was always of interest to the local residents but Mr Blasting held a particularly fascinating allure. This was largely owing to his immense fortune, although his purchase and subsequent refurbishment of Mount Dou had also caused much speculation among the town's unattached fairies. It was unfortunate, therefore, that any fledgling thoughts of connubial bliss had to be abandoned when Blasting steadfastly and politely refused all invitations to interact with Rouche's social elite.

After an exhaustive search Blasting had come to Rouche having finally found a mountain that was not only security-spelled but would also suit his purposes - none of which included marriage. Mount Dou, a long-since defunct quartz mine, was an ideal property in which he could develop his latest project, a weapon that, if successful, would make him the wealthiest and, he believed, the most visionary weapons' maker on Eris.

After a considerable amount of renovation, the mountain now housed a sophisticated complex where the most destructive weapon of all time was being built. The name given to this weapon was Terminus, and Blasting hoped that the power of Terminus would far exceed the reputed power of the Torrimaya Axe - once his team could establish the correct, magical formulae. More importantly, on completion of the project, Blasting expected to become the most powerful being on the planet - a title he felt he rightly deserved.

While Flight Lieutenant Wand was having lunch at the Rouchefort Villa, Theodore Blasting was in his living quarters, somewhere in the depths of his mountain. He had recently finished a light meal of opportuna fish with salad, accompanied by a small goblet of Rouchefort Bojolly, a white wine with citrus undertones and the merest hint of vanilla.

Antique crossbows, sword-staffs, knives, spears, wands and axes of all shapes and sizes, decorated the room's walls. A replica of the Torrimaya Axe, made entirely from gold, was in a glass display case, on a shelf above a faux fireplace. The supposed facsimile had been commissioned by Blasting shortly after he'd purchased Mount Dou. Blasting frequently admired the finely crafted golden axe and had high hopes that it would soon replace his current good-luck charm, which sat next to the golden axe. Blasting's long-standing talisman was a small, antique, sculpture of the dwarvish God of War, Bez. This rotund, rather unattractive dwarf had cost Blasting a small fortune but he had, over the years, believed that the war god had contributed to his fortune. With the advent of the Ani-Bara tunnel, however, Blasting felt Bez had not been earning his keep.

Blasting was sitting with his personal aide and bodyguard, a fairy of extremely muscular build called Kinins. The pair was sorting through the pile of reports and documents that had been delivered by the afternoon courier.

'I've been away from the factory far too long,' Blasting muttered, as he finished reading the monthly report from his factory based in Vinster-on-Sterm.

'Marsham is a company dwarf. He has your best interests at heart,' Kinins said.

'Unlike King Egbert,' retorted Blasting, as he threw his napkin onto the plate in front of him. 'How many times, Kinins, have I implored our weak, ineffectual monarch to curb foreign imports?'

'Many, sir,' replied Kinins, in a tone that suggested he knew what was coming.

'I've tried to reason with him, really I have, but has he

listened? Does he care? Is he interested in domestic industry?'

'It seems he does not have your best interests at heart, sir,' said Kinins.

'Precisely! He seems not to have any of our manufacturers' interests at heart. And where does this lead?' Blasting looked at Kinins. 'Hmm?!'

'It paves...' Kinins started, knowing full-well that he would be interrupted.

'Exactly! It paves the way for cheap, foreign imports, designed and made by the gods alone know who! All that low-quality rubbish coming in. Weapons that wouldn't last a skirmish, never mind a battle. That damned tunnel! Egbert and his cronies have had this coming for years.'

For centuries the Blasting family had been well-known and respected, on both continents, for manufacturing weapons of elegance, precision and quality. With the construction of the Ani-Bara tunnel, however, many now felt Blasting's weapons were too pricey, not least because cheaper Nibaran imports were flooding the market.

Despite the political and economic advantages of the hundred and fifty mile underwater link, from Blasting's perspective the tunnel was responsible for generating nothing but a significant drop in his profit margin. He had lobbied the King for tighter controls on the weapons' market and had even asked the King to promote Cashen's own weapon manufacturing industry but Blasting had been unsuccessful in his attempts to maintain his superior position within the armaments industry.

Kinins opened another document.

'The daily report is here,' he said, placing the document at the top of the pile in front of Blasting.

Blasting picked up the parchment.

'Another order cancelled. It seems the Eskeesnos were unimpressed with our quote.' Blasting slowly scrunched the parchment, with one hand, until it was the size of an egg. 'They shall get exactly what they pay for,' Blasting said, in a low voice. 'Kinins, I think it's time to set phase two of my plan into motion.'

Blasting hurled the scrunched up parchment across the room.

Kinins nodded and stood up.

'Shall we see if Dr Tellurium is awake first?' suggested Kinins.

'Excellent idea,' said Blasting, brightening at the prospect. 'Is that agent still snooping around outside?'

'Operations reported that he left for town some time ago,' said Kinins.

'Shame, we could have tested the new poison dart slingshot.' Blasting rose from his chair. 'Keep tracking his movements.' Blasting put on his coat. 'Have you seen my wand?'

* * *

Dr Simon Tellurium had recently awoken from a drug-induced sleep. He felt heavy-limbed and was sitting on the edge of a double bed trying to clear his fuggy head. Despite the room's tasteful décor, the absence of windows was causing a rising sense of apprehension in the geochemist as he attempted to establish the answer to two important questions.

'Where on Eris am I? And what *is* that smell?' he muttered.

Tellurium vaguely recalled drinking two Furnace Dippers at Iffies the night before and briefly considered the possibility that he had in fact drunk more than he recollected. He could not, however, remember what had happened after he'd left the inn. Tellurium's hazy thoughts were interrupted when the room's only door unexpectedly opened and Theodore Blasting, entered.

'Ah, Dr Tellurium, you're awake,' said Blasting. 'Was it the smell? I do apologise. *Antiaris toxicaria* can have a slightly noxious odour while it's being prepared. It comes through the air ducts. I'm told this will be the final batch, so the stench should soon pass.'

Using every ounce of strength he could muster, Tellurium stood up.

'*Antiaris toxicaria*?! That's lethal!' said Tellurium.

'Only on the tip of a dart,' Blasting said.

In a matter of seconds Tellurium made a series of judgements about the individual who had walked into the room. The fairy looked like one of the caricature drawings Tellurium had seen being painted by unfulfilled, and often unemployed, artists in Halvar Piazza. Tellurium recognised the tailor-made suit from Grebes and Hawkes, and the shoes were obviously by Goochi, but the hair, he thought, what was going on with that hairstyle? It was straw-blonde and combed into an unnatural style which made it look like some kind of furry creature had curled up for a nap on top of the fairy's head.

'I'm sorry but, who are you?' Tellurium asked.

'Where are my manners?' Blasting smiled, but did not hold out his hand. 'My name is Theodore Blasting.'

'*The* Theodore Blasting?! Of Blasting Weapons? Manufacturer of the Z100 mini-crossbow?!' said Tellurium.

Blasting turned to face Kinins, who was standing just outside the door with his arms folded across his chest.

'You see, Kinins. I told you the Z100 would be perfect for the dwarf who has everything. Of course it would be useless as a long-range weapon but stick it in a small wooden crate with a bottle of cologne and it makes the perfect Torrimaya Day gift,' said Blasting, with a tinge of sarcasm.

'Um,' said Tellurium, looking over Blasting's shoulder in an effort to see past the well-built fairy, 'are we in your factory?'

'No, we're not in Vinster-on-Sterm anymore, Doctor,' said Blasting.

Tellurium was feeling increasingly uncomfortable as his legs struggled under the weight of his own body.

'Then where are we and why am I here?' he asked.

'You are here, Doctor, to help me solve a small conundrum with regard to a certain project,' said Blasting, ignoring the 'where' part of Tellurium's question.

'Couldn't you have just sent me a letter?' asked Tellurium, who, realising this might seem a little confrontational, added, 'I mean, it would have saved you all this trouble.'

Blasting walked towards Tellurium.

'When I say a small conundrum, what I mean is, I want to know why my team of scientists remain unable to imbue my weapon with magic,' Blasting paused, 'a weapon, Dr Tellurium, not too dissimilar I suspect, from that of Project Green Pastures and its Rataquian counterpart.'

Blasting, who was at least three feet taller than the geochemist, stood in front of Tellurium and smiled down at the now very nervous dwarf.

'How? What? I mean. I have no idea what you're talking about,' said Tellurium, unconvincingly.

'Come now, Dr Tellurium. Let us discuss this like civilised folk.'

Before sitting down in one of the two armchairs next to the bed, Blasting smiled, and carefully retrieved his wand from its holster, which was inside his coat. Tellurium stared at the wand which, he thought, looked terrifyingly expensive. Blasting sat down and rested the wand on his lap. After a brief urge to urinate, Tellurium managed to walk the few steps to the chair opposite his captor and sat down.

'Can I be frank?' said Blasting.

'You can be whoever you want to be,' said Tellurium, who continued to stare at the wand and had clearly misunderstood the question.

Blasting glared at Tellurium.

'Do you think this is a game, Doctor?' Blasting pointed the wand at Tellurium. 'Because Kinins will tell you, I do not like games.'

'No, I mean, I thought...I'm sorry.' Tellurium said, looking up at Blasting.

Blasting lowered the wand and frowned at Tellurium.

'You have information I want and should you wish to return home or, for that matter, retain your corporeal form then it is most definitely in your best interests to answer my questions.' Blasting crossed his legs.

Tellurium's mouth went dry. Simultaneously he wanted a pee, a drink of water, and a large brandy- preferably as far away from his current location as was possible.

'I can't tell you anything,' said Tellurium, truthfully.

'Shall we start with something simple? Have you found an infusion formula?'

Tellurium opened his mouth in one last effort to deny all knowledge of the weapon.

Instead he said, 'I-uh-nrm-mm ...'

Blasting looked down at the wand in his hand.

'I am a patient fairy, Dr Tellurium, so I shall give you one final chance.' Blasting looked up and stared, steely-eyed, at Tellurium. 'What can you tell me about the infusion formula and the magical processes involved?'

Tellurium's throat tightened.

'I... I...' rasped Tellurium.

'I don't have time for this,' Blasting flicked his wand. Tellurium shuddered. 'Shall we start again? Has the Project Green Pastures team discovered a means by which the weapon can be imbued with magic?' repeated Blasting.

Tellurium tried to keep his mouth closed. He tried *very* hard but he found it increasingly difficult, so much so that sweat started to trickle down the side of his face as he clenched his jaws shut. It was, however, a matter of seconds before his lips started to tingle and his jaw began to ache. He stared at Blasting, who looked on with mild amusement. Eventually the pain of resistance became too much and the words tumbled out.

'The outer shell has been constructed but we haven't

discovered the override-spell or any other enchantment for that matter.' As soon as he finished, Tellurium covered his mouth with both hands.

Blasting held up his wand and then slowly lowered it. With this gentle movement Tellurium's hands were forced onto his lap.

'Why not?' asked Blasting.

'I don't know,' said Tellurium, marginally embarrassed that he really didn't know the answer.

Blasting leaned forward in his chair and peered, through narrowed eyes, at the humiliated dwarf.

'You don't seem to know much do you? Do you even know what the next step is in solving the enchantment problem?' asked Blasting.

'More research,' sighed Tellurium, resigning himself to the truth-charm.

'Oh? What kind of research?' asked Blasting, genuinely surprised at Tellurium's answer.

'I… don't…Mrmrm' Tellurium muttered.

'Do not try to fight the truth-charm, Doctor. You cannot win,' Blasting said. 'What exactly were you going to research in an attempt to solve the enchantment problem?'

In a flurry of words, Tellurium told Blasting that he had recently spoken to an archaeologist who suggested that it was *vaguely* possible that the ancestors of the Torrimaya Trio, who had been involved with the original Torrimaya Axe, were somehow relevant. The consultant, Tellurium said, had a book that might shed some light on the matter.

Blasting beamed, victorious.

'You see,' he said. 'It's so much easier when you don't resist. Now, what's the name of this book?' Blasting asked.

Tellurium frowned, 'Myths and something, no Dwarves and Myths and something.' He paused. 'I can't remember,' Tellurium finally said.

'Then who is the consultant?' asked Blasting.

'Professor Bauxite,' replied the well and truly defeated

Tellurium.

'Kinins, I want that book,' said Blasting as he stood up, 'and if I can't have the book, I want this Professor Bauxite.' Blasting paused, 'Actually, I want both the book and the Professor.'

'Are you going to release the dwarf from the truth-charm?' Kinins asked.

Blasting stood in the doorway and looked at Tellurium.

'No,' Blasting said. 'Not yet.'

Blasting and his aide left the room.

As the door closed, Tellurium groaned and put his head in his hands. 'What have I done?!'

INTELLIGENCE JIGSAW
Putting the pieces together.

General Macjooste asked Talula to wait outside his office while a military carriage was sent to fetch Norman and the Professor from the University, both of whom arrived at HQ half an hour later.

'Will we get into trouble for this?' whispered Talula, to the Professor as he sat in the chair next to her.

'Oh my word, no,' the Professor replied. 'I just thought it might be best if you two spoke directly to the General about both the encounter outside Norman's home and the vanishing barge. Always best to hear this sort of thing from the dragon's mouth, as it were.'

'Do you think I should tell the General about my theory?' asked Talula.

The Professor peered at Talula over his spectacles and shook his head.

'No, I think perhaps it's best to stick to the facts for the moment,' he said, with a serious air.

The office door opened and General Macjooste greeted the Professor, who introduced Norman and Talula. The General instantly noted Norman's resemblance to Dr Tellurium but said nothing.

During his interview with Norman and Talula, no new information was revealed to the General. Towards the end, however, Norman and Talula both mentioned that the dwarf attackers had been wearing strong cologne. From this small, yet vital, detail the General deduced that the failed kidnap of Norman had indeed been carried out by the same Rataquian dwarves who had been followed by canine agent Doyle. Norman's attempted abduction, therefore, had most definitely been a case of mistaken identity - although, for reasons of national security, the General said nothing of Dr Tellurium's disappearance, nor did he mention that LUSU was already aware of the vanishing barge.

'You've both been a great help,' the General said, as he

stood up to see the pair out. 'I'll have someone look into this high-level use of magic immediately.' The General opened the office door. 'Take care, Mr Shale, and should either of you witness any other unusual activities please come to the main gate and ask to see me. I shall make sure you're brought straight to my office.'

No sooner had the General said goodbye to Norman and Talula, then Captain Meejum arrived with yet another update. She reported that the owner of Mount Dou was Theodore Blasting and that the tycoon had been staying at his mountain residence for the past several months. The General was surprised by this revelation and was disturbed that all wands pointed to the arms' manufacturer as the one responsible for the abduction of both Dr Tellurium and Dr Vincenzo.

'Thank you Captain. Keep me posted,' said the General.

'Yes, sir,' said Captain Meejum, who saluted and left.

Captain Florina poked her head around the office door.

'Blasting's been lobbying the King for years,' muttered the General. 'Ever since the tunnel opened.'

'Are you alright, sir?' said Florina, as she stepped in and closed the door behind her.

'Theodore Blasting is our culprit,' said the General.

'Ah,' said Florina.

'He's been blethering on about cheap weaponry being imported from the Nibaran continent for years. Pestering the King to promote the sale of Cashenian weapons to our allies,' said the General, tossing a file into his in-tray.

'But everyone knows His Highness is an advocate of peace,' said Florina.

'Aye, and the King only gave the go-ahead for Project Green Pastures on the proviso that such a weapon should only act as a deterrent.' The General sighed. 'I never thought Blasting would go this far to increase his profits.'

'But how could he possibly know about the project?' asked the Captain.

'How indeed?' said the General, as he tidied some papers on his desk. '... Unless ...'

The General stopped what he was doing, looked up and fixed a stare at the elf. Florina recognised the look and knew that the General was not directing his gaze at her but was instead using her as focal point for his thoughts.

'Unless?' she said, after a moment or two.

'Unless he's paying folk from both projects to feed him information,' the General finally said.

The Captain looked shocked at the suggestion.

'You mean a mole?' she said.

'Mole or moles. I dinnae see how else Blasting could have known to take both Tellurium and Vincenzo.'

'But who? Everyone was thoroughly vetted everyone before they joined the project.'

'Aye, and the Rataquians would have done the same.' The General picked up Captain Meejum's written report and opened the front cover. 'Blasting's getting his information from someone though, which puts us all in a tight spot.' He closed the report, and handed it to Florina. 'In the meantime I want Tellurium and Vincenzo back here before things escalate. Contact Wing Commander Adler. Ask him to ready a rescue team and tell him to come here within the hour for a briefing.'

'Yes, sir,' replied Florina, taking the file. 'Shall I produce copies of Meejum's reports for the Wing Commander?'

The General nodded that she should.

'And have an agent sent to Blasting's factory. I want to know if there's been an increase in his sales,' the General added.

'Right,' said Florina. 'Perhaps an impromptu Health and Safety inspection?'

'Excellent idea. And I think we should set up surveillance for all personnel on the project,' said the General.

'*All* personnel?' asked Florina.

The General focused on his assistant once more.

'I'll make a list,' he said. 'For now send some canine agents to Dr Foxglove's residence and to the senior engineers and thaumurtologists on the project.'

'Yes, sir,' said Florina.

'And get me the files on all project personnel,' said the General.

'I'll get right on it, sir,' said Florina. 'Anything else?' she asked.

'I'd better speak to Professor Bauxite. I've kept him waiting long enough,' said the General, as he followed Florina to the door.

HISTORY
And its real-world application.

Professor Bauxite, who was reading a dog-eared copy of *Weapons Review: The Crossbow Edition*, looked up and smiled at the General as he came out of his office.

'Professor,' said the General, holding out his hand. 'My apologies for keeping you waiting.'

'Not at all, General,' said the Professor, as he stood up and shook the General's hand.

'Do come in,' said the General.

The General closed the office door and gestured for the Professor to take a seat.

'What do you think of young Norman?' asked the Professor.

'I can see that it'd be easy to mistake Norman for Tellurium - at night,' said the General, rearranging his wings as he sat in his chair.

'Quite so,' said the Professor, with a nod of confirmation. 'Their personalities, of course, are quite different. Norman's not nearly as,' the Professor paused, '*self-confident*, as our Dr Tellurium,' he said, peering over his glasses at the General while at the same time raising his eyebrows.

'Aye, Dr Tellurium's certainly no' shy,' the General smiled.

'Norman, on the other hand, is very bright and quite charming in his own way. In fact I took him on as my assistant this morning.'

'Really?'

'Yes. I think he has great potential. Sharp as a butcher's knife when it comes to the written word and keen too. Before he left he asked if he could go to my office and make a start on sorting some things.' The Professor looked up at the Wand of Office on the wall above the General's head. 'I don't suppose he can do too much damage,' he said.

'I'm sure he'll be fine, Professor. He has a fine

memory, which will prove useful in your line of work.'

'Speaking of memory, I had a brief chat with Dr Tellurium yesterday. I'm sorry I didn't mention it earlier but I'm afraid *my* memory isn't quite what it used to be.'

'Was it to do with the project?' asked the General.

The Professor nodded.

'It was about the magical formula for the weapon,' said the Professor.

'You told Dr Tellurium you had a formula?' said the General, with an air of concern.

'Goodness me, no. I simply told him I had a theory. I only briefly touched on it because he was on his way home for the evening. I suggested that he stop by my office this morning to discuss things in more depth but, I suspect you're going to tell me that he has been *unavoidably detained*,' said the Professor, looking at the General with furrowed brows.

'Aye, well, you are indeed correct and I'd appreciate it if you'd keep Dr Tellurium's disappearance to yourself for now,' the General said.

'Oh, dear. Yes of course. Mum's the word,' the Professor said, with a nod.

'So, tell me, what exactly is this theory of yours?' asked the General.

'Well, I was glancing through Dr Tellurium's thesis again and, a book entitled *The Myths and Legends of Eris's Dwarves and Fairies, by J.R. Hornblende*, came to mind.'

'Oh?' said the General.

'It's a very old book, one that isn't widely known within contemporary academic circles, but Hornblende's take on some of Eris's legends have often proven useful when I've been looking for a different perspective on the past.'

'Do go on,' said the General.

'As I recall, Hornblende's interpretation of the legend was that the magical power associated with the Torrimaya

Axe was directly linked to the Torrimaya Trio.'

'The Torrimaya Trio?' The General looked intrigued.

'Hmm,' mused the Professor. 'Of course we've all heard of Halvar the Just who imbued the Torrimaya Axe with magic but, as a consequence of the limited documentation we have regarding the battle of the Valley of the Green Pastures, all we can say with any certainty is that Halvar's senior dwarf forgemaster would have been commissioned to design and manufacture the axe. We can also assume that it was a pixie who placed the axe on the valley floor and recited the detonation incantation because this was common practice at that time,' said the Professor. 'Unfortunately no names have ever been attributed to these two members of the trio,' he concluded.

'And how might this trio relate to the problem of finding the magical formula for our weapon?' asked the General.

'Well, Hornblende proposed that the magic of the axe could *only* be triggered when the Torrimaya Trio, or the descendants thereof, were somewhere in the vicinity of the weapon.'

'And how exactly would that work?' asked the General.

'It's all to do with Ironstyne and Dar Wyn's theory of ancient relatives and magical detonation,' said the Professor.

'I'm sorry?'

'The theory of ancient relatives and magical detonation,' repeated the Professor. 'It's a pre-Wand Wars theory whereby, Explosive Energy, equals, masses of charms, squared or, as it was sometimes referred to, $EE=mc^2$,' said the Professor.

'Right,' said the General, who, despite the repetition, was none the wiser. 'I've never heard of this theory.'

'Indeed, why would you? The inability to fuse magic into any weapon larger than a small slingshot means this ancient theory has long since been redundant.'

The General looked across his desk at the Professor in

anticipation of further explanation. The Professor scratched his beard and gazed up at the Wand of Office.

'Ahem,' the General coughed politely.

'You see,' the Professor finally said, 'Using $EE=mc^2$ would mean that one could, potentially, create a devastating weapon such as the Torrimaya Axe, by squaring, for example, a mere handful of explosive and detonation charms.'

'Why not use spells?' asked the General.

'No need to take the risk. The units of magic, or *uom*, in a charm are comparatively small against a spell, once the charms are *squared* the explosive power can become extremely potent, arguably more intense than a spell.'

The General looked across his desk at the Professor, who pulled out a notebook from his inside jacket pocket and flicked through the pages.

'You're telling me that explosive charms can be more potent than, say, a fire spell?' asked the General.

'Theoretically, yes,' said the Professor, glancing at his notes before looking up at the General. 'Let me put it this way. A fire spell is, if I remember rightly, one hundred *uom*, whereas a simple explosive charm is twenty-five *uom*. Using the formula $EE=mc^2$ means that one explosive charm can be squared, hundreds, possibly thousands of times, in order to produce a blast far more powerful than a fire spell, which is, of course, what is reported to have happened at the battle of Valley of the Green Pastures when the Torrimaya Axe was detonated.'

'I see,' said the General, whose wings twitched, ever so slightly at this theoretical prospect.

'In addition to this, if I've remembered the theory correctly,' the Professor continued, 'the power of the weapon will intensify over time if the fairy infusing the weapon with his or her magic has also included a continuation charm.'

'You mean a magical weapon of mass destruction is like a good brandy that improves with age?'

'I hadn't thought of it in those terms but that's as good an analogy as any, in so far as, ancient magic grows in strength over time. Of course anyone can drink an old brandy but I believe only nominated individuals will be able to access the magic of an object or, in this instance, a weapon, that has been imbued with magic using the $EE=mc^2$ formula combined with a a continuation charm.'

'This is incredible,' said the General, who really was struggling to believe what he was hearing.

'Of course it would make complete sense that the ancestors, and only the ancestors, of the original trio would be able to detonate the explosive magic of the Torrimaya Axe. Equally, it's entirely plausible that Halvar would have created a magical fail-safe by using an infusion-prevention charm which could have been spread across the planet when the axe was detonated.'

'Let me see if I've understood this. You're telling me that the reason we can't imbue magic into our own weapon is because Halvar the Just used hundreds, possibly thousands of charms, to create a devastating weapon of mass destruction, then he used a continuation charm that allowed only specific individuals to access this explosive magic, and, just for good measure, he also used an infusion-prevention charm to make sure no one else on the planet could recreate another super-weapon?'

'It's certainly the best-fit theory to our current conundrum,' the Professor nodded.

The pair sat in silence while the General tried to process the information.

'This theory of yours is quite remarkable,' the General finally said.

'But without any real evidence the only way we might be able to prove it is to gather together the ancestors of the Torrimaya Trio,' said the Professor.

'Would this even be possible given that we have no names to work with?'

'I'll grant you it would be a challenging task but I think

it's definitely an avenue to explore. Of course, if we had the Torrimaya Axe I might first suggest trying to unbind Halvar's ancient magic. That said, we have no way of knowing how many charms Halvar infused into the axe. As you said, there could be hundreds, or possibly thousands of charms and, as every fairy knows, trying to unbind a slew of charms is nigh-on impossible, especially when one doesn't know the precise formula.'

'You are, without doubt, the only dwarf I've met who is so well-versed in magic.'

'Thank you,' said the Professor, oblivious to the possibility that this may not have been the compliment he had assumed it was.

The General inhaled deeply through his nose and then exhaled.

'There are quite a few 'what ifs' in your theory, Professor, most of them I dinnae want to consider at this stage of the project,' the General said.

'At this stage General, this is merely conjecture, and, as I mentioned to Dr Tellurium, my first suggestion would be to try and track down the descendants of the original trio, who may, if we're very lucky, provide the trigger to the ancient magic.'

'So Tellurium knows about the trio?'

'Yes, I'm afraid he does. I'm so sorry,' said the Professor.

'You weren't to know,' said the General. 'Did you mention the rest of your theory to him?'

'No, I didn't have time to discuss it in any depth, although I also mentioned the possibility of ancestral magic to Dr Foxglove. She said she wanted to know more but had to dash off,' said the Professor.

'But you haven't told her what you told me?' the General asked.

'No, I thought it best to discuss the finer points of the theory with you first.'

'Aye, well, I'd ask we keep this theory just between ourselves,' said the General.

'Of course but, do you think we should at least begin searching for the ancestors?' asked the Professor.

'How long would it take to trace the descendants?' asked the General.

'Hmm. If I gather together a crack team of PhD students I think I'll have some preliminary findings within the next couple of days. I've already considered how best to start the process.'

'Unfortunately time is not on our side, Professor. Do you really think you will be able to find the information we need at short notice?' asked the General.

'Ah, well, top secret projects can often be a great motivator for the up-and-coming dwarf, and some of my students are extremely competitive,' smiled the Professor. 'Despite Dr Tellurium's popularity with much of Assay's academe, there are always younger students trying to outshine their older peers.'

The General nodded.

'It's the same everywhere. And can your students be trusted to keep their research confidential?' asked the General.

'I assume you will be asking them to sign the KYMS01 security parchment?' said the Professor.

'Of course,' replied the General.

'Then there should be no problem with confidentiality.'

'And I'd like to take a look at this Hornblende's book, if you have it,' said the General.

'I wouldn't mind checking it again myself. I haven't seen it in a while. Perhaps if I set Norman onto the task he'll be able to find it for me.'

The General looked over the Professor's shoulder and was quiet for a moment.

'Is it possible that King Egbert is the descendant of Halvar?' he finally asked.

'It's a possibility, of course, but with so many

documents missing from this particular period in our history, there has never been any evidence to suggest this might be the case,' said the Professor.

'Presumably you'll need access to the royal archives,' the General said.

'I was going to ask if you might arrange this,' Professor Bauxite said. 'The royal library is quite extensive I believe.'

'I'll be meeting with the King shortly and will arrange for your immediate access.' The General stood up, as did the Professor. 'Thank you, Professor. I hope this gives us the edge we need.'

'I make no promises, General, but I shall round up my students and set them onto the task,' said the Professor.

* * *

No sooner had Captain Florina returned from escorting the Professor to the main gates, then the General stepped out of his office.

'Captain, I don't suppose you have any more wake-up formula do you?' asked the General, pointedly refusing to use the acronym.

'R&D sent a batch for the entire office,' replied the elf, as she took a vial from the drawer in her desk and handed it to her boss.

'Thank you,' said the General. 'Could I possibly take a few?' the General asked.

Florina looked at the General and seemed to struggle with the question.

'Lady Macjooste sent a message, sir,' Florina finally said. 'I'm to make sure you don't have too many stimulants, sir. She said you don't always look after yourself properly when you're on a mission and has asked me to…'

'Yes, yes, Captain,' the General said, 'but please don't forget who pays your wages.'

The young Captain looked worried and glanced at the open drawer.

'Um…' she said.

'Oh for … dinnae worry,' said the General. 'I'll ask you when I need another one.'

Florina responded with a look of relief.

'Yes, sir. Thank you, sir.'

NORMAN AND THE PARCHMENTS
A trip to the University's library.

The cloudless summer morning had drifted into a muggy afternoon by the time Talula and Norman left military HQ. Dense grey clouds loomed over Mount Mukai.

'He's been kidnapped,' whispered Talula, as they walked towards Halvar Piazza.

'Who? Dr Tellurium? How on Eris could you possibly know that? General Macjooste never said a word,' said Norman.

'I know but did you see his expression when we told him about the cologne?'

'What expression? He didn't even blink.'

'Precisely,' said Talula.

Norman rolled his eyes.

'You're in the wrong business,' he said.

'What do you mean?'

'You should be a spy,' Norman said.

Talula considered this for a moment, then looked at Norman.

'Do you think they have many female spies in the military?'

'I have no idea but I'm going back to the Professor's office to start tidying up.'

'Thank the gods for that!'

'Sorry?' said Norman, momentarily offended.

'I didn't mean that you're leaving. It's just hard work walking at a snail's pace that's all,' Talula said, by way of an apology.

'Oh,' said Norman.

'It's not your fault. Anyway, I should be studying for my AVC test.'

'Of course,' said Norman, trying to pick up his pace after Talula's comment about snails.

By the time the pair had arrived at Halvar Piazza, Norman was sweating profusely and Talula was frustrated at having to walk so slowly.

'Good luck trying to sort out the Professor's office,' said Talula.

'Thanks, and I still owe you that drink, so shall I meet you at Iffies later? You never know, we might even see Dr Tellurium there.'

Talula stopped in her tracks.

'You must be joking!' she said.

'What? We might. Oooh look, that's the number eight. Must dash. See you later,' said Norman, as he hurried across the square to catch the horse-bus.

* * *

On his arrival at Professor Bauxite's office Norman unlocked the door, stood in the doorway, and took stock of the colossal mess. Norman decided that his first job would be to devise some kind of workable system. The books, he thought, would be easy to organise but first he'd need to free up some space. He put his satchel in the wheelbarrow full of boots by the door and started rearranging the columns of books on the floor into subject headings.

Norman soon discovered that there was a substantial quantity of library books, most of which were long overdue. As the returns pile grew it became apparent that more than one trip would be needed to take them all back.

Norman looked around the office and spotted the wheelbarrow.

'Unless…' Norman began to remove the boots and load the wheelbarrow.

* * *

Norman balanced the last possible book on the heap, put his satchel strap across his shoulder, and looked around the room to survey his handiwork. He had managed to create a small, but discernible, path to the sitting room.

'It's a start,' he whispered.

Norman shunted the wheelbarrow into the corridor, locked the office door, grabbed the handles of the wheelbarrow, and lumbered off. Oblivious to the stares of both staff and students Norman carefully pushed the wheelbarrow, with its squeaky wheel and mountainous cargo, along the corridors. As he trekked through the tunnels, slowing at the corners in an effort not to drop anything from the load, Norman thought about his fortuitous new job and the responsibilities it involved.

The library run was one of the duties Professor Bauxite had assigned Norman. Others may have viewed this as a menial job but for Norman the task was akin to winning the most coveted prize in dwarfdom, *The Golden Cup of Bez*, which was given to the dwarf who could split a hair with his axe, where the hair was affixed to a pole fifty yards away.

Despite his role as Dr Clastic's assistant, Norman had not had the opportunity to visit the library before and decided to use his first visit to kill two newts with one conker. Once he had handed over all the books, he thought, he could then explore, and begin to familiarise himself with the library's layout.

Norman smiled and thanked the pixie and the dwarf students who held open the library's main doors. Unsure of where to go, Norman glanced around the entrance until he saw an overhead sign that read *Staff Returns*. He took the squeaky-wheeled barrow across the stone floor, towards the librarian behind the counter. The middle-aged dwarf stared at the quantity of books presented to him.

'Where did all these come from?' asked the librarian, as he stood up and peered over the counter.

'Professor Bauxite sends his apologies for the overdue loans,' Norman said, ignoring the terseness in the librarian's tone. 'He's only just hired an assistant.'

The librarian looked from the books to Norman.

'Which would be you, I assume,' he said, in a somewhat patronising tone before sitting down again.

'I'll make sure the Professor returns everything on time in future,' said Norman, as he placed the topmost book from the pile onto the counter.

The dwarf librarian opened *Digs in Tropical Climes, by Augustus Furtwangler.*

'This is so overdue I doubt you were born when it was issued.'

As Norman unloaded the wheelbarrow the librarian muttered a variety of sarcastic comments, all of which Norman ignored.

'What time do you close?' asked Norman, as he put the last book on the counter.

The dwarf looked across the pile of books.

'Eight o'clock,' he said, and pointed his pencil at the wheelbarrow. 'You can't leave that thing in here. It's a health and safety hazard,' he said, with an officious air.

'Thank you. I was just going to move it,' said Norman.

Norman wheeled the barrow out of the library, parked it in a nearby alcove and went back through the main doors, into the main hall. This was the highest room on campus and extended at least a hundred feet into Mount Mukai. The library was famous for its innovative design and, as Norman looked up to the ceiling, he was amazed to see, inserted through the rock, solid tubes of glass which created a polka-dot effect in the high ceiling and afforded a surprising amount of natural light.

Lighting elsewhere in the library, and around the University campus, was provided by the recently installed state-of-the-art Finnician glow worm lamps. The *Lampyris Narcissus* was a breed of glow worm found only in the Finnice Tropics, in the country of Toorquet. Unlike the common variety of glow worm, whereby the female's tails light up in order to attract a mate, the tails of the male Finnician glow worm would glow whenever they detected motion. They glowed bright white and the light they produced could last for several hours. The male *Lampyris Narcissi* were, in essence, show offs and wanted to be admired by everyone, irrespective of species.

Norman looked around at the library's expanse of wall-mounted shelves, which were divided into arched sections and separated by columns with the obligatory ornamental scrolly bits at the top. There was a multitude of free-standing bookcases taking up most of the ground floor and directly in front of him was a section that accommodated long, wooden study tables. Behind the tables was a central staircase leading up to a mezzanine, home to even more shelves, heaving with books and parchments. This, Norman thought, was paradise.

Norman heard the library door open and, as he turned to see who had come in, he noticed a map on the wall near the entrance. He went over to look at the floor plan and spotted a small scroll that had been drawn at the bottom of the plan. Within the scroll, the words *You Are Here* were written in a bold print. Norman scrutinised the locations of the various sections and thought the Ancient Parchments section (formerly the main library) would be an interesting destination for his first visit.

The overhanging signs took Norman through the geology, mining and engineering sections, where he scanned the titles of books as he passed by. He marvelled at the amount of knowledge contained within the reams of pages. The soles of his boots tip-tapped on the floor as he walked among the maze of shelves. He was struck by the peace and tranquility, which was broken periodically by the sound of riffling pages, a cough, or a stifled sneeze. Norman briefly envied those who had been chosen to study in such incredible surroundings.

He strolled through the geochemistry, astronomy and mathematical sections, until he reached the area labelled, *Myths and Legends*. He looked up, in search of a sign that would point him in the right direction, but saw nothing. He carried on, in the hope he was heading the right way, until he arrived at a small, arched entrance, over which a plaque said *Ancient Parchments*. On the wall to his left was a sign asking its reader: *Have You Registered Your Visit To This Section With The Librarian?* And below this was yet another sign, that said: *Do Not Touch Parchments Without Gloves!*

Norman peered through the archway into a small reading room. He saw a mahogany table against the far wall, on which hung a large canvas depicting a gruesome dwarvish battle. There were two comfortable-looking chairs either side of the table. In the wall to his left was a closed door through which, Norman assumed, was the Ancient Parchments section. Norman hesitated. He was a law-abiding dwarf. He had no real reason to go to this section but it seemed unnecessary to walk all the way back in order to register his visit when all he wanted was a quick look.

Norman stepped through the archway. He stared at the door for a moment, glanced back the way he had come, then looked once more at the door. He took a deep breath, thought, *In for a yorit, in for a florin*, and opened the door. Norman's stomach knotted with fear and excitement. Had someone seen him? He stood in the doorway, half expecting to be caught but, when no one came to haul him back, he stepped into the room and closed the door behind him.

The room was cooler and more dimly lit than the main hall. The smell reminded Norman of Mr Libro's second-hand bookshop in the city's antiques' district, where Norman had always thought the books smelled of ancient adventures. The map at the main entrance had indicated this area was once the main library. There had been no further information to enlighten the reader as to when the changeover had been made although, judging by the gloomy interior and ancient décor, Norman assumed it must have been a long time ago.

As his eyes adjusted, Norman looked up at the overhead lighting.

'Magic glowbes. This place must be really old,' whispered Norman, noting the antique lights.

Straight ahead Norman could see banks of shelf units

that were divided by a long, central aisle. Directly in front of him was a table on which was an open ledger. While stepping closer to examine its contents, Norman took a clean handkerchief out of his trouser pocket and, armed with this improvised glove, he turned the pages and started to read.

The ledger was a record of the parchments and documents which, Norman assumed, were kept in this room. As he scrolled through the neat, hand-written rows, he realised that each unit had been assigned a number. He then discovered that unit ten held parchments relating to the Wand Wars.

'Oh,' Norman whispered. 'I'd love to see those.'

Norman scanned a few of the parchment titles: *9439-Wand Wars: Defence of the Western Borders; 9440-Wand Wars: Fall of the West Coast Settlements; 9441-Wand Wars: The Effects of Magic on Livestock.* He shoved the handkerchief into his pocket and headed off to find bookcase ten.

All the units displayed neatly-engraved brass plaques, with the relevant number facing the central aisle. Number ten was at the end of the room, attached to the far wall. Norman took his time examining the numbers assigned to the parchments on the shelves. He longed to open one of the neatly stacked, leather-wrapped, documents but knew he would have to both register with the librarian as well as find some gloves. When Norman finally found parchment number 9441 a rush of satisfaction coursed through him. There it was. He stared at the leather-bound scroll. His curiosity itched at the thought of discovering what had happened to the livestock caught in the cross-fire of a magical skirmish but Norman resisted the temptation and, as the initial excitement began to wane, he decided it was time to go.

Norman stood back from the unit and marvelled once more at the sight of all that ancient history. He smiled with satisfaction and was about to leave when he noticed a document on the floor, tucked under the lip of the bottom shelf.

'I'm pretty sure that shouldn't be there,' he muttered, as he stooped to retrieve the scroll, remembering to use his handkerchief.

The reference number was 9889. Norman looked at the numbers on the scrolls in front of him.

'Too low,' he said. 'You belong higher up.'

Norman gently placed the parchment back on the floor and went in search of the ladder he had seen leaning against another unit. Careful not to crash into anything, Norman positioned the ladder against the shelves in unit ten. He used the handkerchief to hold the parchment in one hand, then proceeded to climb up to what he hoped would be the right place. He scanned the numbers as he climbed but the denominations were still too low. Finally he reached the top shelf.

'9867, 9868.' Norman looked to his left. '9887,' he whispered. 'Just... over... here ...'

Norman stretched his arm to the right spot but couldn't quite reach. He leaned to his left, nearly lost his balance, so he pulled himself upright. He examined the shelf to see if there was anything he could hold onto but there was nothing other than the shelves of the unit.

Unwilling to climb down without having completed the task, Norman shuffled his left foot a fraction in the vague hope that this would extend his reach. As he did so, the ladder wobbled, Norman lost his footing altogether and dropped parchment 9889. He grabbed onto the top shelf with both hands, the ladder fell and Norman was left dangling by his fingertips with his legs wildly thrashing about in mid-air. As Norman scrambled to find a foothold, the bookcase started to make a loud grating noise. He thought the entire bookcase was about to fall but instead it started to move inwards, into the wall.

'Aarrgh!' Norman was losing his grip.

As his feet slipped on the tumbling parchments, the

shelves jolted to a standstill. Norman placed a foot on one of the shelves but the unit began to move again. This time it turned, as if on a turntable. Norman was sweating. His fingers were sliding off the edge.

'Noooooo!'

The bookshelf completed a half circle. The dim light faded as Norman and the parchments moved into darkness. The whole unit then moved back into the wall before coming to a grinding halt just as Norman's fingers slipped off the shelf. A light flickered on. Norman fell to the floor with a thump. A parchment fell on his head.

For a short while, Norman, lay on the ground and stared at the ceiling. He turned his head to see if there was any further threat to his personal safety. Once his heart had stopped pounding, and he was satisfied that he was not going to be attacked by a dragon, a hail of poison darts, or fall into a pit of spears, he stood up and dusted himself down.

Norman had been deposited into a room far smaller than the one from which he had been unceremoniously ejected. Whereas the other room had walls, shelves and looked like a library, this room appeared more like a cave. The walls were unpainted and the stone floor was rough and uneven. The moving bookshelf appeared to be its only entrance.

'Well, this room wasn't on the map,' Norman muttered.

Norman examined his surroundings. A circular, wooden, light fitting was suspended on three, short chains from the centre of the ceiling. Like the lights in the Ancient Parchments' section, the chandelier was magically powered.

The room was cool and dry but Norman could see no visible means of ventilation. The walls of the cave were stacked, floor to ceiling, with units containing thin, wooden boxes, all of which had little knobs on the front.

In the centre of the room was an unassuming wooden desk with a plain, wooden chair tucked neatly underneath.

A large, leather-bound book sat squarely in the middle, a bedraggled quill lay to one side of the book, and a dried-out ink well sat in one corner.

Norman produced the handkerchief from his pocket and stood behind the desk. Using the handkerchief, he gingerly opened the book and saw:

Assay University Librarye
Historical Parchments
Index

Norman closed the ledger and went to the stack of boxes to his left. He pulled the knob of a random box and a drawer slid open. Inside, he found three papyri wrapped in some type of material he didn't recognise.

'I should have gloves,' he said, staring at the scrolls, 'but if I'm really careful, I'm sure no one will notice if I just take a peak.'

Norman used his handkerchief to take out a single papyrus and carefully placed it on the small table. He rummaged in his satchel until he found a pencil, the non-carbon end of which he used to hold one end of the papyrus while he unrolled it using his handkerchief.

Norman began to read.

QUEEN PETRA RETURNS
The Rataquian ambassadorial residence is attacked.
Neither of these two facts are related.

In Vinster-on-Sterm, the oppressiveness of the afternoon had turned into a stifling evening. Thick, dark clouds covered the sky and at Trifolium Palace the staff were in the throes of closing the window shutters, as per the instructions of the head of housekeeping who insisted that her knees were never wrong when it came to predicting an impending storm.

It was almost nine o'clock and, in the King's office, General Macjooste was apprising the King of recent events. The meeting had only just started when Alfonse announced Queen Petra, who promptly marched into the room.

'Oh this heat is exhausting, and remind me to leave the children with you the next time I go away,' said the Queen, while unbuttoning her cape.

The King and the General stood to greet the Queen.

'Petra, I wasn't expecting you home so soon,' said the King.

'Oh, General, do forgive my rudeness. I'm not staying. I just wanted to let Egbert know that we are all home, safe and sound,' said the Queen, as she took off her cape and folded it over her arm.

The General gave a slight bow.

'Your Highness.'

The Queen came to a stop in front of her husband and they kissed twice, once on either cheek.

'Alexandra had a bouncing baby boy the day before yesterday and has taken to motherhood marvellously. She has plenty of help so I thought it best to get out of the way, especially because our daughters were starting to get a little, how shall we say, *fractious*.' The Queen threw her husband a brief but knowing look which she quickly transformed into a smile as she turned to face the General. 'Hamish, how are Maria and the girls?'

'Very well, thank you, Your Highness,' the General replied.

'We really must do lunch sometime soon,' said the Queen.

'I shall let Maria know when I see her, Your Highness' the General said.

'Which, judging by the lateness of the hour, will not be tonight,' the Queen said, with mock disapproval.

The General smiled in return but said nothing.

'How was your journey?' asked the King.

'Long and tiring,' replied the Queen. 'Oh you have Tico-Ticos. Alexandra was disappointed I hadn't brought any. I must send her some. Don't eat too many Egbert. Remember your waistline.'

'I may be a little while. I shall come looking for you when I'm free,' the King said.

'I shall leave you both to your discussion,' said the Queen. 'General, send my regards to Maria and the girls.' Petra kissed her husband again, discreetly shifted her dress away from her feet and walked towards the door. 'Alfonse, my husband is making you work far too late again. What will that friend of yours say? It's a wonder he hasn't packed his bags and moved out. Make sure you take him some Tico-Ticos by way of an apology.'

Alfonse bowed, followed the Queen out of the room, and closed the doors. The King and the General sat down.

'Do you think the Sterminians have heard about the kidnappings?' the General asked.

'King Marco keeps his ear to the ground. I wouldn't be surprised if whispers had reached the Sterminian court.' The King sighed. 'Which means that Petra will almost certainly have heard something - a more likely explanation for her premature return.'

The General smiled, 'Aye, Maria's the same. It upsets her that I don't tell her what's going on.'

'So you stay at the barracks,' King Egbert said.

'It seems the safest option,' the General said.

'One does what one must in order to keep a marriage from crumbling,' said the King, as he reached for his brandy. 'Now, where were we?'

The General informed King Egbert that an agent, posing as a Health and Safety inspector, had paid a visit to Blasting's factory but that nothing untoward had been discovered.

'I heard his sales had slumped in recent years,' the King said.

'According to our agent, there was every sign that business was flourishing. There were dozens of crates of battle-ready weapons waiting to be dispatched,' replied the General.

'Oh?' said the King. 'Did we discover the destination of these weapons?'

'Unfortunately not,' replied the General.

The King and the General discussed possible states or factions that could have ordered such large quantities of crossbows, throwing axes and myriad other weapons but drew no definitive conclusions.

'Even the trolls on the western borders have been quiet in recent months,' said the General.

The King nodded.

'I am, if nothing else, grateful that not all our merchants have responded to the growth in foreign trade in the same way as Blasting. Kidnapping the competition's staff is rather extreme, and extremist behaviour of any kind can be both unpredictable and dangerous.'

'Aye. If only we knew who Blasting was getting his information from,' added the General.

'Until we discover the identity of this traitor we must try to get ahead of the game.'

'I've dispatched a rescue team in an effort to avert at least one political crisis,' the General said. 'The sooner we get Dr Tellurium and Dr Vincenzo back, the happier I'll be. As for Blasting, with any luck the team will be able to arrest him and we can put all this behind us.'

'Have we heard anymore from our fairy on the ground?' asked the King.

'Flight Lieutenant Wand communicated that Colonel Rouchefort has agreed to our request for support and has offered the Rouchefort estate house as a temporary base of operations,' said the General.

'Excellent,' said the King.

'And Wand mentioned that the Roucheforts have a secret weapon of their own.'

'*Another* secret weapon?' said the King, visibly alarmed.

'No, nothing like that,' the General said. 'But the Roucheforts do have triplets in the family.'

'Triplets!' The King's eyes widened as he looked at the General.

The General nodded.

'Three daughters, Your Highness.'

'Good gods! How old are they?'

'Early adolescence,' replied the General.

The King raised an eyebrow, shook his head, and shifted in his chair.

'My sympathies go to their father,' he said, as he took a sip of brandy. 'You know Hamish, I don't think I've heard of triplets since childhood and even then I only recall the one story.'

'The Triplets of the Black Castle,' the General said.

The King smiled.

'And if any of the story is based on truth, then I'm glad the Roucheforts are on our side.' The King put his glass on the coffee table. 'The Colonel was a favourite of my father's you know, although I only ever met him a few times.'

'I went to the Academy with his eldest son, Max. He was a good soldier. We served together for two years and patrolled the western borders during a particularly fierce spate of troll fighting. Max did his tour and then a more *appealing* opportunity presented itself.'

'A female?' said the King.

'A particularly beautiful female and mother of the triplets,' the General said. 'Now Max helps with the family business.'

'Pity. We could do with a man who can run a business while raising *female*, adolescent triplets,' said the King.

The General agreed and politely resumed the subject at hand.

'As for the next stage of Green Pastures, the Professor has gathered a team of PhD students who are currently working with the royal librarian.'

'Remind me why we are searching for Halvar's descendant,' said the King.

'Professor Bauxite thinks that the ancestors of Halvar the Just, the dwarf forgemaster, and the pixie incanter, might hold the key to the trouble we've been having with the weapon's magic,' the General said.

'Ah, yes. A fascinating theory. Have they found anything yet?' the King asked.

'The Professor said there might be difficulties tracing Halvar's descendants because much of the documentation of the final battle is missing,' the General said.

'Let us hope something can be found in the palace library,' offered the King. 'And have we any idea how the rescue team is going to find its way into Mount Dou?'

'The security-spelled entrances might prove problematic but the Roucheforts might have some suggestions,' replied the General.

There was a single knock and an anxious-looking Alfonse entered.

'Your Highness, forgive the interruption but there has been an incident at Lord Esodo's residence in Fortnum Park Square,' said the King's secretary, his wings twitching.

'An incident?' asked the King.

Through the open doors the General saw a uniformed

pixie.

'An explosion, Your Highness,' said Alfonse.

The General jumped up from his chair and marched to the door, with the King hot on his heels. The soldier saluted.

'Report,' the General said to the uniformed pixie.

'Lord Esodo's residence was hit less than half an hour ago by unknown assailants. Two incendiary devices were thrown through a first floor window. A servant came to the Fortnum Park outpost and Sergeant Boe sent a crew to help with the fire but, by the time we a got there with the fire wagon, it had been put out.'

'So quickly?' the General asked.

'The Ambassador must've used magic to extinguish the fire, sir,' said the soldier, expectantly.

'Was anyone hurt?' asked the King, ignoring the report of the illegal use of magic.

'No, Your Highness, everyone escaped unharmed,' replied the soldier.

'Go back to the Ambassador's residence and tell your sergeant I'm on my way,' said the General.

'Yes, sir.' The pixie saluted and dashed off.

'I shall come with you. Dammit Hamish! Blasting has to be stopped before he kills someone!'

The General and the King hurriedly marched the length of the wide, high-ceilinged corridor. The King told Alfonse to ready a carriage, while the General barked orders at several sentries and told them to make sure that no one entered or left the palace.

By the time the King and the General had reached the grand staircase even Queen Petra had heard the commotion.

'Egbert? What on Eris is all the fuss about? I heard shouting,' the Queen said, as she descended the main staircase and followed her husband outside and down the steps.

'I'm afraid there's been an explosion at the Rataquian

ambassador's residence,' said the King.

'An explosion?' said the Queen, horrified. 'Is anyone hurt?' A carriage rolled up to the steps and the Queen lifted her dress away from her feet. 'I shall come with you.'

The King gently took his wife by the shoulders.

'Petra, my dear, no one was hurt and there really is nothing you can do. It will be much safer if you stay here...'

'Nonsense,' replied the Queen. 'You and Hamish will have those frighteningly serious faces. Constanza and the children will be terrified. I shall bring them here, where it's safe.'

'Petra, please. This is fast becoming a diplomatic nightmare which must be handled with kid gloves. Stay here with Alfonse and I shall tell you what has been going on over a glass of brandy when this has been dealt with.'

The King kissed his wife on the forehead and stepped into the carriage. As the carriage pulled away, Petra hoiked up her dress and started to climb the steps.

'Alfonse, I'm going to get my cape. I want a carriage here by the time I return,' said Petra.

'But His Majesty said...' started Alfonse.

'Never mind what His Majesty said. This calls for a female touch. I can feel it in my wings. Now hurry. I don't want them causing too much damage before I arrive.'

JAMES WAND AND THE ROUCHEFORTS
Blasting stays one step ahead.

After lunch James had returned to his room at the Grape and Goblet to file a report with Captain Meejum. While he awaited further instruction from General Macjooste the Flight Lieutenant considered the events of that afternoon.

Lunch with the Roucheforts had been an interesting experience, not least because there had been a largely female contingent around the table. Apart from the Colonel and his wife, the party had included: the Colonel's youngest daughter Maisy, his son Max, and Max's wife Celeste. Max and Celeste's triplet daughters - otherwise known as the Trips - were introduced as Amber, Ruby and Jade. Coffee was served in the drawing room where the latest addition, Maisy's newborn babe, Ferdinand, had been brought down from the nursery for inspection.

'If he's like all the others,' the Colonel had said, 'then it won't be long before we'll need a temporary binding charm for the little sprite.'

The Trips had protested against this suggestion, insisting that no magic was necessary as they could look after their cousin and see that he didn't cause any trouble. At this point Ferdinand had hiccoughed and the action had produced a small bubble, which then floated above the baby's smiling face. His mother, Maisy, had quickly popped the bubble and everyone had turned an anxious face to James.

'Out of the mouths of babes,' James had said with a smile, much to the relief of those present.

James, the Colonel and Max had then retired to the Colonel's study where it transpired the ageing military fairy had been keeping tabs on Blasting and his staff since their arrival two and a half years ago. The Colonel had, he insisted, not exactly been spying on Mr Blasting but was trying to keep his mind active by using some of his former LUSU skills. Max had laughed and pointed to a lockable cabinet which was filled with information on most members of the Rouche community.

'Just a hobby,' the Colonel had said, while searching for the notes he kept on Blasting. 'Stops me from getting under everybody's wings at the vineyard.'

The Colonel told James that, apart from the initial flurry of activity when Blasting had first moved in and refurbished the property, the only other observation that he and other Rouche residents had noticed was the amount of staff Blasting seemed to keep - a surprisingly large number given his marital status. Max added that earlier in the week, while checking the vines in the field nearest to the foothills, he had noticed two Rataquian fairies, with their distinctive purple wings, flying towards the base of Mount Dou.

'I'd be careful,' the Colonel had said, as James was leaving. 'I wouldn't be surprised if Blasting has a surveillance system up there. Tommo, our local goatherd, says every time he steps onto Mount Dou a patrol comes out of nowhere just to say hello. Every time, he says. It doesn't matter which direction Tommo's coming from, there's always someone watching.'

* * *

The Flight Lieutenant was cleaning his wand when he was contacted by Captain Meejum and given further orders, which sent him hurrying back to Rouchefort Villa.

The Colonel's eyes had lit up when James relayed General Macjooste's request for support in setting up a base of operations for the rescue team that was flying in from Vinster. A courier was immediately sent asking Max to prepare for the arrival of several guests at the vineyard's estate house - which was a more private location and much closer to Mount Dou.

It was now past nine o'clock at night and the rescue team was due to arrive within the hour. James was sitting in an enclosed carriage, outside Rouchefort Villa, waiting for the Colonel to take him to the estate house. A creamy full moon sat low in the sky and the sweet scent of the jasmine perfumed the warm, evening air. James listened to the chirping of cigaradas and his mind turned to the usefulness of the small creatures.

The distinctive sound of the *Grylloidea Cigarada* was also accompanied by small puffs of smoke generated by the insects' wing-rubbing action. At some point in weapons' manufacturing history, it had been discovered that placing a hundred cigaradas in a perforated box and then shaking it offered a very effective smoke screen in a conflict situation. James briefly wondered whether the team had packed any for the mission.

The Colonel emerged from his home with a servant, who was carrying a small wooden chest. The Colonel gave instructions to fasten the item securely and then stepped into the carriage.

'Forgive the delay,' said the Colonel, as he sat opposite James.

The Colonel tapped the roof of the carriage with his silver-topped cane and they set off into the darkness.

'Wing Commander Adler and the team have been briefed but I don't know the area well. I thought I might go for a quick scout before they land,' said James.

'No need. I've brought maps and I'm going to ask Max if the girls can give us a hand.'

'You mean the Trips? With all due respect, Colonel, we can't involve civilians, especially children.'

'I wouldn't dream of involving the girls in the mission,' said the Colonel, overlooking the fact that he too was a civilian. 'But they know Mount Dou better than anyone. Of course if Max says no, then you'll have to make do with a map.'

'The Trips know Mount Dou? How is it they haven't been caught by Blasting's security?' asked James.

The Colonel started to chuckle.

'Dear boy. Do you know anything about triplets?' he asked.

'I know they're rare,' replied James.

'Rare, yes, but do you know what three identical fairies can do?'

'I'm afraid, Colonel, you have the advantage. We briefly touched on the subject of triplets at the Academy, although mostly in relation to their rarity,' said James.

'Sounds about right. I didn't encounter triplets at any point during my sixty years with LUSU.'

'Then I shall consider myself fortunate to have encountered them so early in my career,' said James, with a smile.

The Colonel took on a more serious air.

'Triplets come along maybe once in three or four generations, not per family but per country.' The Colonel looked at James. 'Flight Lieutenant, would you agree that the power of a senior military fairy depends on both natural and environmental factors?'

'Um... I...erm...' muttered James, who was reluctant to comment on this outdated view of military aptitude.

'Well, I firmly believe that good breeding, good training and an aptitude for spell-casting all go a long way towards producing a skilled, military fairy,' said the Colonel. The carriage hit a rut and shook the Colonel and James in their seats. 'But with triplets, it's a completely different box of imps.'

'How so?' asked James, disregarding the equally inappropriate reference to Eris's smallest, magical race.

'Triplets are born with magical abilities that most top-grade spellcasters only ever dream of achieving. The girls can already outstrip me and their father, not that we ever tell them that, and they would be able to circumvent many of our traditional spells or charms. More incredible still, when triplets cast spells as a unit they do not lose their life-force.'

'You mean...'

'They are a force to be reckoned with and are quite capable of looking after themselves,' said the Colonel.

'But they're still young. Max is fiercely protective, as am I, and much of the Trips' education is dedicated to learning how to restrain and control their magic.'

'But it's obviously difficult keeping your eye on them all the time. Doesn't it worry you knowing that they roam Mount Dou?' asked James.

'Young fairies must have some freedom and they have to learn that the world can be a dangerous place. The girls know the rules and they understand the consequences. I'm confident that if they thought they were in any real danger they would find an *appropriate* way to handle the situation.'

'The Trips might know a lot about Mount Dou's terrain but I still feel uncomfortable about involving them in any part of the mission.'

'They might not be able to help us yet. Max may not give his permission,' said the Colonel.

'Understandably,' said James who, despite his genuine reluctance to include the young fairies in any way, briefly considered what an asset to LUSU the triplets could be.

* * *

'Kinins,' said Theodore Blasting, 'the day is almost over and I'm not sure whether to call it a good day or a bad day. What say you on the matter?'

Blasting and Kinins were walking through a brightly lit tunnel towards the security operations room.

'Perhaps it is neither one nor the other, sir,' replied Kinins.

'Oh? How so?' Blasting asked.

'We may have been unsuccessful in extracting much information from Dr Tellurium...'

'Or *any* from Dr Vincenzo,' interrupted Blasting. 'We should have known he would have spell-protected himself.'

'Or, as you say, any information from Dr Vincenzo but, thanks to Dr Tellurium we do have a new lead for the weapon, and,' Kinins took his fob-watch out of his waist coat pocket. 'If phase two went according to plan, the Ambassador's residence should currently be ablaze.'

'Finally some good news,' said Blasting. 'When will that be confirmed?' asked Blasting.

'Soon,' replied Kinins.

Blasting and Kinins approached the double oak doors of the security operations room, either side of which stood two troll guards. As Blasting and Kinins drew closer, the trolls opened the doors.

'Kinins, if you were the head of the King's forces, what would be your next move?'

'I would attempt to rescue the scientists,' replied Kinins, unfalteringly, 'and I would want to know how much you know.'

'I agree, so perhaps it's time to set phase *three* of my little plan into motion,' said Blasting.

Blasting and Kinins walked through the open door into a spacious room, in the middle of which were ten desks in a semi-circular formation. Suspended above the desks were rectangular, crystal screens all of which contained images. Fairies were sitting in front of the screens monitoring Mount Dou, inside and out. Kinins had designed the state-of-the-art security system with the help of a former military fairy tracker, who firmly believed that a bowl of magically-imbued water was outmoded and offered a poor quality image for its operator.

In the middle of the semi-circle stood a green-winged fairy. He walked from one monitor to another. Every so often he checked the clock on the far wall and wrote something in the ledger he was carrying. The supervisor noticed Blasting and Kinins standing by the door and went to greet them.

'Good evening, Mr Blasting, sir. There hasn't been any activity outside, not even the goatherd,' the supervisor said.

'And what about the agent? Do we know where he is?' asked Blasting.

'I'm waiting for a report from the pixie I sent to the Rouchefort villa,' said the supervisor.

Blasting nodded and turned to face Kinins.

'The only good thing about the Roucheforts is their grapes,' said Blasting. 'I knew they couldn't be trusted.' Blasting inhaled deeply. 'Kinins, it seems a rescue plan is indeed underway and the Roucheforts are helping the King's agent.'

'We have some time yet,' said Kinins.

'Not much,' said Blasting. 'I want you to prepare for our departure first thing tomorrow morning. You know what to do.'

'And the two scientists?' asked Kinins.

Blasting consider this question for a moment.

'It might be considered churlish not to leave the King's forces someone to rescue, and yet...' Blasting paused, 'they are of no further use, so perhaps you could see to them before we leave.'

Kinins nodded.

'I shall deal with them tomorrow morning, sir,' said Kinins.

INTELLIGENCE GATHERING
The Red Wings and three teenage fairies.

The drawing room at Max and Celeste's estate house had been hurriedly rearranged to accommodate a squadron of an elite unit of LUSU, the Red Wings. Wing Commander Adler and five heavily armed fairies, all of whom were dressed entirely in black, had arrived shortly after ten o'clock. Small badges, depicting a fairy with red wings in flight, could be seen on the lapels of their jackets. Their backpacks contained an impressive array of weapons, tools, gizmos and gadgets.

Flight Lieutenant Wand introduced Wing Commander Adler, Squadron Leader Dash and Flying Officers Silas, Ryan, Raza and Pitou, to Max and the Colonel. While the team partook of the refreshments laid out on one of the tables, the Colonel retrieved the maps from the wooden chest he'd brought with him and laid them out on a large table.

Before Max left the team alone to plan their mission, the Colonel discreetly asked if the Trips might assist. Max categorically refused to allow his daughters to become involved with the mission, a decision everyone had accepted with good grace. No one had been entirely comfortable with the idea and Adler had been appalled at the thought of the children being consulted.

James Wand, the Colonel, Adler and the rest of the team were now studying a map of Mount Dou looking for any potential nook or cranny that might serve as a point of entrance.

'The two spell-protected entrances are here, and here,' said the General as he pointed them out on the map.

'Which means we need to find and create our own entry point,' Adler said.

'Then we're better off higher up,' said Pitou. 'Here, look. If we go half way up we can find a thinner layer of rock and tunnel as we go.'

'The tunnelling-powder can probably penetrate up to

twelve feet so if there's an indentation in the mountain's surface we should be fine,' said James.

'Let me see the old quartz mine map again,' said Adler. 'Of course we don't know how much of the interior Blasting has altered but it looks like there's an indent here which...'

There was a noise. It sounded like a suppressed sneeze. All six of the armed fairies grabbed their wands from their holsters and assumed different positions. They pointed their magical weapons at the window and saw the merest breath of a movement from one of the closed curtains.

'Come out!' screamed Adler. 'Now! Slowly! Hands in the air!'

James dashed over to the window just as three identical fairies came out from behind the curtains. They held up their hands and looked pale with fright.

'Hold your fire!' James cried out.

The drawing room door burst open as Max rushed in to see what the shouting was about.

'What..? Girls!' said Max, horrified to see his daughters in the room.

'It was Amber's idea,' said Jade.

'Snitch...' whispered Amber.

'Quiet!' Max stormed over to his daughters.

'If you hadn't sneezed...' whispered Amber to Ruby.

'Silence! Out!' Max pointed towards the door. His face was puce with rage and his wings bristled with anger.

James glanced at Colonel Rouchefort, who was now standing by the doorway looking concerned. The girls filed out past their grandfather with their heads lowered. The last girl, Amber, mumbled something as she walked by the Colonel.

'Stop right there young lady,' said Max. 'What did you say?' The girl stopped but did not turn around or reply to her father's question. 'Amber Isabella Rouchefort, I asked you a question,' Max said, in a quiet but severe tone.

Amber slowly turned around and looked at her

grandfather, who nodded once to confirm she should answer her father's question. Amber glanced at the other fairies in the room before looking at her father.

'I said there's a third entrance,' she mumbled, her cheeks now flushed with embarrassment.

There followed the kind of speechlessness that often accompanies a revelation of such magnitude. All the fairies in the room stared at Amber, who had offered a gem of information at precisely the right time, or the wrong time, depending on one's perspective. The rage drained from Max and was instantly replaced with a look of disbelief. The Colonel glanced at his granddaughter and signalled for her to join her sisters in the hallway.

'Max, might I have a quiet word?' the Colonel said, as he followed Max out of the room.

James, Adler and the rest of the team put their wands back in their holsters and re-grouped around the table with all the maps.

'I hope this little family dispute doesn't stop us finding out where that entrance is,' Raza said under his breath.

* * *

The Colonel and Max closed the drawing room door and stood in the hallway with the triplets.

'You three go and find your mother and bring her to the study. Don't think this is over and believe me when I tell you I'm not just furious, I am deeply, deeply disappointed with your behaviour,' said Max.

'But Father...' said Amber.

'Go and find your mother,' said Max, holding up his hand to indicate that this part of the conversation had ended.

As the girls trooped off in search of their mother, Max walked into the sitting room, directly opposite the drawing room.

'I do my best. They know the rules.'

Max went to a drinks cabinet and poured himself an apple brandy.

'This is not your fault Max,' said the Colonel. 'They're children, they're curious and you know how excitable they can get when visitors come to the estate. Don't be too hard on yourself, or them for that matter.'

Max downed the brandy and poured another.

'It's alright for you. You don't have to discipline them. You have all the fun.'

'You're right, of course you are,' the Colonel said. 'Being a grandparent is far easier than being a parent. But don't forget I had just as much worry, if not more, when you and your brothers and sisters were growing up. Children are most definitely a handful.'

Max downed the second glass and turned to face his father.

'I can't even begin to think of a suitable punishment for those three,' Max said.

'I understand your anger, Max.' The Colonel continued, still attempting to placate his eldest son.

The Colonel went to the drinks cabinet and helped himself to a glass of Belleberry liqueur, a sweet digestif made from summer fruits and herbs.

'What am I to do with them?!'

'Perhaps under the circumstances we might consider this a learning experience for the Trips as well as an opportunity to provide Wing Commander Adler with some useful information.'

'I should clip their bloody wings!' Max said, just as his wife and daughters came into the room.

Ruby started to cry and Jade ran off down the hall. Max looked at his sobbing daughter and then at his wife.

'Max!' said his wife, visibly horrified.

'Celeste,' Max said, 'I didn't mean it.'

The Colonel slumped into a chair with his drink.

'Girls, go to your rooms,' said Celeste, in a gentle voice.

Amber put her arm around the sobbing Ruby's shoulder and the pair went in search of Jade.

'Celeste...' started Max.

Celeste held up her hand and looked at her father-in-law.

'I'm so sorry Colonel, would you mind if I had a moment alone with Max?' she asked, in a calm tone.

'Not at all, my dear,' said the Colonel, as he stood up. 'And at the risk of sounding like an interfering old goat,' he said from the doorway, 'might I remind you, Max, that titbit of information from the Trips may prove very useful - a fact you may want to take into consideration when discussing their punishment.'

'What information?' Celeste asked Max.

The Colonel closed the door behind him and Max immediately started to bluster about the embarrassment his daughters had caused him in front of members from the country's most well-respected wing of the air force. Celeste listened to her husband's rant and was finally able to ascertain exactly what had happened.

Celeste, then suggested that clipping the girls' wings, or binding their magic was not appropriate for what amounted to an error of judgement borne out of curiosity. And, she continued, given that the girls also had information that might help the Red Wings it was perhaps more suitable, she said, to ground the girls for a week. Despite Max's initial protestations against this punishment, Celeste reminded her husband that his own adolescence had been riddled with far more disturbing infractions and that his initial response to the girls' act was probably punishment enough.

'I'm disappointed with you Max,' said Celeste. 'The girls have proven to be nothing but trustworthy and respectful given their age and powers. You should be proud of them. I'm not saying that what they did was right but your reaction was clearly frightening enough, never mind that awful threat.'

Max looked at his wife. Celeste held her head high and steadfastly held his gaze.

'I'll go and talk to them,' Max said.

'*We'll* go and talk to them.' Celeste smiled, and drew nearer to her husband. 'And perhaps we can find out where that entrance is for the team as well.' Celeste leaned in and kissed her husband on the cheek.

* * *

It was late by the time Adler and his team discovered the whereabouts of the third entrance. Armed with this valuable information a rescue plan was formulated and everyone turned in. No one slept well that night, least of all the Trips, who wondered if they should have told their parents about some of the other things they had learned from their time spent exploring Mount Dou, outside … and in.

THE AMBASSADORIAL RESIDENCE
Queen Petra's diplomatic interference.

Under cover of darkness the royal carriage raced through Vinster's streets. King Egbert and General Macjooste arrived at the Rataquian embassy to find that Cashenian troops had cordoned off most of Fortnum Park Square. There was a fire wagon parked in the embassy's driveway. Half a dozen Rataquian soldiers, each holding an ornamental, yet perfectly operational sword-staff, stood to attention in a line across the main entrance. The royal carriage was waved through the embassy's gates and the King and the General were greeted by the sound of the Ambassador barking orders to his staff, who were loading two carts with trunks and soft furnishings, in the torch-lit courtyard.

'Lord Esodo!' said the King, as he hurried from the carriage towards the Ambassador. 'I came as soon as I heard. Was anyone hurt? What on Eris happened?'

'Your Highness. General Macjooste,' said the Ambassador, with only the barest hint of a nod. 'We leave now.'

Situated on the west side of Fortnum Park, Fortnum Park Square was home to several foreign diplomats, many of whom now stood watching, with concern, the events that were unfolding at No 1.

'Ronaldo, please,' said the King. 'You cannot possibly think we are responsible for this attack.'

'This is no time for biscuits!' replied the Ambassador, defiantly.

At the sound of carriage wheels, everyone turned to see another royal coach being waved through the gates.

'Oh good gods,' muttered King Egbert.

Queen Petra shooed the footman away, swept past her husband and stood directly in front of the Ambassador

'I'm glad to see you are unhurt, Lord Esodo. Where is Constanza?'

'We leave now,' repeated the Ambassador, with fire in

his eyes. 'We are not wanted here. I take my family home now!'

'Let's all just take a moment, shall we?' said the Queen, as she scanned the courtyard. 'Constanza and the children must be scared half to death. I think it might be best if I take them to the palace where they can recover in safety.'

'With due respects, Your…' started the Ambassador.

Queen Petra gave a twitch of a smile to the Ambassador and then something caught her eye.

'Ah, there she is. Excuse me Ambassador,' said the Queen, as she left the Rataquian fairy standing with his mouth open.

King Egbert bowed his head to the Ambassador.

'My deepest apologies, Lord Esodo. My wife is a force of nature, one I rarely have the resources to fight. She does not mean to offend and she genuinely has your wife's and children's best interests at heart.'

'This is outrage!' boomed the Ambassador, as he stormed off towards his personal carriage. 'Constanza Arianna Esodo! We leave now!'

'Ambassador Esodo,' said the Queen, as she twirled around to greet the enraged fairy, 'Could I possibly prevail upon you to calm your emotions for just a short period of time?'

From inside the Esodo's carriage could be heard the heartfelt sobs of his family.

'Constanza,' said the now worried Ambassador, as he opened the carriage door and climbed inside.

While the Ambassador was with his family, King Egbert approached his wife.

'Petra, you really shouldn't have come. It's not safe, nor particularly politic at the moment.'

'Which is precisely why we must reassure the Ambassador that we can keep his family safe. I take it we can arrange for an escort back to the palace?' the Queen enquired.

'Please, Petra. You really should leave this to …'

'Ssh,' interrupted the Queen.

Ambassador Esodo stepped out of the carriage and, head lowered, walked towards the King and Queen.

'Your Majesties,' said the Ambassador, as he bowed. 'I am sorry for my outburst. As you can imagine…'

Once again Queen Petra did not let Ambassador Esodo complete his sentence.

'Ambassador Esodo - Ronaldo,' she said, with a warm smile. 'You have nothing for which to apologise. Now please, I absolutely insist that you come to stay at the palace where I can look after Constanza and the children while you and my husband find out who did this.'

The Ambassador glanced at the King, then looked at the carriage from which the sound of hiccoughing sobs was emanating.

'I must stay to arrange departure,' said the Ambassador, in a more subdued tone.

'I shall stay with you, Lord Esodo,' said the King.

'Excellent. Then I shall speak to General Macjooste and he can arrange for an escort back to the palace. I shall see you later, Egbert,' said the Queen, as she strode off and left the two utterly defeated fairies standing in the courtyard.

'My wife, she say that Her Highness not take no for answer,' said the Ambassador.

'Some may see this as a flaw but I hope, Ambassador, that on this occasion you will forgive my wife's forthright nature and accept that we are all truly sorry that you have suffered such a terrifying ordeal. General Macjooste and I will do all that we can to get to the bottom of this and perhaps we may even find a way to work together to stop the individual responsible for this despicable offence.'

The Ambassador watched General Macjooste order his troops to surround the Ambassador's and the Queen's carriages. Before getting into the royal carriage, Queen Petra briefly spoke to Lady Esodo's personal attendant who enlisted the help of two elves to arrange for some of the family's personal belongings to be sent to the palace.

'You know who has done this?' asked the Ambassador, as he watched the two, heavily guarded, carriages drive through the gates.

'Perhaps we, too, should return to the palace. I have news that may be of interest to you,' said the King.

By now, Lord Esodo's anger had completely dissipated and, even in the torch light, King Egbert noted that the Rataquian fairy had aged slightly, most certainly as a consequence of magically extinguishing the fire.

'You have three daughters, yes?' asked the Ambassador.

'I do,' replied the King.

'What you do if you are me?' the Ambassador asked.

'I would use every ounce of magic in me to protect my family,' replied King Egbert, sombrely.

Lord Esodo considered the King's answer, nodded once, looked down at his shoes and then looked at the monarch before him.

'I tell staff to stop to packing. I come to palace and you tell me what you know.'

'Thank you, Ambassador,' replied the King.

With this tentative accord struck there was a deafening clap of thunder, followed by two streaks of lightning. The air cooled as large droplets of rain fell from the clouds. The impending storm dispersed the onlookers, while the Ambassador's staff hurried the fully-laden carriages back to the stables.

'The gods fight instead tonight, no?' said the Ambassador, looking skyward.

'Rather them than us,' whispered the King.

TALULA LOOKS FOR NORMAN...
and Professor Bauxite's wheelbarrow.

Iffies was rammed with dwarves, fairies, goblins and elves. Talula was sitting in a corner of the inn, nursing half a flagon of Triple Axe. She had been waiting for Norman for over two hours. Talula's friend, Margaleet, had paid an impromptu visit and had kept Talula company for the first hour but it was getting late and Talula was feeling tired. She wasn't sure whether she should wait any longer or go upstairs to her room.

At first Talula had been slightly miffed that Norman hadn't turned up but, as the evening wore on, his absence had increasingly begun to niggle rather than offend her. Talula may not have known Norman for long but he definitely struck her as a dwarf who kept his word.

Over the conversational hubbub Talula heard a loud voice.

'Oi! Axe!'

A uniformed dwarf of King Egbert's army elbowed his way to the bar and found himself a stool.

'Jack,' replied the owner of the inn, while pulling a flagon of Triple Axe.

''Ere 'bout that ta-do at Fortnum Park Square?' said Jack.

'Wot the toffs bin up to now?' said Axe, as he placed the flagon in front of Jack.

'Some kinda 'splosion at the Rataquian embassy. No one hurt mind but some o' the lads reckon the King and Queen turned up.'

Talula did not wait to hear the rest of the conversation. She left the inn and raced over to Norman's house.

* * *

'My, my,' said Professor Bauxite, as he entered his office. 'Progress indeed.' The Professor was pleased to see a relatively debris-free path lined with tidy columns of books on the floor. 'Well done Norman. I've a feeling you'll be worth every florin. Now let's see if we can find that book, shall we?'

The Professor had left his students with the palace librarian, Mr Antequam, and had come back to the University in search of *The Myths and Legends of Eris' Dwarves and Fairies*. Given that the book was a family heirloom the Professor wasn't sure whether he'd brought the book to the University or if it was in his library at home. He did, however, have a vague recollection of referring to it in the not-too-distant-past and the University had seemed the more likely choice.

A short time after his arrival there was a knock on his office door.

'Enter,' said the Professor, while standing on a stool and checking the spines of the books on a top shelf.

'Professor Bauxite, sir.'

The Professor carefully climbed down from the stool to greet the late-night caller.

'Miss Ewesage, how nice to see you again. How may I help you?'

'I was hoping to find Norman here. He said he'd meet me at Iffies but never showed up and he's not at home. I heard about the explosion at the Rataquian embassy and,' Talula paused, 'I just wondered, what with everything that's happened recently…'

Professor Bauxite nodded and gestured for Talula to come into the office

'Yes, the palace librarian told me what happened. A very serious business indeed. Come in, come in. I'll make us both a nice cup of tea. I'm sure Norman is fine … wait … where's my wheelbarrow?'

The Professor looked at the space near the door where his wheelbarrow should have been. Talula stopped in her tracks and waited while the Professor continued to stare at the empty space next to her.

'I'm afraid I can't answer that question,' Talula eventually said.

The Professor looked from the space to the path that

Norman had created. He bent down to read the spines of some of the books stacked on the floor and then stood upright. He looked at the space once more, frowned and scratched his beard.

'He's in the library, with the wheelbarrow, returning books!' he said, triumphantly.

'Are you sure? Is the library even open?' Talula asked.

'Ah, yes, fair point,' said Professor Bauxite, as he looked up at the clock above the door. 'So where can he be and what on Eris has he done with my wheelbarrow?'

'If we find the wheelbarrow I'm pretty sure we'll find Norman,' said Talula.

* * *

Norman was reading a papyrus entitled, *Ladye Orquidea Wythe Ijolite Clann*, when his stomach started rumbling. The gurgling sound caught him off guard and he momentarily mistook the noise for some kind of small animal. Norman had become so absorbed in the ancient texts that, as a consequence of his stomach's interruption, he instantly realised that he'd completely lost track of time.

'Balderdash! What time is it?! I said I'd meet Talula.'

Norman pulled his shirt sleeves down over his hands and rolled up the papyrus, careful not to let his fingers touch the delicate document. Once he had put the papyrus back in the correct wooden box Norman picked up his satchel, slung it over his shoulder, and went to the bookcase, to one side of which was a wooden lever.

'Right, let's see if I can get out of here.'

Norman pulled hard on the lever and finally managed to yank it all the way down. After a brief, worrying, silence the mechanism made a loud clanking noise and the bookshelf began to move.

* * *

Professor Bauxite suggested that he and Talula begin their search for Norman at the library in case there was a late night opening of which he had been unaware.

'I don't always get a chance to read the memos,' the Professor said, as the pair made their way through the tunnels.

'I see,' said Talula, making a concerted effort to walk as slowly as the Professor.

When they finally reached the library it was abundantly clear that the facility was closed. No light came through the glass doors which, when Talula tried them, were firmly locked. Parked in an alcove just outside the library, however, was Professor Bauxite's wheelbarrow.

'It seems he's definitely been here,' the Professor said. 'The question is, where is he now?'

Talula thought she heard a noise coming from inside the library and pressed her face against the glass. Through the darkness she could make out the shadowy shapes of bookshelves and tables but couldn't see any movement.

'I'm sure I heard something,' she said.

'Mmrf!'

'Norman?' Talula said, as she continued to peer into the gloom.

'Really?' said the Professor.

From the stacks appeared a short, shadowy, figure, who promptly bumped into a table near the entrance.

'Ow!'

'Yep, that's definitely Norman,' Talula said, relieved to hear Norman's voice.

'Marvellous,' said the Professor. 'Now how are we going to get him out of there?'

'Um,' said Talula, as she turned to face the Professor, 'I don't suppose you happen to have a pair of long-handled tweezers on you?'

'Tweezers?' said the Professor.

'Talula? Professor?' Norman had reached the library doors and looked through the glass. 'What are you doing here?' he shouted.

'Looking for castles in the sky! What do you think we're doing here?!' Talula replied.

'Why would you need tweezers?' asked the Professor, still perplexed by Talula's request.

'What?' Norman shouted.

Talula looked at the Professor and sighed.

'It's not something I've done in a long time but I might be able to pick the lock,' said Talula.

'My word, you are indeed a pixie of many talents. As it happens, I carry a variety of miniature tools all neatly contained in a handy leather pouch. It's served me well over the years but I can't remember seeing a pair of tweezers,' said the Professor.

While Professor Bauxite searched his jacket pockets, Talula took a small cylindrical item from inside her pouch. She shook it once and, from one end of the tube, came a bright, white, light.

'What a fabulous pocket torch,' said the Professor.

'Finnician glow worm. A friend gave it to me last week,' replied Talula, as she bent down and looked at the door's keyhole.

'Talula, I'm really sorry,' shouted Norman through the door.

'Can you please stop shouting!' shouted Talula, 'I need to concentrate!'

'Bless me. I don't think I've ever used these,' said the Professor, as he pulled a pair of long-handled tweezers from the leather pouch - which also contained a miniature saw, a pair of small scissors, a tiny hammer, a brush, and a well-used, sharp blade.

Talula stood up and the Professor handed over the tweezers.

'Thank you,' she said.

Talula put one end of the torch in her mouth, cracked her knuckles and crouched down to face the keyhole.

* * *

Back in the Professor's office nothing was said of the ease with which Talula had picked the lock or, for that matter, was much made of Norman's presence in the library. Instead Norman was profusely grateful for Talula's and the Professor's concern. Norman apologised, several times, and insisted that he would never again do anything so thoughtless.

'So, I think my work here is done and I need to go home. I hope you don't mind if I go. No offence but I'm pretty tired,' said Talula.

'Quite right too. It's almost midnight,' said the Professor. 'Before you leave Norman, I don't suppose you found a book entitled *The Myths and Legends of Eris' Dwarves and Fairies, by J.R. Horneblende?*'

Norman considered this for a moment and then shook his head.

'Sorry, Professor, I haven't seen it here but I have a copy at home if you want to borrow it.'

Professor Bauxite looked at Norman, stunned that the young dwarf also had a copy of the incredibly rare book.

'My, my. This day has certainly been full of surprises. Thank you, but perhaps you might try to find my copy when you come in tomorrow,' said the Professor.

'Yes, sir, and shall I tell you what I found in the library?' asked Norman.

'Not tonight, Norman. We shall, however, discuss your late-night sojourn, tomorrow,' said the Professor, peering over his glasses.

Norman felt that he really ought to tell the Professor of his incredible find in the library, and had he done so then perhaps the following sequence of events may not have occurred. Instead the young dwarf looked down at his boots and felt guilty for causing his newly-made friends so much trouble.

THE RED WINGS MAKE THEIR MOVE
A mountain, some frogs, and two rescue missions.

Due to the nature of their work LUSU field agents were frequently forced to use magic. The risks associated with this practice were obvious, which was why, at the beginning of their careers, agents were not only trained in armed and unarmed combat but were also instructed in the art of charm-fare, whereby charms, rather than the more life-force depleting spells, were used to aid their missions. Agents also had an array of magically infused gadgets, gizmos and serums at their disposal, all of which came from HQ's R&D department.

Early the next morning, Wing Commander Adler and his team, had cast chameleon-charms, crossed with detection-avoidance charms, before leaving the Rouchefort estate house and flying to Blasting's mountain.

As the sun crawled its way up the eastern side of Mount Dou, so the Red Wing unit crept around the western side, looking for the third entrance. The handicap of working with a magically camouflaged team had been overcome with the use of a thick, magical rope that was able to adapt to any spell or charm, which, in this case, meant it could be felt but not seen.

'This must be it,' came Wand's voice from behind a boulder.

'I can see two fairies and three trolls in the doorway,' whispered Adler, who could be heard unclipping his holster and drawing his wand. 'The trolls have crossbows. We'll use quick-fire freeze-charms. Dash, aim for the fairy on the left. Wand…'

At the sound of several small rocks tumbling from above the entrance onto the path below, Adler stopped.

'Wait. What's that?' he whispered.

Two of the troll guards went to investigate. As they approached the source of the sound, a large boulder came crashing down in front of them, bringing with it an army of frogs. There were hundreds of them and the writhing mass of amphibians struggled to escape from the swarm of armed guards who had come racing out of the entrance.

'Looks like there's more than five guards, sir,' Raza whispered.

'Is that a pile of frogs?' Wand asked.

'It's a distraction, is what it is,' said Adler.

'Never look a gift frog in the mouth,' Raza said.

'We don't have much time. Everyone know what they're doing?' said Adler.

'Yes, sir,' whispered the squadron in unison.

'Let's go,' said Adler.

Adler and the unnoticeable team took full advantage of the frog invasion and crept through the chaos, into Mount Dou.

Fairy and troll guards, alerted to the kerfuffle at the mountain's non-security-spelled entrance, had been sent to join their colleagues. The sound of their boots bounced off the walls of the white-tiled corridor as they ran to the entrance.

Adler and the team hugged the white walls, invisible to the guards.

'Disengage charms,' whispered Adler, when the corridor finally fell silent.

The team became visible, as did the magic rope, which everyone unclipped from their belts. Raza gathered the rope and put it in his backpack.

'Everyone ok?' asked Adler, aware that even a minimal use of magic could tire his team. 'Have you got your WUF handy?'

The team patted their breast pockets to check for the vials of golden liquid and nodded acknowledgement that their energy shots were to hand.

'Wand, Dash and Silas, you three check that tunnel to the right for the scientists. The rest of you follow me and we'll try to find Blasting. Rendezvous here in twenty minutes. Wands set to stun and use your chameleon-charms only when necessary.'

The fairies unholstered their wands and walked away from the sound of cursing, stomping and zapping as the guards at the entrance continued to deal with the frogs.

* * *

Celeste and Max were having their morning coffee on the veranda when the Colonel joined them.

'Adler's team have left I see,' Max said.

'A few last minute changes to the plan but they were up and out before dawn,' replied the Colonel.

'I shall be glad when this is all over,' sighed Celeste.

'No Trips this morning?' asked the Colonel.

'I thought it best to let them sleep,' replied Celeste.

The Trips, safe in the knowledge that their parents wouldn't miss them until at least midday, were not in their beds but had in fact risen early and had left shortly before Adler's team.

The young fairies were currently crouched behind three large rocks, several feet above the third entrance, watching the guards as they tried to clear away the seething mass that had fallen with the boulder.

'Frogs?' said Amber to Ruby.

'It was all I could think of,' replied her sister, defensively.

'But frogs?' Amber repeated.

'Stop it you two. A distraction is a distraction. The team should be in so we can fly home before Mum and Dad find out and have a hairy head fit. Come on let's go,' said Jade, the most cautious of the three.

'Hold on, it's all very well chucking a few frogs in the entrance but what about Mr Blasting?' said Amber.

'No!' said Jade.

'I'm kind of with Jade on that one,' said Ruby.

'What's wrong with you two?! That lot will have no idea where to find anything. It took us ages to figure out where everything was. We can't just abandon them. There are loads more guards, *with* poison-tipped arrows, and

I've a pretty good idea where those scientists might be,' said Amber.

Jade and Ruby stared at their sister incredulously.

'Mum and Dad would definitely clip our wings,' said Jade.

'And how can we help the Red Wings without letting them know it's us? After last night, even if we made ourselves invisible, everyone would still know it's us,' added Jade.

'Fine, I'll go on my own,' said Amber, as she stood up and adjusted her wings.

'No!' said her sisters, simultaneously grabbing at Amber's sleeves and pulling her down out of view.

'Let me go! I'll be in and out quicker than you can say abracadabra,' Amber said.

'Really?' said Ruby, 'Abracadabra? We're not babies anymore you know.'

'Says the one who produced frogs as a distraction,' said Amber. 'Look, I'll be back super-quick. I'll point them in the direction of those scientists and…'

The triplets heard cursing and loud zapping coming from the entrance below.

'Alright! Alright! I'll help,' said Ruby.

'Amber Isabella Rouchefort, you're the most annoying fairy ever! But Dad would kill us if anything happened to you. We stay in constant touch do you hear! I'll stay out here and keep watch. You two go inside.'

'Finally, some common sense,' said Amber.

Ruby shoulder-punched her sister.

'Ow!'

'Don't push it,' said Ruby.

* * *

Wand, Dash and Silas opened four doors along the corridor in search of Doctors Tellurium and Vincenzo. None of the rooms contained the scientists. As they came to the end of the corridor Wand suddenly stopped.

'Did you hear that?' Silas whispered.

'Ssh,' replied Wand.

A barely audible tapping sound was coming from the second-to-last door in the corridor.

'Engage chameleon-charms!' whispered Wand.

Unable to see each other, Wand, Dash and Silas employed the four-step-pause technique as they slowly made their way towards the sound. When they reached the door the tapping stopped. The three fairies stopped and listened. There was a click and the door opened.

'Oh please gods!' came a terrified voice from inside, 'I don't know anything! Let me go.'

'Disengage,' said Wand.

Dr Tellurium stared at the three military fairies as they appeared before him and entered the room.

'Took you long enough!' Dr Tellurium said, and promptly covered his mouth with his hands.

Wand held his forefinger to his lips indicating that Dr Tellurium should stay quiet. As Silas escorted the geochemist from his room, so another bout of tapping led them to Dr Vincenzo's room at the end of the corridor.

'What's that noise?' whispered Tellurium.

'Ssh!' said Wand, as the sound led them out of the corridor back towards the main tunnel.

* * *

In the main, white-tiled, corridor, Wing Commander Adler and the other Red Wings came to a junction. As they stopped to assess the situation they too heard a quiet tapping sound.

'What ...?' Raza's question was interrupted by what sounded like a suppressed sneeze.

Adler turned to face his team who momentarily looked bewildered. Within seconds, however, the military fairies grinned as they simultaneously realised that they had heard that sneeze before.

'Sir?' whispered Raza, 'What should we do?'

Wing Commander Adler had been on more secret ops than he could shake a wand at. He'd been captured and tortured by ruthless mercenaries and, bar a few scars, had lived to tell the tale. He'd rescued kings, queens, princes and, inevitably, princesses. He took immense pride in his minimal use of magic and could disable a troll with a toothpick. Adolescent fairies, he thought, shouldn't be too hard to handle.

Adler gesticulated for his team to keep an eye on the corridor then looked at his feet and shook his head. When he looked up again he faced the direction from which the sound of the suppressed sneeze had come.

'Ahem, Miss Rouchefort? Is that you?' Adler said, as quietly as he could.

A few yards ahead of the team, a hushed, but heated, exchange was taking place.

'Sir, I think we have incoming,' whispered Raza, as the sound of running footsteps came towards them.

'Engage chameleon-charm,' Adler whispered. 'And you, Miss Rouchefort, stay exactly where you are until I give the all-clear.'

No sooner had the team blended into the tiled wall then a dozen trolls, armed with crossbows, jogged by and headed towards the other end of the tunnel. Once the trolls' footsteps could no longer be heard Adler piped up again.

'Disengage,' he said.

The team reappeared.

'Sir,' said Raza, 'should we follow them?'

A female voice shouted, 'No, not that way!' quickly followed by a murmured, 'Oh blast.'

'Miss Rouchefort,' said Adler, 'We know it's you. If you really want to help then perhaps you could tell us where we can find Theodore Blasting.'

After some inaudible whisperings the team nearly lost their wings with fright when the female voice began whispering right next to them. She remained invisible.

'Blasting's gone to that big contraption of his. Turn left here and look for the stairwell. He's got some kind of egg-shaped escape pod on a launch pad half way up the mountain and loads of guards seem to be heading that way. Be careful though cos he's been working on a lethal poison and the crossbow arrow tips have probably been dipped in it. Oh, and mind out for fairy guards on the stairwell cos they've got postings on every floor.'

In the momentary silence that followed, the team looked at one another and then at their commanding officer, who had been listening very carefully to the voice in front of him.

'Anything else?' Adler asked.

'If you can get past the guards near the escape pod you might want to try flying out that way. You'll never get back out the way you came in.'

'I'm sure we'll…' started Adler.

'Flight Lieutenant Wand and his team will rendezvous with you somewhere else,' the disembodied voice interrupted.

'And where might this new rendezvous be, dare I ask?' said Adler, trying to sound like he was still in control of the situation.

'We found a cave at the foot of the mountain. It's not big but no one ever goes there. It's almost directly below Mr Blasting's launch site.' The voice hesitated and added, 'You won't tell our father will you, Commander?'

'And your sister will arrange the rendezvous with Wand will she?' said Adler, aware that if Max Rouchefort ever discovered that his daughters had helped the team there would almost certainly be a court marshal.

'She said she's been guiding him that way already and my other sister said Blasting is at the pod so you'd better get a move on.'

'Go home, Miss Rouchefort,' said Adler, as the team started moving towards the junction, 'Go home now and leave the rest to us.'

There was what sounded like a *hrmpf!* and then silence as the team hurried towards the junction.

Theodore Blasting was indeed at his escape pod on a launch pad half way up the mountain. The pod looked something akin to a giant, silver dragon's egg. What it lacked in aerodynamic properties it made up for in being able to accommodate Blasting, Kinins, his senior thaumurtologist, the weapon, a chest full of personal possessions, lab equipment and twelve fairies, all of whom had been hired to instantly transport the pod away from the mountain.

'You!' barked Blasting, to a fairy with purple wings, 'Do you know where we're going?'

The fairy nodded that he did and waited for Blasting to step through the door into the pod.

'Sir, the weapon is on board,' said Kinins, who was following his boss.

'Have you dealt with Tellurium and Vincenzo?' asked Blasting of his aide.

'I… um… no, sir. I hadn't planned to leave quite so early this morning,' said Kinins, who had, only minutes earlier, been told of the frog incident and had immediately gone to arrange for their hurried departure.

'Damn it Kinins…!' started Blasting.

'Halt in the name of the King!' came a voice from the stop of the stairs.

'At least see if you can deal with this,' snapped Blasting, as he hurried inside and made for the lower decks.

Kinins and the fairy with the purple wings stood at the doorway and fired a quick succession of freeze-spells. The spells missed the rescue team but turned the surrounding rock to ice. Adler's team returned fire with flame-spells directed at the guards who had come storming up the stairwell.

'Cover me!' shouted Adler.

Flying Officers Raza, and Pitou tried to fend off the attack coming from the pod, while Ryan fired at the fairies on the stairs. A stray zap caught the tip of one of Raza's wings and he cried out. Without warning there came a flash of white light that blinded everyone on the stairwell and the launch pad. Kinins and the purple-winged fairy quickly fumbled their way inside the pod and closed the door.

'Raza!' shouted Adler. 'Are you..?' before he could finish the sentence he, and the rest of the team, vanished.

* * *

'Mum and Dad are going to cut off our wings!' shouted Jade to Amber.

'What else could we do?! They'd all have died if we'd left them in there!' retorted Amber.

Wand, Dash, Silas, Dr Tellurium, and Dr Vincenzo, all looked on in silence at the young female fairies.

'Jade's right. We're going to be in so much trouble,' said Ruby.

'Quiet!' bellowed Adler, who had reappeared - along with Silas, Pitou and Raza - into the middle of the squabble. 'What on Eris is going on!'

The triplets jumped and turned to face Wing Commander Adler.

'Oh, First Lieutenant Raza,' said Jade, 'You're hurt.'

'In the name of everything that's sacred! What on Eris do you three..!'

Adler stopped mid-sentence. Ruby's bottom lip started to quiver and her eyes welled up with tears.

'I surrender,' the exhausted Wing Commander said, as he slid down the wall of the cave.

MEANWHILE, BACK AT THE PALACE
Mr Antequam and Professor Bauxite make an interesting discovery. Queen Petra organises lunch.

Professor Bauxite and Mr Antequam were the only two dwarves awake in the library. Half a dozen History and Chronicles' PhD students were curled up on chairs, exhausted from the all-night search that they had been conducting in an effort to establish whether the King was the descendant of Halvar the Just.

Early in the proceedings Mr Antequam informed the keen young dwarves that he'd never found any documentation in the royal archives linking King Egbert to Halvar the Just but, the librarian admitted, the royal library held a vast collection, which also meant that he hadn't actually read everything. Professor Bauxite added that they might not find anything at all, largely because much of the relevant documentation was either missing, or hadn't been written in the first place.

This prompted the student dwarves to search the oldest parchments first so that they could work their way forward along the royal family trees, a complex task that had not only required vast quantities of dandelion coffee but had also caused more than a few debates.

Hundreds of names were cross-referenced with Cashen's myriad ancient fairy tribes and current Cashenian aristocracy. This lengthy process managed to settle several long-standing arguments with regards to a few unanswered genealogical questions although the student dwarves found no records documenting Halvar's family after the Wand Wars. It was as if the warrior chieftain's family had never existed.

While the students were delving into the library's extensive collection of documents, Professor Bauxite and Mr Antequam had looked for the other two ancestors from the Torrimaya Trio. As the sun rose over Mount Mukai the aged dwarves' search finally paid off as they discovered someone they believed to be a direct, living, descendant of the pixie incanter.

'You know, I would never have bought these records if I hadn't been looking for confirmation of a specific linen-making family from northern Cashen,' said Mr Antequam.

'Oh?' said the Professor.

'The family is applying for a royal warrant to make linen for Her Highness and I wanted to check the family's history.'

'How fortuitous, Mr Antequam,' said the Professor, who paused and then smiled. 'I really shouldn't be surprised that our young pixie has a role to play in all this. From what I can see she seems both loyal and brave, rather like her ancient relative.'

One of the library doors opened and the two dwarves looked up from the parchments spread out on the table before them.

'Good morning, General,' said the Professor.

'Professor. Mr Antequam,' said the General, glancing at the sleeping students littering the chairs.

'Our young team finally succumbed to slumber about an hour ago. Unfortunately, none of them is yet any closer to discovering who Halvar's descendent is. The absence of key documents and chronicles is proving problematic,' said the Professor.

'You did say this might be the case. Have you discovered anything at all?' enquired the General.

'Indeed we have,' said the Professor. 'It would seem our young Talula is more than just a tricksy pixie with an armoury of useful skills,' said the Professor.

'I'm sorry?' said the General.

'Tuläher Daye Forêt, General, when translated from ancient Cashenian, means Tuläher of the Forest and is a name we found linked to an old linen-making, pixie family - the Toile De Lins - at the northern tip of the Valley of the Green Pastures,' Mr Antequam added.

'What makes you think Miss Ewesage is descended

from this particular Tuläher?'

'Mr Antequam keeps a marvellous library, General. Indeed, we are very fortunate in that he recently acquired records written by an order of fairy nuns who served as midwives, in the Valley of the Green Pastures, up until as recently as six hundred years ago. A rare find indeed Mr Antequam,' said Professor Bauxite, with an appreciative nod in Mr Antequam's direction.

'I confess I haven't had time to open them,' said Mr Antequam, with a mildly embarrassed air.

'Are you sure it's her?' the General asked.

'Our suspicions were aroused when we stumbled upon several parchments written by a dwarf chronicler named Johansen. We don't have all the records but our findings suggest that Johansen documented the Toile De Lin family's history for well over two hundred years after the Wand Wars,' said the Professor.

'This is the family I have been researching,' interrupted Mr Antequam.

'Luckily for us,' smiled the Professor. 'This chronicler meticulously describes the family's linen business and one of the parchments even includes a comprehensive family tree. We were then able to cross-reference the family tree with registers of births and deaths.'

The General raised his eyebrows.

'I'm still not sure how you know Talula is a related to this family,' said the General.

'It's all in the name, General. In one of the documents, which was written a mere two centuries after the Wand Wars, reference is made to what appears to be something akin to a memorial service for those who died during the battle of the Valley of the Green Pastures. The name Tuläher comes up time and time again. More importantly, in one particular branch of the Toile de Lin family there is a continuous line of girls who have been named a derivative of Tuläher, which, we now believe to be the name of the pixie incanter,' said the Professor.

'The branch in question is that of the Daye Forêt family and this is what Johansen recorded.' Mr Antequam picked up a parchment from the table and began to read. '*The young female pixie was most serious in her demeanour. She was handed the axe by the fairy chieftain, who bowed and then left Tuläher Daye Forêt's descendant to place the axe on the ceremonial table in the centre of the valley.*'

The General folded his arms and considered the Professor's discovery.

'So how did Talula end up here if her family is from the Valley?' the General asked. 'And as far as I know her last name is neither Daye Forêt, nor Toile de Lin.'

'Daye Forêt is the family name of the original pixie incanter, whereas the Toile de Lin side are linked by marriage. We have one more check to make before we can absolutely confirm Talula is the incanter's ancestor but the death register indicates that a couple who went by the name of Daye Forêt died shortly after their arrival in Vinster. At the same time a female pixling, who was found in a basket outside the city's infirmary that same day, was sent to the Pixie's of Mercy orphanage. We still have to dot the Is and cross the Ts, General, but I can say with some considerable certainty that Talula was that baby and is the descendant we have been searching for,' said the Professor.

The General unfolded his arms and put his hands in his trouser pockets.

'Very impressive work, sirs,' the General said, with a smile. 'We are one step further in…'

Before the General could finish his sentence, Queen Petra was announced and swept into the room.

'Morning everyone,' she said, rather loudly.

The six student dwarves, startled into wakefulness, fell off their chairs, stood up and bowed when they realised who had entered. One of the students bowed too far and stumbled in the process. He turned bright red with embarrassment and mumbled an apology. Professor

Bauxite and Mr Antequam bowed with far more decorum.

'Your Highness,' said the General, with a slow nod of his head.

'How are we this fine, clear morning? The storm has cleared the air and, I hope, everyone's heads,' said the Queen, looking at the parchments and books that were strewn on the library's reading tables.

'There's been some interesting progress,' replied the General, 'but there've no' been any leads on Halvar's living relative.'

'Have you asked your wife, General?' asked the Queen, with a look that suggested he might have started there in the first place.

'What a splendid idea, Your Highness! Lady Macjooste is a keen amateur genealogist, Mr Antequam,' explained the Professor, 'and told me she had found some interesting documents the last time she was at her in-laws' Carrtile estate in the Highlands.'

'Excellent,' beamed the Queen. 'I am on my way to see Chef Cappo so I shall tell him to expect more guests. Lady Esodo and the girls will be missing home so I think we shall have a Rataquian-themed lunch. Professor Bauxite, Mr Antequam, you are of course both invited. Does anyone have any special dietary requirements?' the Queen asked, looking from Mr Antequam, to Professor Bauxite and then to the General.

'Ahem,' Mr Antequam, looked slightly uncomfortable.

'Mr Antequam?' said the Queen.

Mr Antequam bowed.

'I am most honoured to accept your invitation to lunch, Your Highness. I do not wish to put anyone to any trouble but I'm afraid I have one or two small requests.'

Mr Antequam, it turned out, was not only a vegetarian but also suffered with intolerances to several foods, including yak's milk, opportuna fish and wheat, three of the main ingredients in the Rataquian rice dish the Queen had planned to serve for lunch.

'Well,' said the Queen, 'then I shall ask Chef to make something especially for you. A nice salad perhaps?'

Mr Antequam hated salad.

'That would be most kind, Your Highness,' said Mr Antequam, with a small bow.

'Jolly good,' said the Queen. 'For now, I shall have Alfonse send you all some breakfast.' The Queen turned to leave and walked towards the library doors. She stopped suddenly and then turned to face the room, 'Oh, and shall I ask Maria to bring those interesting documents with her when she comes?'

'An excellent idea, Your Highness,' beamed the Professor.

'Let's see if we can get to the bottom of this once and for all shall we?' The Queen smiled, and everyone bowed as she left.

THE RETURN OF THE ABDUCTED SCIENTISTS
Dr Tellurium is questioned.

The Red Wings had escorted Doctors Tellurium and Vincenzo from Rouche to Vinster-on-Sterm, courtesy of the Rouchefort's six-horse, relay coaches. The vehicles were designed primarily for speed rather than comfort, which meant the travellers arrived at military headquarters not only exhausted but feeling more than a little achey and stiff.

Lord Esodo was informed of Dr Vincenzo's safe return and the Ambassador made a brief visit to the infirmary to reassure Dr Vincenzo that he was in safe hands. The Ambassador was relieved to discover that Dr Vincenzo had protected himself with a series of charms, the purpose of which was to prevent anyone from eliciting any information in the event of capture. Unfortunately the thaumurtologist had incurred several injuries as a result of his 'non-cooperation' when questioned by Blasting. The Rataquian scientist was treated for cuts, bruises, a hairline fracture in his wing and was then taken to a private room so that he might recover from his ordeal before being taken home, under military escort.

Flying Officer Raza, whose wing had been zapped in the crossfire on Mount Dou, was also sent for treatment whereupon the young Lothario insisted, to the pretty fairy nurse dressing his wound, that it was only a graze and that he would be happy to show her the rest of his scars if she would let him take her out to dinner that night.

Dr Tellurium was physically unharmed during his ordeal but before he was seen by the medical staff he was interviewed by Captain Meejum - who decided that things might progress more quickly while Dr Tellurium was still under the influence of Blasting's magic.

'So you definitely told Blasting that further research was required and you're sure he's building his own weapon?' Meejum repeated her question.

Dr Tellurium, threw his hands in the air in frustration.

'That lunatic had me kidnapped solely to find out why he couldn't imbue magic onto his own weapon! So, *yes*, I'm sure!'

Tellurium brought his hands back down and glared at Captain Meejum, who forced a small smile.

'I'm sorry, sir. I'm sure this has been a very difficult...'

'Difficult?! *Difficult*?! What's *difficult*, Captain, is fathoming exactly how that mad fairy even knew about the, *top secret*, project. And what's even more *difficult*, is coming to terms with the fact that I almost lost my life because of a theory! A bloody theory! Are you taking this down?!'

Captain Meejum resisted the temptation to look away from the angry dwarf sitting opposite her.

'I think it's rather more than a theory, Dr Tellurium,' said Meejum.

'Really? Unless we can establish the exact formula I'm afraid I still see it as just a theory!'

'I understand you're frustrated,' said Meejum, 'and I am sorry to have to ask you these questions but you also mentioned a book. Did you tell Blasting the title of this book?'

'No, I didn't tell him the title of the book,' Tellurium retorted. 'Something about Myths and Legends. You'd have to ask Bauxite about it.'

'And had you mentioned anything to anyone else prior to your abduction?' Meejum was trying to draw things to a close.

'No I didn't *mention* anything to anyone else! It's a *top secret* project!' Tellurium folded his arms and glared at the floor. 'Dr Foxglove knows more about the project than I do, can't think why they didn't take her instead,' he grumbled.

Captain Meejum blinked and paused.

'Right,' she said, and looked down at her notes.

Tellurium looked up at the Captain.

'For gods' sake, get this spell out of me!' he whined.

* * *

During his visit to the palace library General Macjooste had received two couriered reports. One was from Captain Meejum, detailing her interview with Dr Tellurium. The other was from Adler and was far less comprehensive, not least because the commander had completely omitted the fact that the Trips had come to the team's aid during the rescue mission in Mount Dou.

Shortly after receiving the two reports, the General had briefed the King. In the spirit of entente cordiale, King Egbert had revealed Professor Bauxite's Torrimaya Trio theory to Lord Esodo. The King decided that the Rataquians could do little with this revelation, if only because most of the information regarding the original descendants was safely stored in the palace archives and was therefore beyond the reach of Rataquian genealogists and/or historical researchers.

By ten thirty that morning, General Macjooste had returned to his office and was currently re-reading the files of the senior personnel working on the Green Pastures project. The documents revealed nothing new, LUSU agents, however, had been ordered to delve even deeper into the backgrounds of the project team.

Several canine agents had also been sent to stake out the homes of senior project team members and the dogs had been told to report any suspicious activities. Agent Doyle led the surveillance operation and had chosen to watch Dr Philomena Foxglove's residence, not far from Fortnum Park. Nothing untoward *seemed* to have happened overnight but at one point in the evening Doyle could have sworn that he'd lost the scent of Dr Foxglove, and yet he was certain she hadn't left the house. Doyle had snuck into the garden and spent the best part of an hour sniffing around to see if he could detect the project manager's distinctive rose and jasmine perfume but, just as Doyle was about to report the incident he finally got a whiff of the fragrance. Satisfied that she was in the house

Doyle returned to his surveillance location (a doorway across the street) and the rest of the night passed without incident.

The following morning the dogs tailed their respective suspects to their workplaces, that is to say military headquarters. Once the canine agents had been debriefed they were dismissed for a well-earned snooze.

'We should have done this to start with,' the General said, to his empty office. 'I blame myself. My father always says that with prosperity comes complacency.'

There was a knock on the door.

'Sorry to trouble you, sir,' said Captain Florina, as she poked her head around the door.

'Captain?' said the General.

'I hope you don't mind but I stopped at your home on my way to work this morning. Lady Macjooste has sent some clean clothes, sir.'

General Macjooste was momentarily silenced by a rush of guilt.

'Um,' he finally uttered. 'Thank you Captain.'

'Shall I send Lady Macjooste a bunch of flowers, sir?' asked the young elf.

'Yes. I mean, no. I mean, I think this is going to take more than flowers,' said the General, somewhat thrown by the personal nature of the conversation. 'Thank you anyway. Could I possibly trouble you for a cup of...'

'Kettle's just boiled, sir, I'll be two shakes of a dragon's tail,' said Florina, unfazed by her boss' response. 'Oh, and Lady Macjooste asked me to remind you to have a shave before lunch.'

The General stared at the door as his assistant left to retrieve the items of clothing and make his coffee.

'But... I've...' the General rubbed his face. 'Right ... Another shave...Um... where was I?'

BLASTING PLANS THE NEXT PHASE
Queen Petra hosts lunch.

On the banks of a turquoise-coloured pool that was surrounded by leafy palm trees, a dozen recently-aged fairies were resting after the huge reserves of magic they'd used to instantly transport Blasting's giant pod from Mount Dou to his isolated oasis in the southern province of Rojizo, in Rataq. The fairies spoke in hushed tones about families and mates back home and avoided discussing the limited amount of time they would have to spend the vast sums they had been paid for their magic.

In a clearing, set back a short distance from the pool, stood three large tents. At first glance these looked like any other desert tents, as erected by the nomadic Rojizo elfin tribes, whose camel trains travelled back and forth along the Old Salt Road of the Gogobee Desert in order to sell such goods as salt, silk, and silver spoons handcrafted by the elves of Arjondell.

The three tents at Blasting's oasis, however, were no ordinary temporary dwellings. On closer examination it was clear that no expense had been spared in creating a luxurious home-away-from-home. A dense clump of palm trees provided shade from the piercing sun and swathes of white silk wafted in a warm, gentle breeze. In tent number one a full contingent of staff was preparing vast quantities of food. Within the second tent was an impressively well-equipped, temporary laboratory.

On either side of the entrance to the third tent meanwhile, stood two burly, purple-winged, fairies, dressed in the traditional garb of the Gogobee desert-fairy warriors. They had long, curved wands tucked into their black silk waistbands, and wore black boots, especially designed with small, internal pockets in which could be hidden two small daggers, the tips of which were dipped in scorpion poison.

This was Blasting's personal tent. The floor was carpeted with intricately detailed handwoven rugs, on which were with the traditional designs of the pixies of Atolia. To one side of the tent was a desk on which stood a glass-fronted display case containing Blasting's solid gold replica of the Torrimaya Axe. The statue of the war god, Bez, was nowhere to be seen.

In the middle of the tent were four sofas, positioned in a square, all of which were smothered in cushions. On one of the sofas sat Blasting, who was discussing recent developments with his senior thaumurtologist, Dr Stobel, who sat opposite her employer.

In her home country of Stermin, Dr Stobel had been struggling to attract the funding she needed for an experimental spell-extraction technique which she'd designed and developed. Despite trying to convince investors that the procedure had enormous medical potential, the controversial procedure was considered by many to be a form of torture and therefore illegal under Eris's Bi-continental agreement. When, therefore, Blasting had asked to meet her to discuss the technique, and then offered her an unlimited budget, as well as a large fee, if she came to work for him, Dr Stobel had said, *Yes please. Where do I sign*?

Accepting Blasting's terms and conditions had seemed like a remarkably good idea at the time. There were, however, circumstances Dr Stobel could not possibly have foreseen. Uprooting her laboratory from Mount Dou at extremely short notice and transporting it to the middle of the dessert had, for example, not been mentioned when she'd signed the contract.

'… Yes, well, it's not beyond the realms of possibility that we might need the descendants of the Torrimaya Trio, especially if the ancestor of Halvar the Just is linked to the ancient enchantment. If this is the case then, technically, I would be able to extract his inherited spellage. The ancient magic contained in his spellage could then be infused into Terminus,' said Dr Stobel.

'Excellent!' said Blasting. 'This is exactly what I

wanted to hear.'

'So, does this mean that you know who the descendants of the original trio are?' Dr Stobel asked.

'I have someone keeping their ears to the ground,' said Blasting, not wishing to reveal too much to Dr Stobel.

'Mr Blasting, sir,' a purple-winged fairy-guard opened the tent flap and entered. 'A message for you,' he said, handing Blasting a note

'I shall be in my lab if you need me.' Dr Stobel stood up, bowed slightly and left the tent.

* * *

While Blasting was in the Rataquian desert, working on the next phase of his plan, Queen Petra was talking to Lady Esodo about wine.

'Of course it's entirely up to you, Constanza but a small glass of the Rouchefort Rosé over lunch may not do your girls any harm, as long as they eat something first. I know it's not the same as the Rataquian Cielo Uva Rossa,' said the Queen, rolling her 'r' perfectly, 'but the rosé is a little lighter and just one glass might help calm their nerves.'

The Queen and Lady Esodo were in the Mukai drawing room, waiting for everyone to join them before lunch.

'Your Highness is most thoughtful to go to so many troubles,' smiled Lady Esodo.

'I shall of course leave it up to you,' replied the Queen. 'I always allow my eldest two a small glass with their main course, and I will most certainly be having a drop or two this afternoon,' she added with a conspiratorial smile.

The drawing room doors were opened by attendants and the females of the Macjooste family were announced.

'Oh Maria,' said the Queen, as she stood to greet the General's wife. 'How lovely to see you. It's been an age.'

Lady Esodo also stood and the Macjooste fairies curtsied to their queen.

'Your Highness,' said Lady Macjooste. 'It really has been too long.'

'My goodness, Maria, Hamish will be mounting guards at your front door to prevent young suitors from whisking off your beautiful girls,' said the Queen, with a smile.

'Please don't suggest that to Father, will you?' said the taller of the two.

'I'm afraid he might think of it all by himself,' the Queen said, with a smile. 'Now will you two do a little something for me? Please go and find the others, and no dawdling. There'll be plenty of time for gossip after we've eaten.'

As requested, General Macjooste's daughters went in search of the royal children and Lady Esodo's daughters.

'Constanza, you've met Maria haven't you?'

'Of course, Lady Macjooste, a pleasure to see you again,' said Lady Esodo, with a bow of her head.

'Please, call me Maria. I'm so sorry to hear of the dreadful attack on your residence. You must have been terrified,' replied Lady Macjooste.

'We are much calmer now and Her Majesty has been most generous in her hospitality,' said Lady Esodo.

'You are very kind to say so Constanza but, I'm sure you would have done the same had the roles been reversed. We are all fairies of the world here and I think it's probably fair to say that if there's one thing worse than a husband who's prone to knee-jerk reactions, it's teenage daughters being caught up in their father's knee-jerk reactions and being swept along in the ensuing drama.'

The Queen looked at her guests, searching for confirmation that she was not alone in this experience.

'Ronaldo is of course Rataquian. Rataquian male fairies are always emotional. It is in their blood. They overreact when they are stuck in traffic,' added Constanza, waving a hand in the air for emphasis.

'Hamish has gone to quite the other extreme and won't tell us a thing. I understand he wants to protect us but I'm not sure it's always wise to wrap our girls in velvet wings,' said Maria. 'Besides which, have you seen the new iBox?'

The Queen and Lady Esodo nodded.

'I'm not sure I'm happy about the use of techo-magic. Who knows what those imps might hear. What if they get stolen? All that private information in one place. I'm surprised Hamish lets them in the house, Maria,' said the Queen.

'Of course, he's had the imps security checked and all messaging has to be stopped after supper but, the girls are constantly communicating with their friends through something called Imp Chat. It seems to be nothing but a forum for gossip and misinformation, which I think is far worse for young folk.'

'Ronaldo have taken girls' boxes from them now,' said Lady Esodo. 'There were many tears but their father he blame boxes for attack.'

'Does he really?' said the Queen. 'Gracious me.'

With that, the doors opened and the three husbands, accompanied by Professor Bauxite and Mr Antequam, entered the room. From the corridor could be heard a gaggle of chattering female voices heralding the arrival of the younger members of the party.

* * *

Queen Petra had arranged for lunch to be served alfresco, as was the custom in the Esodos' home province of Imbria. A long table had been placed under two old Willow trees near the river and the leafy, umbrella-like branches shaded the party from the sun. Dozens of servants relayed to and from the palace, with an array of especially prepared Rataquian dishes. A number of bottles of wine, including several of the Rouchefort Rosé, were kept cool in the River Sterm using a metal cage designed by the palace sommelier. Mr Antequam was served three different types of salad, and an omelette, all of which were delicious much to the librarian's surprise.

The meal proved the perfect opportunity for the younger fairies to distance themselves emotionally from recent events. Queen Petra was pleased to observe that the royal children, as well as Lady Macjooste's daughters, had taken the Esodo girls under their wings. The young fairies sat at one end of the table, where the main topic of conversation revolved around plans for General Macjooste's youngest daughter's upcoming twenty-fifth birthday ball. The young fairy was currently being bombarded with much advice and there was some considerable discussion on a variety of ball-related subjects.

While the girls discussed dresses and whispered the names of potential, eligible, dance partners, Professor Bauxite quietly conversed with Lady Macjooste.

'Of course, I'm only an amateur, Professor, and confess I was sidetracked during my most recent search,' said Lady Macjooste.

'Ah, yes,' nodded the Professor, 'easily done I'm afraid, although some diversions can prove fruitful in the long-run.'

'This is true, however, I was hoping to produce a completed genealogical chart for my father-in-law, as a Torrimaya Day gift,' said Lady Macjooste. 'There are countless anecdotes about the role the family played during the Wand Wars, although it's unlikely many of them are true, so I thought I would try to set the records straight.'

'But Lady Macjooste, going back that far is rarely done by anyone other than a PhD student of Fairy Genealogy! In some cases it can take decades to research and generate a completed fairy family tree,' said the Professor, genuinely startled at Lady Macjooste's ambitious project.

'Oh I'm so relieved to hear that. I started the project almost two years ago and have been berating myself for not having managed to get further back than nine thousand years,' said Lady Macjooste.

'My word!' said the Professor. 'Most dwarf genealogists will only go back two or three thousand years because of the difficulty in finding parchments any older than this.'

'So I've discovered,' said Lady Macjooste. 'I asked several of the city's most reputable genealogists to take on the task but they all refused. I'm ashamed to say I thought it would be far easier than it has in fact turned out to be,' said Lady Macjooste. 'Even with the help of the myriad information archived at the Macjooste family's Carrtile estate.

'Have you found anything at all?' asked the Professor.

'The estate librarian is a sweet old dwarf but, Mr Pergamir's memory isn't quite what it used to be. During our visits to Hamish's parents I'm rarely able to dedicate much time to the project and, even when I do have time, I am often hampered by the jumble of poorly shelved records. I frequently second a member of the household staff to help re-shelve the documents I've examined.'

'So exactly where are you in the proceedings?' asked the Professor.

'I've traced Hamish's family back to the Wing Dynasty, when some of Cashen's regions were ruled by members of a tribe referred to as the Rhowe,' said Lady Macjooste, 'which I read somewhere, may have connections to the Rao tribe, although I've yet to prove this.'

'But that's only a thousand years after the Wand Wars!' said the Professor.

'Indeed. But, during my last visit, I was sidetracked by a chest full of scrolls that I think may relate to a forging family of dwarves from the Torrimaya mountain range.'

'My word. A rare find indeed. Do you know how the Macjooste family came by these scrolls?' asked the Professor.

'I'm afraid I don't, Professor,' replied Lady Macjooste. 'However, my mother-in-law allowed me to bring the scrolls home so that I might examine them further. Unfortunately my knowledge of ancient Cashenian is woefully inadequate which means I have hit a dead-end. Her Majesty says the scrolls might help your quest, so they are waiting for you and Mr Antequam in the palace library,' said Lady Macjooste with a modest smile.

'Lady Macjooste, I cannot thank you enough for such an opportunity,' said the Professor.

'My pleasure. Perhaps when you are done with them you could tell me if they were of any use to you.'

Lord Esodo, who was sitting opposite General Macjooste, leaned forward to speak.

'So, General, you too have very clever wife,' Lord Esodo said with a nod. 'And your Queen, she knows what she is doing, no?'

'Lord Esodo, sometimes I wonder if it is the females who have more sense than us males. And, despite the occasional evidence to the contrary, Queen Petra has more diplomatic skills in the tip of her left wing than most of us males put together,' said the General, with a smile.

'Ah,' said the Ambassador, as he shrugged and raised his hands, 'as with so many females. Et sic de mundo, as my ancestors say.'

The General sipped his nectar and nodded.

'As you say, Ambassador, it really is so often the way of the world.'

* * *

Not long after the coffee and Tico-Tico biscuits had been served, King Egbert, General Macjooste, Ambassador Esodo and the two elderly dwarves, thanked the Queen and excused themselves from the party. For the Queen and the other fairies the serenity of the setting proved ideal for a relaxing afternoon. Blankets were brought from the palace so that the girls could sit or lie by the river's edge, make daisy chains and share intimate stories out of earshot from their ever-watchful mothers.

REVELATIONS
The Macjooste scrolls.

Professor Bauxite and Mr Antequam agreed that the alfresco lunch had provided a much needed break in their attempt to unearth the identities of the Torrimaya Trio. Now, however, the pair was keen to scrutinise the scrolls loaned to them by Lady Macjooste. The two elderly dwarves returned to the palace library to find the students huddled around a mystery chest that had been delivered just before lunch.

'Gloves first,' said the Professor, 'And Hibbs,' he added, addressing one of the students, 'would you be so kind as to clear the reading tables so that we can examine the documents Lady Macjooste has kindly loaned us.'

It was immediately apparent that someone had gone to great lengths to ensure that the records would withstand the test of time as most of the documents were in excellent condition for their age. The team delicately and painstakingly began to examine the chest's contents and was captivated by what they found. Included in the cache were dwarf clan financial ledgers, fairy tribe chronicles, journals, and several detailed designs for a range of tools, including axes. In the corners of many of the records were variations of the wand and broken wing symbol, a mark indicating that these were writings from the post Wand Wars period.

There was much scritching and scratching of quill on parchment as the dwarves translated the ancient Cashenian texts and made notes. Subdued conversations took place at one table or another throughout the day until the orangey-pink glow of the setting sun shone through the library windows. One of the students yawned and his peers quickly followed suit. Professor Bauxite broke the soporific silence.

'Mr Antequam, would you agree that we have been more than lucky in our discovery of the descendant of the Green Pastures pixie, Tuläher?' asked the Professor, scanning a small, leather-bound, book on the table before him.

'I would indeed,' replied the librarian, poring over a drawing of an axe.

'Would you therefore consider that our chances of finding another member of the Torrimaya Trio today are extremely unlikely?' continued the Professor, who was now checking a ledger, which lay next to the small book.

'Such good fortune rarely happens twice in one day,' said the Mr Antequam, as he looked up.

The Professor looked between the two texts and then wrote something in a notebook on the table.

'Have you, or has anyone for that matter, come across any references to a Forgemaster Sæl?' asked the Professor, as he looked up from the documents.

'Sæl? Do you think he could be the forgemaster?' asked Mr Antequam.

Some of the students stopped what they were doing and graduated towards the reading table.

'Professor, sir,' piped up one of the students. 'There's something in this ledger that has a forgemaster by the name of Sæl in it.'

'Could you bring it here, Hibbs?' asked the Professor.

'Let's clear a space shall we,' said Mr Antequam.

Hibbs's peers carefully removed several parchments from the reading table so that room could be made for the second ledger. The Professor took a moment to translate the information during which time there was much foot shuffling from the students. Hibbs chewed his nails.

'We now have four documents where this Forgemaster Sæl is mentioned,' the Professor finally said, 'but first, Mr Antequam, would you read from the ledger Hibbs discovered so that I may compare translations?'

Mr Antequam scuttled to the other side of the table to look at the entry and, after making his own notes, began to read aloud.

'*Forgemaster Sæl, Ijolite senior forgemaster. Level of*

the highest order to the clan. Axe-maker to the chieftain. Forgemaster Sæl declared absent,' read Mr Antequam.

'I have much the same translation. Now would you be so kind as to read this entry,' said the Professor, pointing to the first ledger.

'Faunal Bazzite, Ijolite high-level chronicler. Faunal Bazzite declared absent. I'm not sure I see the connection,' said Mr Antequam.

'I believe these entries may, partially, explain what happened,' said the Professor, as he trundled to the other side of the table and began to read from a third ledger. 'Here we have, *Forgemaster Sæl, Ijolite senior craftsman. Level of the highest order to the clan. Axe-maker to the Rao chieftain. Requested permission,* or perhaps it says *the right,* it's open to interpretation,' the Professor added, *'Requested permission to leave clan, with his family, to accompany Ladye Orquidea. Permission granted.'*

'Lady Orquidea?' said Hibbs, 'That sounds very similar to Lady Orchid.'

'An excellent observation, Mr Hibbs,' said the Professor, walking back to his original spot in front of the leather-bound book. 'Given the timeline, in conjunction with the reference to a chieftain, my best guess would be that Lady Orquidea is in fact Lady Orchid, whom we have always recognised as Halvar the Just's wife. This would almost certainly mean that Forgemaster Sæl is the forgemaster of the Torrimaya Axe.'

The students' eyes widened and their excitement gave them all a burst of energy.

'But what of that document?' asked Mr Antequam, pointing to the small, leather-bound, book.

'This, Mr Antequam is a journal of the aforementioned Faunal Bazzite, and must have been written subsequent to the Sæl family's departure from the Torrimaya Range. It seems that this is more of a journal than a tribal history, and this particular extract has given me several clues as to who the descendant might be. Let me first read you this and then I shall explain all.'

The Professor cleared his throat and began to read to the excited dwarves.

'*The entourage has finally settled far south of the Torrimaya range and we camp near a hamlet the local dwarvish clan refer to as Svjarte. Forgemaster Sæl has been offered a place on Ladye Orquidea's council, a great honour indeed.*

'*Forgemaster Sæl's family has constructed a temporary foundry and they are being asked to repair all manner of items by the local community. There is talk of settling here permanently although Ladye Orquidea misses her son who, having made camp in the hills further north, has yet to join us.*

'*The forgemaster's youngest son has recently approached me asking what qualifications are required for chronicling. It seems he feels unsuited to the forging trade as he is unable to grasp some of the fundamentals needed to make an axe. I sympathise with the young dwarf. Fortunately chronicling is an equally noble trade for a dwarf. Sadly there are some who do not always recognise this. My own father once said that a dwarf is not a real dwarf unless he is able to make his own axe...*

'Now, before we all head home for a rest, let me tell you about this young dwarf I recently met by the name of Norman Shale,' said Professor Bauxite.

THE MYTHS AND LEGENDS OF ERIS' DWARVES AND FAIRIES,
By J.R Horneblende.
Professor Bauxite goes missing.

While Professor Bauxite had been working at the palace, Norman had taken full advantage of his new employer's absence to tidy the office. Using the University library's system as a point of reference, the young dwarf had organised several hundred books into subject headings. He had then affixed rectangular labels to the shelves indicating where each subject could be found. Norman had managed to return all the library books he could find and had then cleared one of the shelves so that future borrowed library books could be separated from the Professor's own.

After completing this monumental organisational task Norman had gone home feeling exhausted, but satisfied. As Norman lay in bed he reminded himself that Talula was coming to meet him for lunch the following day and that his next administrative task would be to tackle the mountain of parchment-work on the Professor's desk.

Unfortunately Norman overslept the next morning. By the time he arrived at Assay University it was rush hour. Hordes of cacophonous students stampeded through the corridors as they hurried to their lectures and Norman vowed never to be late again because he didn't like crowds, and the heat was beginning to make him feel a little nauseous.

Norman sighed with relief when he finally spotted the sign for Barchan Tunnel East. He ducked down the side exit, leaned against the wall and took a few deep breaths before taking the office key out of his jacket pocket. The office was two doors along and, as he approached number 27B, Norman could see that the door was slightly ajar. He knocked and tentatively pushed open the door.

'Professor? Are you here?'

Norman's question was greeted with silence. He

walked into the office and immediately noticed that the wheelbarrow had been moved and that dozens of books had been pulled from the shelves. Norman considered two possible reasons for the mess: either Professor Bauxite had no respect for Norman's efforts or someone had been looking for something without the Professor's consent. Neither prospect reassured Norman about the scene before him. Norman suddenly remembered the petty-cash tin that he'd hidden under the Professor's sofa for safe-keeping and dashed through to the back room. He dropped to his knees and, much to his relief, found the dented metal box with a faded painting of Mount Mukai on the lid.

* * *

Norman spent the morning tidying up and found space on another shelf for the majority of the documents and scrolls that had been taking up so much space on the desk. He'd just finished putting some of the tools back into the canvas bag behind the door when Talula appeared in the open doorway. It was just after midday.

'Wow, this place looks completely different. It looks like a proper office,' said Talula, as she looked around the room.

Norman was packing his satchel and looked up at Talula.

'Oh, I was hoping it was Professor Bauxite,' Norman said.

'There's manners for you,' she replied.

'Sorry, I mean, I've been waiting for a message from the Professor and was just about to go and see if he was at home.'

'Why?' Talula asked.

'Last I heard he was at the palace so I used some money from petty-cash and sent a courier with a message but I didn't hear back so I sent another one to his house, and I still haven't heard anything,' said Norman.

'Had it occurred to you that he's busy?' Talula asked.

'Of course. I mean it's not like he has to let me know

175

where he is every minute of the day I just thought… what if something's happened to him?'

'Like what?' said Talula.

'I don't know. He knows Dr Tellurium and there's that whole weapon of mass destruction theory of yours. What if he's been kidnapped too?'

'Not that long ago I seem to remember *someone* thought I was a bit odd for suggesting a member of Assay University's staff might've been kidnapped.'

'I never said you were odd,' Norman said, defensively. 'And that was before we'd met the General, and had that interview, and found out the Professor and the General knew each other, and the Professor asked me to find that …'

'Woah! Slow down,' interrupted Talula, 'aaa-and breathe.' Norman looked into Talula's eyes and inhaled deeply. 'That's better. Now, who delivered the message to the Professor?' asked Talula.

'A pixie?' said Norman, marginally confused by the question.

'Useful,' said Talula, sarcastically. 'What did the pixie look like?'

'I don't know. I used one of the couriers from the staff room down the hall. He had red hair, if that helps.'

'Hmm.' Talula frowned.

'What, hmm? What's wrong?' asked Norman.

'Snoop Fox is the only local pixie I know with red hair and he was hanging around Iffies last night.'

'Who's Snoop Fox?'

'You don't know who Snoop Fox is?' asked Talula, incredulously.

'Should I?' replied Norman.

'You live in the Murks, dodgiest part of the city, you must have heard of him. Snoop grew up there!'

'I don't know anyone in the Murks, apart from Mr and Mrs Wimble, and that's only because they're my landlords.'

Talula stared at Norman.

'How is it possible to …'

'Talula,' interrupted Norman. 'Who is this Snoop Fox and what does he have to do with Professor Bauxite?'

'Sorry. Snoop is a pixie with friends in lower than low places. Whenever Snoop hits the streets criminal activities are sure to follow,' said Talula.

'And you *know* this pixie?' said Norman, visibly worried.

'No! I don't *know* him, know him, I know *of* him. My mate, Margaleet, told me that Snoop used to be a royal courier but got sacked when he got caught with his mitts in the head courier's cash box. Apparently he was dishonourably discharged from royal duties and couldn't get a job anywhere in the city so he started working for the Disattos,' explained Talula. 'You have heard of the Disasttos haven't you?'

'Of course I've heard of them. They're Vinster's biggest Below Ground criminal network,' replied Norman. 'Anyway, what was this Snoop Fox doing at Iffies?'

'No idea. Margaleet popped in while I was waiting for you...'

'I'm really sorry about last night,' interrupted Norman.

Talula rolled her eyes.

'I know,' she said. 'Anyway, Margaleet popped into Iffies last night, so we had a drink. Snoop was sitting next to our table. I vaguely overheard him talking to a couple of fairies about a book.'

'Fairies? Book? What book?' asked Norman.

'I don't know. I didn't think I needed to pay too much attention.'

'Do you remember anything?' asked Norman.

Talula looked down as if studying the floor.

'There was a female fairy and a male fairy. The female was wearing a dark blue, almost black, silk cape. She kept looking around the inn. I'm guessing she wanted to blend in but she seemed a bit twitchy and the expensive-looking cape actually made her stand out. As for the male fairy, he was wearing a black cape with a hood,' said Talula, as she looked up. 'Which isn't that unusual a dress-code at Iffies. I did hear the male fairy say he'd pay top florin if Snoop found the book he wanted.' Talula looked apologetically at Norman. 'Sorry, I didn't get the title, it was really busy last night. I couldn't hear much. The three of them were there for about an hour, maybe less.'

Norman put on his jacket.

'We need to find that book,' said Norman.

'What book? Where are you going?'

'The one the Professor mentioned last night. It might be at the Professor's house,' said Norman, as he walked towards the door.

'You think these fairies are after this book then?' asked Talula.

'I don't know for sure but I was reading it last night and then when I came in this morning there were books and stuff all over the floor. It looked like the office had been ransacked.'

'Oh.' Talula frowned. 'So what was in this book then?'

'I'm not sure if it's even relevant. It's just a book on myths and legends but there's a chapter about the Torrimaya Axe and, well, I don't know, I just have a feeling it might be linked to the super-weapon theory and I ...' Norman looked at his boots.

They were covered in scuff marks and one of the shoelaces was undone. He didn't bend down to tie it up.

Talula had delivered messages to some of the meanest characters in the city; dwarves who'd poke your eye out with a fork as soon as look at you, fairies who wouldn't hesitate to use an entrapment-spell down a dark alley then steal all your money, and trolls who'd throw you down a well just to see how deep it was.

'You are quite possibly the most un-dwarfy, dwarf I've ever met,' Talula said. 'You're clumsy, you have no clue when it comes to the real world, and you consistently ignore the first rule of survival in Vinster.

'What rule is that?' asked Norman.

'Never get involved in someone else's fight,' replied Talula.

'This isn't a fight,' said Norman as he picked up his satchel and put the strap on his shoulder. 'You coming?'

Talula sighed.

'You *say* it's not a fight, but in the end there's always *some* kind of fight,' she mumbled, as she followed Norman out of the office.

'What?' asked Norman, as he closed the door.

'So where does the Professor live then?' asked Talula, tactfully.

A SHED, AN EXPLOSION, AN AXE
And another kidnapping.

Norman and Talula left Assay University and took the number eight horse-bus, which would take them all the way to Queensbridge. On the bus the pair said very little about recent events, reasoning that it was best not to let anyone hear a conversation that included words such as kidnap, weapon of mass destruction or General Macjooste. Instead Talula espoused her views on the new iBoxes and how they'd never catch on, not only because they were a bit on the pricey side but also because imps could be fickle creatures and had a tendency to get stroppy if they felt they were being overworked. Eventually, however, Talula couldn't resist passing on some information that she thought might be useful to their current quest.

Talula looked around to make sure the other passengers weren't listening. The goblin sitting behind Norman was engrossed in a copy of the Vinster-on-Sterm Times. Three female dwarves and an elf were discussing the recent price increase of fish at Fillingsgate market, and a pixie mum was holding onto her two young pixlings to stop them from, literally, climbing the walls of the cart.

Talula leaned in and whispered to Norman.

'Fig the fruit merchant, told Belle the seamstress, who told Bob the rag man, who I was chatting to this morning, that someone's been flashing a lot of cash and paying top florin for a slew of Disatto fairies.'

'I don't follow,' whispered Norman, who really hadn't understood the series of events leading to Talula's concluding statement.

'It *means* that some of the Disatto fairies are selling their magic on the black market to someone here in Vinster. Which makes sense, cos' the likes of Snoop Fox don't usually hang around Iffies,' whispered Talula.

'Why not?' asked Norman.

'Because soldiers go to Iffies far too often for the likes

of Snoop,' said Talula.

'Right,' said Norman. 'And what does this Snoop Fox do exactly?' Norman whispered.

'He's a lifter for the Disattos,' whispered Talula.

'Halvar Piazza!' shouted the driver, as the cart pulled into the bus stop.

The goblin behind Norman folded his newspaper and waited for the horse-bus to come to a complete stop before waddling to the front and getting off.

'You mean he steals things?!' Norman whispered.

Talula nodded confirmation. The horse-bus pulled away and trundled down the street.

'You know that painting by Tamian Urst that went missing from the city gallery a couple of years ago?' whispered Talula.

'The one that just had tiny, multi-coloured, fairy wings all over it?' whispered Norman.

Talula nodded conspiratorially and mouthed, *Snoop.*

Norman stared at Talula, who looked furtively over her shoulder.

'Windig Hill!' shouted the driver.

'If it's not nailed down, Snoop'll nab it,' whispered Talula.

'How do you *know* these things?!' said Norman, unnerved by the idea that he, potentially, now knew the name of the pixie who had committed one of the most talked about crimes in Vinster since the Fillingsgate murders.

'Come on,' said Talula, as the horse-bus came to a stop.

＊ ＊ ＊

At the top of Windig Hill was a cul-de-sac with just two cottages. The first cottage had two miniature, wooden wheelbarrows parked outside - one either side of the front door,

'This is it. One Windig Hill,' said Norman, looking at the number on the white picket gate.

Talula opened the gate and started walking down the

path.

'Never been to this part of Queensbridge before,' said Talula. 'Good to know for my test.'

'Something's not right. The front door's not closed properly,' said Norman.

'I'll admit, it's a bit suspicious,' said Talula, as the pair came to a stop in front of the door.

The complete lack of noise coming from inside the house prompted Norman to push the door open.

'Hello? Professor?' Norman said.

The pair waited a few moments.

'Doesn't seem to be here. What now? Shall I get the General?' asked Talula.

Norman looked through the door into the house and then at Talula.

'You have a quick look inside and I'll look around back. He might be doing some gardening or something.'

'Gardening? Really?' said Talula.

'Unlikely but, stranger things have happened... recently, in fact.'

Norman left Talula to check inside the house. Norman's stomach churned as he scurried past the front windows to the side of the house.

'I'm not cut out for this,' Norman muttered, trotting towards a wooden door, which he assumed led to the back garden. 'Please gods, nothing's happened to the Professor.'

Norman undid the latch and closed the door behind him. He stood at the back of the house and glanced around the Professor's very tidy, long wide garden, which was separated from his neighbour's by a low, stone wall. At the end of the garden were several trees. In front of the trees was a small shed. There was no sign of the Professor. Norman could see that the shed's door was closed but he decided to check the potential hideaway to make sure the Professor wasn't inside.

'He could be asleep,' Norman muttered, as he walked

down the stone path. 'He's been working hard these past few days.' Norman stepped over a fallen flower pot. 'But then why was the front door open?' Norman reached for the latch on the shed door. 'And if he'd been....'

BANG! WHOOOOOOSH!

Norman was hurled backwards onto the lawn.

Weeeeeeeeeeeeeeeeeeeeeeeeeeeeeeeeeeeeeeee...!

Something flew skyward.

eeeeeeeeeeeeeeeeeeeeeeeeeeeeeeeeeeeeeeeeeeeeeeeeeeeeeeeeee..!

Norman curled up into a ball and covered his head with his hands...

...eeeeeeeeeeeeeeeeeeeeeeeeeeeeeeeeeeeeeeeeeeeeeee...!

...and waited.

...eeeeeeeeeeeeeeeeeeee! THUD!

After a moment's silence Professor Bauxite's neighbour, and cleaning dwarf, opened her kitchen window and leaned out.

''Ere! What you doin' blowin' up the Professor's shed!' hollered Mrs Poto. 'Bloomin' student 'speriments! You lot had better clean up after you!' she added as she closed the window.

* * *

Blasting was sitting on one of the heavily cushioned sofas in his exclusive hideaway in Rataq. A very old, and extremely big, book entitled, *The Myths and Legends of Eris' Dwarves and Fairies, by J.R. Horneblende*, was on the coffee table in front of him. The fairy was nonchalantly tapping his wand on his right thigh. Opposite Blasting, Professor Bauxite was sitting on another sofa. His face was pale and weary.

'...And this theory of yours all started with a tale from Hornblende's book?' said Blasting, pointing his wand in the book's direction. 'How fascinating.'

'I've told you everything I know. What more do you want from me?' asked Bauxite, deeply frustrated that he had been unable to resist the truth spell.

'And I am grateful you have shared your knowledge

with me, Professor,' said Blasting.

'I feel I had little choice, sir,' said the Professor, indignantly

'True,' said Blasting, with a smug grin.

'What are you going to do now?' asked the Professor.

'I have of course sent a courier to my aide, who should be searching for this Talula Ewesage and Norman Shale, as we speak,' replied Blasting.

'But I haven't confirmed that they are the descendants,' said Bauxite, truthfully.

Blasting smiled.

'Please, Professor, try not to worry. Kinins will take good care of them.' Blasting stood up. 'Now, you look like you could do with a rest. Guards!' The two dessert warrior fairies entered the tent. 'Take the Professor to his tent.'

* * *

'TA DA!'

An old, battered axe stood on the tip of its handle among the splintered remains of the Professor's shed.

'Norman?!'

Talula had dashed out of the house and was removing bits of shed that had landed on the dwarf.

'I'm fine,' said Norman, hauling himself up from the lawn.

'I said... Ta Da!' repeated the axe.

* * *

'General, sir,' said Captain Florina, 'there has been a massive surge of magic in Queensbridge.'

The General stood up and marched across his office.

'Where in Queensbridge?' he asked, grabbing his cloak from the back of the door.

'The top of Windig Hill, sir,' said Florina.

'That's Professor Bauxite's address. Contact Adler and Wand and tell them to meet me there.'

* * *

'But you talk, and you don't look anything like the

pictures I've seen of the Torrimaya Axe,' said Talula. 'And what's with blowing up the shed?'

Norman and Talula were standing either side of the Professor's kitchen table. On the tip of its handle stood the Torrimaya Axe.

'Pent up magic,' said the Axe. 'And what do you mean I don't look anything like the pictures you've seen?'

'I expected something smaller, you're almost as big as me. And…I thought you'd be fancier,' said Talula, 'and maybe not quite so filthy. How do we know this isn't some kind of trick? You could be a student who couldn't pay Larry the Lender for all we know. I heard he turned a second-year from the University into a pick axe once and forced it to dig up an entire warehouse floor.'

'Really?' said Norman and the Axe, simultaneously.

'That's what I heard,' said Talula, folding her arms.

'I'm so sorry that my appearance does not meet with your expectations,' said the Axe, huffily, 'but first of all, I don't think I was designed to be some kind of trinket to hang above the fireplace and secondly, you try being buried for thousands of years under permafrost, dug up, then chucked in a shed with a pile of rusty old tools. I'd like to see how good *you* look after living under those conditions!'

'Um…?' said Talula, 'I didn't mean…'

'Here I am, reawakened to fulfil my destiny, using all the magic I can muster to ensure you are all brought together but, instead of being greeted warmly, or even tepidly, by the descendants of heroes, I'm told I'm filthy and accused of being a dwarf in disguise! I mean, it comes to something when …'

'Wait,' said Norman, 'what do you mean the descendants of heroes?'

'Which part of that phrase is troubling you?' asked the Axe.

* * *

Kinins was waiting for Snoop Fox at Iffies. He was

sitting at a table, in a dark corner of the inn, with his back against the wall, watching the front door. He'd barely touched the flagon of Triple Axe ale in front of him. As he watched a red-headed pixie push his way through the crowd Kinins felt a twinge in the scar on the tip of his left wing - a sign the table and sat down.

* * *

General Macjooste, Wing Commander Adler and Flight Lieutenant James Wand crept towards Professor Bauxite's open front door. The three uniformed fairies unholstered their wands. The General signalled for Adler to go to the back of the house while he and Wand moved towards the front door.

* * *

'... You mean your magic *forced* me to that axe-making class?!' said Norman.

'*You* made me interfere in Norman's attempted kidnap?! I broke the first rule of survival in Vinster thanks to you!' said Talula. 'Yet *another* reason to hate magic,' she mumbled.

'I'm sorry but it's in my sap! I'm *programmed* to bring the ancestors together. You have no idea how hard it was to get a...'

'I can't even hold a hammer, never mind make an axe. You have no idea how *humiliating*...!?' Norman interrupted.

'Freeze!' shouted the General, as he burst into the kitchen with Wand and Adler, wands pointed.

'NO!' shouted Norman, as he stood in front of Talula and put his hands in the air.

'Norman..? and Miss Ewesage,' said the General, lowering his wand.

'Ah, there's no doubting you are from the Rao,' said the Axe, as it bowed to the General, in a tilt-ey sort of way.

* * *

At Blasting's oasis in Rataq, a new batch of drained-looking fairies were sitting by the water's edge, resting after instantly transporting the Professor from Vinster. From the direction of the lab-tent, Dr Stobel walked between the palm trees towards the pool. She was wearing a long, white, sleeveless dress. Her emerald-green wings shimmered in the sun as she approached the male fairies lounging on the sand next to the water. When she arrived they all stood to greet her.

'Good afternoon,' said Dr Stobel, with a charming smile. 'I see you're all enjoying the sun.'

'Just waitin' for final payment, Miss, then we can shove off and spend it before we die,' said one of the fairies.

'And you undoubtedly deserve to do so,' she acknowledged. 'I wonder, however, if one of you has any spell reserves left?'

Dr Stobel fluttered her wings coquettishly and looked at the faces of the old fairies.

There was much muttering and mumbling as many of the fairies shook their heads and told her no. Finally a blue-winged fairy, who had not aged as much as the others, piped up.

'Woss it worf'?' he asked.

* * *

'Thank you, Miss Ewesage,' said the General. 'Perhaps at a more convenient time you can tell me all about this Larry the Lender.' General Macjooste turned to face the Axe. 'In the meantime, our young pixie raises a fair point. How do you propose to prove that you are what you say you are?'

'Well,' said the Axe, as if settling down to read a bed-time story, 'a long, long time ago, a fabulous fairy chieftain of the Rao tribe - your ancestor,' said the Axe, bowing to the General, 'commissioned an exceptionally talented dwarf of the Ijolite clan - that's your ancestor,' the Axe turned and bowed to Norman, 'to make an axe - that would be me. I was then infused with a ton of magic in order to put an end to both a brutal war and the life of a heinous fairy who, as I recall, went by the sobriquet of The Wing Collector. This remarkable weapon - that would be me again - was then placed in the centre of the Valley of the Green Pastures by one stupendously brave pixie - that would be your ancestor,' the Axe bowed in Talula's direction.

'Wait,' said the General. 'How do you know we are the ancestors?'

'I'm not quite finished,' said the Axe, haughtily. 'Where was I? Oh yes...The aforementioned pixie then incanted a spell that had been entrusted to her by the chieftain and, lo! I did my job and the war was ended, as were the lives of many warriors, good and bad.' The Axe paused. 'Oh, and you might not be able to see under *centuries* worth of dirt but, I also have the Rao insignia on my blade.'

Norman leaned over the table and scraped some of the caked-on mud off the blade to reveal a circular insignia with three triangles in the middle.

'Is it the circle with the mountain and the valley symbol?' said Norman, squinting at the small emblem on the Axe's blade.

'It might not look like much *now* but...'

'Excuse me,' said the General, 'but how exactly do you know *we* are the ancestors?' he repeated.

'It's in my sap. A built-in detection system if you will. The chronicler would have recorded everything, including my magical instructions, which state that I must return to fulfil my destiny if I am needed again. Surely everyone knows about this?' said the Axe, loftily.

'What do you mean fulfil your destiny?' asked the General.

'Clearly not everyone has read the instructions,' muttered the Axe. 'So,' it continued, 'included in Halvar's charm combination was a nifty magical clause in case the world was once again threatened. I am programmed to re-establish a connection with the four descendants and my force was to be used for good. Of course getting a decent signal around these parts has been tricky…'

'Hold on,' said the General. 'Four descendants?'

'Ah, yes, I've been meaning to ask. Where's the descendent of the chronicler?'

The General stared at the Axe.

'There are *four* ancestors?' he repeated.

'Are you certain I'm a descendant of the forgemaster?' said Norman, incredulously.

'What on Eris is going on?!' Talula said.

'What threat is the world under?' asked the General.

'One at a time please!' said the Axe 'Right, so, the magic is aligned in such a way that if anyone were to even attempt to start a magical war, one that would most definitely threaten the continued existence of the planet, then I was to fly into action and save the day, again,' said the Axe. 'It would seem that the time has come.'

'And Blasting is definitely the perpetrator?' asked the General.

'I can't tell you *who* is responsible for this threat, I can only sense the magic,' said the Axe. 'Someone definitely wants to start a war and is developing the capability to achieve that end.'

'And this combination of charms, they weren't…' started Norman.

'An intricate combination of charms? Yes they were,' interrupted the Axe.

'No, I mean…' Norman tried again.

'What was the name of Halvar's chronicler?' asked the General.

'I believe he was known as F….'

Without warning, the Axe fell from its tip and lay flat on the table. A second later every window in the cottage exploded. Everyone dived to the floor and covered their heads.

'Stay down!' the General ordered Norman and Talula.

The three military fairies upended the table to use as cover, unholstered their wands and began firing random freeze and flame-spells through the windows.

'Talula, grab the Axe,' shout-whispered Norman. 'See if you can get out of here.'

The Axe lay on the floor and continued to play dead. Talula crawled across the cottage floor on her stomach.

'What good are you if you can't handle a magical firefight!' whispered Talula, as she reached for the Axe

'Aarrgh!' screamed Adler.

'No!' James Wand cried out.

'I've been hit, General,' said Adler, paralysed.

'So have I, sir,' moaned Wand.

The General continued firing but the unseen forces outside were overwhelming. Talula took the Axe, stood up, raced for the back door, and sped away from the house. A steady stream of spells came from the front garden, besieging Adler, Wand, the General, and Norman. Before a plan could be formulated, four fairies burst through the front door of the cottage. There was a white flash and Norman and the General vanished.

The firing stopped. Adler and Wand lay paralysed, on the floor of the Professor's sitting room among the debris.

'Was that a quick-exit spell?' rasped Wand.

'I'll give them quick exit, when I catch them! Sons of trolls! Ow…' Adler winced. 'You alright Wand?'

'Fit as a fiddle, sir,' whispered Wand, then promptly passed out.

TALULA AND THE AXE
Doyle reveals his secret identity.

Talula hid behind a bush, clutching the Axe, and watched as there was another white flash and the four fairies reappeared - with the General and Norman. They bundled the pair into a carriage, which then charged off down the hill and vanished into thin air before reaching the bottom.

'Saw a barge do that the other day,' Talula said, staring down the empty road. 'Do they use their wands to do that or what?'

'We need a dog endowed with a keen sense of smell,' said the Axe, ignoring Talula's question.

'You can see, talk *and* smell?' said Talula.

'Don't be ridiculous. How could I possibly smell?!' said the Axe.

Talula glared at the Torrimaya Axe's head.

'Don't start with me. I think I've been pretty understanding about all of this,' she said in a voice that suggested she was losing patience with all things magic-related.

'Correct me if I'm wrong but I believe there was a dwarf driving that carriage,' said the Axe, with a supercilious air, 'and if memory serves, it was the female dwarves of the Ijolite clan who produced vast quantities of heather and lavender scent to disguise the pungent odours of their husbands.'

Talula inhaled deeply.

'Cologne!'

'Now we need a dog,' said the Axe.

'The city's full of dwarves dripping in cologne. And that carriage just disappeared. How do you expect a dog to follow a recently-vanished scent?'

'You find me a dog and I'll do the rest,' said the Axe.

Talula looked down the hill, then at the Axe.

'What about the injured soldiers?' she asked.

'Trust me, magic as strong as mine won't go unnoticed,' said the Axe. 'They'll be fine.'

'Right. So we need a dog,' she said. 'As luck would have it, I know the very one.'

Talula sped through the city and didn't stop until she'd reached Iffies.

'Axe,' Talula said, as she walked towards the bar, holding the Torrimaya Axe, 'Have you seen Arthur and Doyle lately?'

Axe, who was polishing glasses, peered over the bar, and stared at the ancient weapon that was almost as big as Talula.

'What you doin' wiv' that?' asked Axe.

'Present for a friend. Got it at a market,' Talula lied.

'Ain't seen nuffin' like that before,' Axe said.

'Paid half a florin for it,' Talula said, as she looked towards the fireplace. 'Don't worry, I see them. Thanks Axe,' said Talula.

Arthur had fallen asleep in a comfy chair. After a night spent watching Dr Foxglove's house, Doyle was now dozing at Arthur's feet. The skinny dog stood up as Talula approached.

'Good boy, Doyle,' whispered Talula, patting the dog on the head. 'I need to borrow you.'

Doyle sniffed the Axe in her hand then looked up at the pixie.

'Follow me,' the dog whispered.

'Seriously?!' said Talula, 'You think you know someone…'

'Sssh!' said Doyle, 'Back alley. Now.'

* * *

'*This* is the Torrimaya Axe?' said Doyle, staring at the Axe who was standing on its tip in the alley behind Iffies.

'Half a florin?!' said the Axe.

'Yes, Doyle, this is the Torrimaya Axe,' said Talula.

'At a market! I've never been so insulted…'

'Can we please stick to the point,' said Talula.

Talula quickly summarised the situation while Doyle kept an eye on the Axe.

'… And if we went back to Windig Hill then maybe you could pick up the scent,' concluded Talula.

'I'm good, I'll grant you,' said Doyle. 'Given, however, that I work for the King's forces…'

'What?!' said Talula,

'*Given* that I work for the King's forces,' repeated Doyle, 'in an *undercover* capacity, I think it would in fact be far better if, instead of attempting to chase a scent that has long-since vanished, I bring you to HQ where you'll both be safe and I can get backup.'

'So you can't pick up the scent?' said Talula.

'Even if I enhance your olfactory senses?' added the Axe.

'You can do that?' said Doyle, momentarily distracted by the possibility.

'I can try,' said the Axe.

'Great, so no chasing scents, which means…' Talula trailed off and fixed her gaze on the Axe. 'I have another idea,' she said. 'But first I need a bag, and I should probably take some cash with me, in case of emergencies. You two wait here while I nip upstairs.'

* * *

Around the turquoise-blue pool of Blasting's oasis, there lounged an ever-growing crowd of recently-aged fairies, some of whom awaited remuneration for their magical services. As a result of the large number of mercenaries loitering on the sands, Blasting's isolated hideaway was looking less like a luxury retreat and more like a convalescent home for retired fairies.

Inside Blasting's ornately furnished tent were the General and Norman, none the worse for wear after their trip, but with their hands bound behind their backs. Blasting was standing in front of his captives, while Kinins stood behind the General.

'General Macjooste, this is indeed an unexpected pleasure. I trust you suffered no ill-effects from the magical transportation? It's such a shame this mode of transport is so costly,' said Blasting, 'I find it a far more efficient way to travel long distances. Wouldn't you agree?'

'What do you want, Blasting?' asked the General, through gritted teeth.

Blasting smirked.

'I'm so sorry I had to bind your magic,' said Blasting.

'No you're not,' the General retorted.

'No, I'm not,' Blasting agreed, 'but I *am* sorry we now find ourselves on opposite sides of this little arms race. It really didn't have to be this way.'

'Are you the one who kidnapped Professor Bauxite?' Norman piped up. 'Where is he? Is he alright?'

'Ah, the descendent of the forgemaster, Mr Shale.'

Blasting looked down his nose at Norman.

'And did you take Dr Tellurium as well?' Norman continued, unabashed.

'He's rather inquisitive for a dwarf in his position, isn't he,' said Blasting, ignoring Norman and fixing a stare at the General.

'What do you hope to achieve? The Cashenian and Rataquian governments know you're the one responsible for the recent attacks.'

'Try not to take it so personally, General,' said Blasting, with a patronising smile. 'I'm a businessman and in recent years my business has seen a marked decline in profits. What does one do when business is slow? One explores every conceivable angle in order expand one's market and boost sales.'

'Or you diversify! You wee scab of a ...!'

'But General,' Blasting interrupted, 'I fully intend to, as you say, diversify. I think you'll find that my plan will work to everyone's advantage. After all, war...'

'No!' interrupted the General.

'But everyone knows that war is good for the economy, General,' said Blasting, with a sly grin. 'As for the Ani-Bara tunnel, the sooner that irksome, financially ruinous, little corridor is closed down, the better!' Blasting added, scathingly.

'You wouldn't dare,' said General Macjooste, glaring at his captor.

Blasting stared into the General's eyes with an equal amount of loathing.

'Wouldn't I?' Blasting said.

Norman watched the pair but failed to think of anything that might defuse the situation.

'May I have a drink of water?' Norman finally said.

Blasting looked away from the General first.

'No!' Blasting barked. 'Oh, and did my team overhear your little conversation at the Professor's cottage correctly? Is it true that you are a direct descendant of Halvar the Just?'

'I doubt it,' replied the General.

'Of course we should have guessed by your name that you are a descendant of the Rao chieftain. *Just. Jooste.* It makes perfect sense when you think of it. It's such a shame that we couldn't have met under better circumstances.' Blasting walked towards the glass-fronted display case that contained the golden axe. He patted the box and turned to face the General once more. 'No matter,' Blasting said, 'I have someone I want you both to meet. Kinins, take them to Dr Stobel.'

* * *

'I'm not getting into a black *sack*!' the Torrimaya Axe protested.

'It's an official courier bag,' said Talula, 'which you have to get into because I can't just carry you around the streets. I'll get arrested if I'm caught with a weapon,' said Talula, as she quickly scanned the alley behind Iffies for any potential eavesdroppers before putting on her royal-blue, Vinster Parcel Services courier jerkin.

'She's right,' added Doyle.

'You mean to tell me that dwarves can't carry their own axes in public anymore? How can they tell which clan they're from?' asked the Axe.

Talula and Doyle looked at each other. Talula sighed and held open the large bag.

'Just get in,' she said.

'I shall only do so under protest at such an undignified mode of transport, and I reserve the right...'

'We really don't have time for this,' Talula bent down, grabbed the Axe by its handle and stuffed it into the bag. 'Your protest has been duly noted.'

'I do have magical powers you know! I deserve better treatment than any old weapon of mass destruction!'

'Until you can do more than talk the hind legs off a badger, I suggest you let Doyle and me get on with the business of finding the General and Norman,' said Talula, as she tied up the bag.

'You should really leave this to the King's forces,' Doyle said.

'Do the King's forces have contacts in the Disattos?' asked Talula.

'Not exactly...'

'And can the King's forces wander around every street in Vinster without raising suspicion?'

'There aren't many places I can't gain access to. I'm a dog.'

'If a dog starts asking questions Below Ground it's likely to get turned into a lamp post,' said Talula as she flung the bag over her shoulder.

'Fair enough,' muttered Doyle.

'I'm sensing the ancestors, apart from you Miss Talula, are no longer in Cashen, if that helps,' the Axe said.

'Great,' muttered Talula. 'Doyle, do you know the Below Ground entrance in the cemetery?'

'I do,' replied Doyle, 'but I'm on assignment.'

'What kind of assignment?' asked Talula.

'Surveillance. Top secret,' replied Doyle.

'Who are you watching?' asked Talula.

'I can't...'

''Cos there were a couple of fairies last night in Iffies that looked decidedly suspicious,' interrupted Talula.

'What did they look like?' asked Doyle.

'I have a friend who lives in one of the tunnels underneath the cemetery. I need to ask her some questions. I'll tell you all about the fairies last night, on the way to the cemetery.'

Doyle looked at Talula, then at the bag with the Axe in it.

'Fine...'

'And I'll tell you everything I find out so that you can take the information to headquarters,' Talula added.

'I said fine. Let's go. We're wasting time,' said Doyle.

TRAVEL PLANS
Blasting's location is discovered.

In the Remote Tracking room, at LUSU headquarters, Captain Meejum and her trackers had witnessed the magical skirmish, as well as the kidnapping of General Macjooste and Norman, on Windig Hill. King Egbert was duly informed of the incident and he immediately ordered troops to the site.

Adler and Wand were found at Professor Bauxite's cottage and the two fairies were rushed to the infirmary. Here the pair were patched up and told to rest, but the concerned soldiers disobeyed medical advice and quickly returned to the LUSU operations room,.

As soon as he arrived, Adler had raised the security state from amber to red alert. The King, Adler and Wand, now stood in the middle of the room, checking every new report from LUSU agents. Meejum's trackers, meanwhile, were desperately trying to locate the General.

'And we have no idea where General Macjooste and the Professor could have been taken?' asked the King.

'The old lady next door mentioned a carriage and some purple-winged fairies,' said Adler, reading from a file, 'but as yet we have no idea where the carriage went.'

King Egbert looked around at the busy scene before him. Dwarves, fairies, pixies, imps and goblins bustled about the room. Macjooste had trained his staff well, thought the King, and it was clear that all resources were being pooled in an effort to discover the whereabouts of the General.

Standing next to the King was Captain Meejum, who said nothing as she read a note.

'Does Blasting have a residence in Rataq?' the King enquired.

Captain Meejum nodded and looked up at King Egbert.

'He does, Your Highness. An oasis in the Rijozo province to the south of the country,' she said, holding up the note.

'And we know this, how?' asked the King.

'We received an anonymous tip-off about twenty minutes ago,' said Meejum.

King Egbert looked down at his shoes, smiled knowingly to himself, and made a mental note to thank Lord Esodo at the first available opportunity. The King looked up at the expectant team.

'Adler, assemble the Red Wings and meet me back at the palace in an hour. I think it's time we spoke to our ally and made this a joint mission.'

* * *

At Vinster's oldest cemetery, behind a tangle of honeysuckle and ivy, was a warped door. Talula lifted the latch and pushed the door inward with her shoulder. Doyle trotted past the waiting Talula who then squeezed through the gap.

'So there was a female and a male, fairy at Iffies last night?' asked Doyle.

'Uh huh,' confirmed Talula.

'Was the female fairy you saw wearing perfume?'

'I'm not in the habit of sniffing folk, as a rule,' said Talula, as the pair jogged between the tombstones towards the centre of the cemetery, 'but she was wearing an expensive-looking cape.'

'That's good but, you'd have definitely known the scent. It's a light floral fragrance with a jasmine top note and the merest hint of rose,' said Doyle.

'Why do you want to know what she smelled like? Do you think it was the fairy you were sent to watch?' asked Talula.

'I'm afraid I couldn't possibly comment,' said Doyle, in a tone that said *Yes I do think it's the fairy I was sent to watch*, without actually confirming that this was indeed the case.

'Wait,' Talula stopped, and sniffed. 'What does jasmine smell like?' she asked, staring straight ahead.

Doyle stopped and looked around the graveyard.

'Over there! Quick,' he said.

'Is this really the time to stop and smell the flowers?' asked the Torrimaya Axe.

Talula and Doyle ignored the muffled voice from inside the bag and raced towards an outer wall on the other side of the graveyard.

'Of course the scent is always better in the evening,' said Doyle, panting slightly, 'but you'll be able to smell something.'

The pair stopped and Talula stood next to the flowering plant trailing down the wall.

'Maybe,' Talula said, as she sniffed the delicate, white flowers. 'I mean…'

'Take another whiff,' insisted Doyle. 'It's important.'

Talula closed her eyes and inhaled the flowers' scent once more.

'It's vaguely familiar but I couldn't say for certain,' she said.

'Try one more inhalation, please.' said Doyle.

As the pair stood in front of the wall a slight breeze whispered through the trees.

'Wait! That's it!' said Talula, opening her eyes. 'It was mixed with… with…' Talula looked around her. 'There! Did you say rose? Over there, look!' Talula pointed to a rose bush at the head of a tombstone.

'Well done! I'll make an olfactory agent of you yet!' said Doyle.

'A what?' Talula and the Axe said, in unison.

'It doesn't matter. Come on. Let's see if we can find out who's behind all this,' said Doyle, as, tail held high, he trotted off towards the centre of the graveyard.

* * *

Talula and Doyle were standing in front of a marble mausoleum, constructed for one of Vinster's most well-known and wealthiest family, the Blastings. The pair looked around to make sure that no one was nearby and, satisfied that they were alone, they walked to the back of the building towards a piece of wood that was leaning against the wall at the base of the building. Talula took the bag from her shoulder, laid it on the ground, and then carefully moved the piece of wood.

'It's a bit of a squeeze,' she said, 'so I'm going to chuck you ...'

'Chuck!' said the Axe.

'... so I'm going to *lower* you through the gap first and I'll be right behind you.'

'Chuck,' the Axe muttered, from inside the sack, 'thousands of years under permafrost...'

'Sssh!' said Talula, as she picked up the Axe and began lowering it down the hole. 'Doyle, you wait here. I won't be long.'

* * *

General Macjooste was strapped to one of three beds in Dr Stobel's lab-tent. The other two beds were occupied by Professor Bauxite and Norman. The General tugged at the straps around his wrists and ankles in a vain effort to break free.

'Do lie still, General,' said Dr Stobel, as she prepared to attach a modified wand, with a needle on its end, to the General's arm. 'It will work far more effectively if you're awake but I will put you to sleep if I have to.'

'I only take orders from the King,' said the General, tugging at the straps one last time, 'and my wife,' he growled.

The thaumurtologist smiled arrogantly as she straightened a copper wire attached to one end of the wand and then fed the rest of the wire into the mouth of a glass bell-jar sitting on a table next to the bed.

'There we are,' she said, in a satisfied tone, as she inserted the needle into the General's arm. 'Now, all we need is a small spell and it will all be over.'

Dr Stobel turned to face the middle-aged, blue-winged fairy she had spoken to earlier, who was standing by the entrance to the tent.

'What exactly are you doing?' Norman enquired, from the bed furthest from the General.

'Oh, how sweet,' said Dr Stobel, patronisingly, as she beckoned for the fairy to join her. 'I'm sure you have absolutely no understanding of medicinal magic,' she said, 'but, suffice it to say, I have discovered a means by which inherent spellage can be extracted from an individual.'

'I thought that was just a theory?' said Norman.

Dr Stobel stopped and stared at the Norman.

'What do you know about it?' she said, with narrowed eyes.

'I read an article somewhere. I seem to remember it said, potential applications include healing hereditary wing-malformation or removing magical curses that had been handed down and were encoded in a family's inherited spellage, and,' Norman continued, 'theoretically it might also be applied to non-magical beings as well,' said Norman, 'which would be great for dwarves or trolls who were cursed, charmed or spelled by fairies hundreds of years ago, although it seems unlikely it would work on non-magical folk because they don't have inherent spellage,' concluded Norman, staring at the ceiling of the lab-tent.

Professor Bauxite chuckled.

'Mr Shale is a real asset to my work, Dr Stobel,' said the Professor.

'Enough!'

Dr Stobel grabbed her own wand and flicked it in the direction of both Norman's and the Professor's beds. They both fell unconscious.

* * *

'Why didn't you tell me you were coming?' said Margaleet, as she poured a cup of imported cherry blossom tea for Talula.

'It was a spur of the moment thing. I was delivering something in the area and thought I'd pop in,' said Talula, as she picked up the delicate Toorquean cup from the coffee table and inhaled the tea's sweet aroma.

Talula looked around Margaleet's underground home. It was spacious and beautifully furnished. Brand new Finnician glow worm lamps lit the sitting room. Hand woven Rataquian rugs covered the floor and pure silk drapes in peacock blues and greens hung across the doorway to Margaleet's boudoir. Talula had to admit that the underground rooms were far more sumptuous and elegant than her own, damp, attic room at Iffies.

'What's up?' asked Margaleet, sipping her own cup of tea.

'What? Can't I come visit you now and then?' said Talula.

'I saw you last night,' smiled Margaleet, 'and you hate coming down here because you say it's full of criminals … *Sooo…* What's up?'

'You've come a long way since the orphanage, financially, if not geographically,' said Talula. 'I don't want you getting into trouble with the King's forces.'

'You worry too much, Talula-Lula. I won't be doing this forever. Don't you worry,' she said, and tapped the side of her nose.

Talula looked at her friend and smiled. Margaleet had always been good with numbers but, Talula thought her beautiful pixie friend was being naive if she imagined the Disattos would simply let her walk away from such an important position. No one, least of all the gang's accountant, could leave the organisation, except, perhaps, as a result of an *unfortunate* accident. Talula sipped her tea and said nothing.

Margaleet leaned back in her chair and looked at Talula. The pair sat in silence staring at each other. It was a game they'd played as pixlings. Whoever broke the stare first had had to steal biscuits from the orphanage's kitchen.

Talula's eyes began to water.

'I've got some friends in trouble and I need your help,' said Talula, after a mere five seconds.

'What do you need?' Margaleet grinned.

* * *

'It's quite remarkable, Mr Blasting,' said Dr Stobel. 'At first I thought he was rambling in his sleep but when I finished the procedure with General Macjooste I began to pick up certain key phrases and realised he was talking in ancient Cashenian.'

Theodore Blasting and Dr Stobel were standing over Norman's bed in the lab-tent staring down at the sleeping dwarf.

'And you're sure they're spells?' asked Blasting, flushed with excitement.

'I only have a basic understanding of ancient Cashenian. I need it for medical terminology, and I can't be a hundred percent certain but, it certainly sounded like spells,' replied Dr Stobel.

'Why would he know any spells?' asked Blasting.

'In nocte... quattuor... simul...telum...' Norman mumbled.

'What did he say?' asked Blasting.

'Erm...' she paused, 'I think he said, in the night, four, square and, possibly, charms.'

'What are the chances it has anything to do with the Torrimaya Axe?' asked Blasting.

'Earlier I heard him say Vallis Viride Pascuis, which translates to Valley Green and Pastures, so it's entirely possible his ramblings are connected to the Torrimaya Axe, especially given his lineage,' replied Dr Stobel.

'Can you extract anything from him?' asked Blasting, looking at Dr Stobel with an expression that suggested this wasn't really a question.

Dr Stobel looked at Blasting and then at the young dwarf lying on the bed.

'Do you mean extract magic?' asked Dr Stobel.

'Yes. I mean, isn't it possible that, as the forgemaster's

descendant, he was infused with magic by Halvar?'

'I'm not sure it quite works like that,' said Dr Stobel.

'What exactly are you sure of?' asked Blasting.

'Um…' said Dr Stobel.

'According to Hornblende's book, several, ancient, non-magical beings were infused with magic, and these beings then passed this magic down through the family line. I'm surprised you didn't know that,' said Blasting, in a superior tone.

Dr Stobel glanced at her benefactor and then back at Norman. As she stared at the unconscious dwarf on the bed, the fairy scientist struggled to come to terms with the depth of Blasting's ignorance of dwarf and fairy biology. Any ten-year-old could have told her that what Blasting had just said was impossible. In fact, the dwarf in front of her had a better grasp of her work.

'I'm afraid I don't, as a rule, use mythology as a point of reference in my work.'

Blasting was wearing a supercilious expression of someone who believed he was right, despite all evidence to the contrary.

'Ah but, you haven't read Hornblende have you?' he said.

'No,' Dr Stobel replied. 'No, I haven't read Hornblende.'

'Then perhaps it might be worth trying to establish, once and for all, whether or not a non-magical being can in fact be infused with magic, and, more importantly, whether or not any potential spellage can be extracted from this dwarf.'

'I suppose I can try,' said Dr Stobel.

'No… no… not…Norman…' muttered the General, as he lay, pale and drained, and still strapped to the bed on the other side of the lab-tent.

* * *

Talula pushed the bag with the Axe in it through the gap under the mausoleum and then climbed out of the hole.

'Well?' asked Doyle.

Talula stood up, brushed herself down, and adjusted her ponytail.

'Margaleet reckons Theodore Blasting has definitely been up to something lately.'

Doyle and Talula looked up at the mausoleum.

'Theodore Blasting? Of Blasting's Weapons?' asked Doyle.

'Is that the name of the descendent of the Wing Collector?' asked the Axe, from inside the courier bag.

'I have absolutely no idea, ' said Talula.

'Is he Rataquian?' asked the Axe.

'As far as I know he's Cashenian,' said Doyle.

'Doesn't matter where he's from, a nutter is a nutter, and Blasting sounds totally bonkers,' said Talula, picking up the Axe in the bag. 'He's hired loads of fairies from the Disattos, which Margaleet says is uber-expensive, and incredibly stupid if you ask me.'

'Let's not forget it's uber-illegal as well,' added Doyle.

'Did you find out where the others are?' asked the Axe.

'Margaleet said she's recently fudged the gang's accounts to hide a large sum of money used to pay for magical-transportation services to Rataq. She wasn't given Blasting's name but she overheard one of the fairies in the office talking about an oasis in the Rijozo province, belonging to a rich, Vinster dwarf in the arms manufacturing business. Can't be many of those in the city.'

'I need to get all this intel to HQ,' said Doyle.

'And we're going on a little trip to Rataq,' said Talula, as she slung the bag over her shoulder.

'What! You can't do that,' said Doyle.

'Why not?' asked Talula.

Doyle sat down, scratched an ear and then looked up at Talula.

'Because…it's just not the way we do things in the

forces,' said Doyle.

'Then it's probably a good thing I'm not in the forces,' she said. 'Look, if the Axe is right...'

'What do you mean '*if*?' interrupted the Axe.

'...*if* the Axe is right,' Talula continued, 'and it's here to save Eris, then the sooner I can get it to where it needs to be, the sooner we can put an end to all of this.'

'How will you know where to go? Have you even been to Rataq before?' asked Doyle.

'Margaleet told me where to find another courier in Tamor she said I can trust. I'm sure I'll be fine.' said Talula.

'What courier? And where exactly in Tamor?' asked Doyle.

'She didn't give me a name, just said to look out for a courier booth in the Sezar Quarter,' said Talula.

'It's too dangerous,' said Doyle. 'Please don't go.'

'If it helps,' said the Axe, 'I can probably pick up the magical frequencies of the descendants once we're close,' said the Axe.

'But what if you get caught?' asked Doyle. 'Why don't you come with me and you can tell the King's senior officer...'

'Doyle,' interrupted Talula, 'I really have to get going, but thanks for all your help.'

'He didn't do anything!' said the Axe.

'Shut up and stop being so rude,' hissed Talula.

'I really haven't done much,' admitted Doyle. 'And I think that female fairy you overheard at Iffies last night is someone we definitely need to bring in for questioning, so I should be thanking you.'

'If she's the one responsible for kidnapping Norman and the Professor then I hope you lock her up and bind her magic forever!' said Talula, as she started walking away from the mausoleum.

'I have a bad feeling in my handle about this,' said the Axe.

'How is that even possible?' said Talula, as she and Doyle picked up the pace and headed for the exit.

VORSPRUNG DWARF TECHNIQUE
The Ani-Bara Tunnel.

It had taken more than twenty years to build the one-hundred-and-fifty mile underwater link between Vinster and Tamor, Rataq's capital city. Vosrprung Dwarf Technique, the best dwarf engineering on the planet, had been used to design and build the multi-lane barge-way, which now operated twenty-four hours a day. The tunnel offered merchants a reliable and, for the most part, safe route by which goods could be transported. There were also four courier lanes that provided a first-class delivery service for international messages.

Despite the occasional incident of piracy, many businesses were thriving as a result of the engineering marvel. Before its completion, however, the tunnel hadn't been popular with some of Vinster's residents. It worried the average working citizen that immigrants - who spoke funny, had their own sets of gods, and cooked strange food - might come over and take all the jobs. As it turned out many of the tunnel's cynics now wondered how they could have lived so long without the diverse choice available for a takeaway on a Friday night. In fact, city folk had become quite proud of their multi-cultural metropolis.

The tunnel brought with it the hope that hatchets and/or wands could be buried, that old wars between various nations might one day be forgiven, if not forgotten, and that the growth in trade would encourage a lasting peace between the planet's two continents.

On the Vinster side of the tunnel there were three terminals, all of which were housed in one large, architecturally-stunning, domed edifice that dominated the dockside. Inside each terminal there were restaurants, cafés, shops and departure lounges that catered to the needs of the tunnel's multicultural users.

Talula stood inside the doors of the tunnel's main entrance. The vast hall echoed with chatter as folk either trundled to the ticket office or descended the wide staircase that was situated directly in front of Talula and led to one of the three terminals.

'What are you waiting for?' whispered the Axe.

Talula looked up at the overhead signs. Terminal three was for the transport of goods. Below this sign was a symbol indicating that there was a courier lane. This was where Talula needed to go.

'Shoot!' Talula whispered, 'I don't have a pre-paid courier docket or any travel papers, and I have to get you through package control and customs. If I'm caught carrying a weapon with no papers, I'll be arrested.'

'I think I might be able to help,' the Axe whispered. 'Just go.'

Talula's stomach tightened as she made her way toward the staircase.

'You'd better not get me arrested,' Talula hissed.

At the bottom of the staircase separate corridors took the traveller to their terminal of choice. Signs suspended from the ceiling indicated that couriers were banned from running too fast in the courier lanes and that there was a fine of six florins for anyone who was caught speeding. At the entrance to terminal three's corridor was an old pixie, sitting cross-legged on the floor, playing a tin whistle. A cap was on the floor next to the pixie, in which were a couple of florins and a handful of yorits. Talula reached into her pouch and threw in half a florin.

Traders of all descriptions lined one wall of the sloping, brightly-lit corridor. Talula walked past a gift stand selling imitation wooden axes, of all shapes and sizes. On the next table was an assortment of gifts, such as hats, bags and flagons with 'I♥Vinster-on-Sterm' engraved on them. The stall-holder watched Talula as she hurried past.

'Ere!' called out the dwarf, 'Wot you got in that bag love? It's glowin'. Where'd you get that then?'

Everyone looked in Talula's direction to see what the

dwarf was talking about. Talula took the bag from her shoulder and held it close to her body in an effort to hide the bright, orangey-red light that was emanating from the Axe in the bag. Talula picked up her pace and headed for the end of the corridor.

'What are you doing?!' she hissed.

The Axe stopped glowing.

'I'm a magic axe! I glow when I'm doing magical things!' shout-whispered the Axe.

'Well stop it!' Talula shout-whispered back.

'Look, do you want my help or not?' said the Axe.

'Oh for…Fine.' muttered Talula.

She hurried to the end of the corridor which widened into a large area with a row of a dozen ticket barriers. Pixies couriers, dwarves, trolls and goblins were queuing with their packages, waiting to be security checked.

'Go to the quietest barrier,' the Axe whispered.

Talula did as she was instructed and went towards the barrier at the far end. A surly-looking goblin was picking at a scab on his chin. Talula came to the barrier.

'Docket and papers,' said the goblin.

'I…' started Talula, still clutching the sack.

From inside the courier bag, the Axe started to glow again.

'You do not need to see this pixie's docket and papers,' the Axe said, quietly.

'I don't need to see your docket and papers,' repeated the goblin.

'Let the pixie go through the barrier,' said the Axe.

'Go on through,' said the goblin, who proceeded to open the barrier.

'Have a good day,' said the Axe.

'You 'ave a good day, Miss,' said the goblin.

Talula walked through the barrier.

'Quick,' said the Axe. 'It won't last long.'

Talula dashed towards the staircase leading down to the tunnel's courier lane.

* * *

Three unmarked carriages were parked in the alley next to the tunnel's main entrance. Uniformed trolls, armed with crossbows, were standing at both ends of the alley. Lord Esodo and a Red Wing squadron led by Wing Commander Adler, alighted from the carriages and filed through a door being held open by a dwarf.

'Afternoon, sirs,' said the dwarf, who was wearing the familiar dark blue uniform and peaked cap of the tunnel staff. 'As instructed, I've sent staff to all checkpoints and they've been told to clear the service canal. I've closed the loading bay to deliveries for twenty minutes and we've prepared the royal barge for you.'

'Thank you Superintendent,' said Wing Commander Adler.

'If you'd all like to follow me,' said the dwarf.

'Can you trust your staff to keep quiet?' enquired Adler, as they trooped down the service corridor.

'Everyone workin' for the tunnel has to sign a contract, sir, which says we reserve the right to cast security charms if there is a suspected emergency or threat to national security,' replied the dwarf.

'I did not know this,' said Lord Esodo.

'Well, it's to protect the public innit,' said the dwarf. 'Say there's a leak in the tunnel and one of my staff tells an outsider, there'd be pandemonium. We can't 'ave that now can we?'

'A leak!' said Lord Esodo.

They all reached a junction at the end of the corridor whereupon the superintendent turned left.

'Oh, don't worry,' said the dwarf, confidently. 'T'ain't never 'appened but, if it did we'd 'ave to get security staff to cast charms on some of the workers to stop 'em blabbin', see.'

The dwarf took out his fob watch and checked the time while they marched towards a loading bay at the end of the corridor.

'Please try not to worry, Lord Esodo,' said Adler. 'I suspect the workers at the Rataquian end of the tunnel are subject to the same contractual obligation.'

'We have no leaks at our end of tunnel,' muttered Lord Esodo, as they approached three lifts.

'We ain't got no leaks at our end neither but, we do 'ave top notch security, and no one will ever know you woz 'ere, you 'ave my word on that,' said the dwarf. ''Ere we are. Mind the gap.'

The superintendent opened an outer metal gate, then an inner wooden gate and gestured for everyone to enter the lift. He closed both gates and pushed one of two buttons. From somewhere in the depths of the shaft a troll cranked a huge handle and the lift began to move.

'So,' said the superintendent, 'you lads off on some kind of secret mission then?'

Quick as a whip Silas said, 'We could tell you, but then we'd have to kill you.'

The military fairies, who were all standing behind the dwarf, suppressed their laughter. One of the team members coughed to disguise a potential outburst. Adler held up his hand signalling for silence.

'I do apologise, superintendent,' said Adler. 'A military joke I'm afraid.'

'A silencing charm would probably do the job,' replied the dwarf. 'You might wanna look into that.

TAMOR
City of culture and the location of Talula's contact.

Blasting looked down at the luxurious hand-woven rug as he paced the length of his tent. Kinins coughed in order to announce his arrival and showed Dr Stobel inside.

'Did you find anything?' Blasting stopped and looked expectantly at Dr Stobel.

'There is definitely no ancient spellage in the dwarf,' said Dr Stobel. 'I tried everything but there's nothing there.'

'So what was he wittering on about then?' asked Blasting, impatiently.

'I suspect it was simply a recollection of a fictional scroll he read at some point and...'

'Yes?!'

'Perhaps you...I mean...*I* got the wrong end of the wand,' said Dr Stobel, aware that Blasting would never accept responsibility for the ill-conceived act. 'He's stopped talking now,' said Dr Stobel, quietly.

Blasting turned away from Dr Stobel and looked at his precious golden axe. He momentarily rested a hand on the case, inhaled deeply, and then turned to face the thaumurtologist.

'What now?' he asked.

'The General's extracted spellage remains stable so I think we're ready to infuse the magic into the weapon,' said Dr Stobel.

Blasting beamed with satisfaction.

'Perhaps you should have started with the good news, Dr Stobel,' he said.

'Um...' Dr Stobel looked flustered.

'No matter. Let us waste no more time.' Blasting turned to face his assistant. 'Kinins, have Terminus brought to Dr Stobel's lab.'

'What shall we do with our guests, sir?' asked Kinins.

'Are they still alive?' Blasting asked Dr Stobel.

'Yes,' replied Dr Stobel, 'but the General's life-force

was drained along with his spellage. I don't know if he'll last the night.'

'Not such a bad thing,' said Blasting, nonchalantly. 'Will the others be of any further use to the project?'

'No, sir. I have everything I need now,' replied Dr Stobel.

Kinins frowned, and looked at Blasting.

'I would suggest that King Egbert will have launched a team to search for the General. Perhaps we should return the trio to Cashen,' said Kinins.

Blasting picked up his wand from his desk.

'When we have imbued the weapon you can take them back to Tamor and leave them near the tunnel entrance. Yes, I rather think that will be a fitting finale don't you Kinins?' he said, with an excited look - which might have been mistaken by some as a fairy quickly descending into madness.

'Yes, sir. And I have done as you instructed. The latest transportation crew has been paid and the camel train will be taking them south very shortly, sir,' added Kinins, ignoring the flicker of insanity in his boss's eyes.

'Excellent. Have we a new flight crew waiting?'

'I have a dozen fairies on standby,' replied Kinins.

'Dr Stobel?' said Blasting. 'Shall we?'

* * *

Talula was exhausted and had stopped at one of the rest points two thirds of the way along the tunnel. She was sitting in a corner of a small café drinking a cup of restorative, Senging tea. There were only three other pixies in the café. All of them were young and she guessed that they, like her, were not yet able to complete the tunnel run in one hit.

'How far is it now?' whispered the Axe.

'Fifty or so miles,' whispered Talula.

'Perhaps a small charm to give you a boost might...'

'Keep your magic to yourself!' whispered Talula. 'Give me five more minutes and I'll be fine.'

The three pixies turned around to look at the female pixie who was whispering to her bag.

Talula smiled.

'Alright lads?' she said. 'Any of you know where the Sezar Quarter is in Tamor?'

The three pixies shook their heads and looked back at their energy drinks.

'You deliver to Sezar Quarter?' said the Rataquian pixie, behind the counter.

'You know it?' Talula picked up the Axe in the bag as she stood up.

'Yes, but is not safe for Cashenens in Tamor right now,' she said, pointing to the jerkin. 'You better to leave package at depot and send message with city pixie.'

'No can do. I've been told to get a signature,' lied Talula, as she approached the counter.

The pixie looked hard at Talula and then at the bag.

'Is not far from tunnel entrance. You see market place, this is Sezar Quarter,' the pixie finally said.

'Why isn't it safe for Cashenians?' asked Talula.

'You no hear?' she asked, 'Cashenen soldiers start fights in bars and take our female fairies without they say yes.'

Talula looked at the pixie for a moment and blinked.

It was not, Talula briefly considered, implausible that the odd brawl broke out in garrison towns or ports. She'd had to dodge many scraps when the King's fleet was docked in Vinster, but General Macjooste was known to come down hard if any military personnel were found guilty of conduct unbecoming a member of the King's forces, especially in other countries.

'Are you sure?' Talula asked.

'This is what I hear,' replied the Rataquian pixie, with a shrug.

'When did this happen?' asked Talula.

'I hear this yesterday from couriers.'

'And who was taken?' asked Talula.

The Rataquian pixie tilted her head slightly and shrugged again.

'I not know who. All I know is Cashenens not so welcome in Tamor right now,' she said.

'Thanks for the information,' said Talula, politely.

Talula put a generous tip in the goblet on the counter and left the café.

* * *

The General, Professor Bauxite and Norman had been removed from Dr Stobel's temporary lab. In their place stood Terminus, secured by its own scaffolding. Around the weapon stood half a dozen Sterminian, Toorquean and Rataquian fairies, who were discussing how best to infuse the General's recently extracted spellage, into the weapon.

Dr Stobel was at the back of the lab-tent. She hovered protectively over the glass bell-jar filled with what looked like dense, swirling smoke. The General's extracted spellage was the palest of blues and Dr Stobel assiduously monitored the density and volume in an effort to establish what the half-life of the magic might be, all the while desperately hoping that the precious contents would continue to remain stable long enough to be infused into the weapon.

'Exciting times indeed,' said Blasting, to Dr Stobel's back.

'Oh, Mr Blasting, you startled me,' said Dr Stobel, turning around to face the fairy who had financed her ethically dubious experiment.

Blasting had his hands clasped behind his back. He leaned over and peered at the jar on the table.

'Is this it?' he asked.

'Mr Blasting, sir,' came a voice from the centre of the tent. 'We're ready,' said an orange-winged fairy.

'Dr Stobel, I believe that is your cue,' smiled Blasting.

'Thank you, sir,' said Dr Stobel.

Dr Stobel took a deep breath and carefully picked up the jar.

'Sir,' said Kinins from behind his boss.

'What now Kinins?!' replied Blasting, clearly irritated at the interruption.

Kinins approached his employer. In a lowered voice so that no one in the lab might hear, he said, 'Apologies, sir, but you asked me to let you know when everything was ready for phase four. If you wish to go ahead then I need to send a courier to the Tamor team now.'

Blasting looked at his aide and nodded.

'Yes, yes, get on with it!' he said.

* * *

Talula completed the rest of her tunnel run in over an hour. At Rataquian border control the Axe, yet again, slipped Talula through customs and the security check, with a simple mesmer-charm.

Talula followed the exit signs until she came to a brightly coloured, corridor that led to a vast staircase, at the top of which was the exit. Talula clutched the black courier bag close to her chest and kept a firm grip on the Axe's handle as she followed the busy stream of pedestrian traffic. At the top of the staircase was another beautifully designed domed hall, in which the new arrivals were greeted by whistles, whoops and shouts from waiting families and friends.

Talula's ears were bombarded by the racket and she was jostled among the crowd as she made her way to the main doors. Talula walked out into the warm night air, followed the instructions given to her by the pixie in the café and headed to the Sezar Quarter which she could already see from the tunnel's entrance.

Talula quickly found herself in the middle of a bustling, night market. Lighted paper lanterns were strung up between the stalls, many of which were selling food. A mélange of smells assaulted her nose and her stomach rumbled in protest.

'I'm starving,' she muttered. 'I'd eat roast stoat right now.'

Vendors hollered in foreign tongues at passersby but Talula resisted the temptation to stop for a snack.

'I hear stoat is good in a stir fry,' said the Axe.

An olive-skinned, Rataquian fairy soldier, coming from the opposite direction, spied the colour of her jerkin and caught Talula's eye. Talula smiled nervously.

'I should have taken this off,' she muttered, without moving her lips.

She felt the soldier watch her as she walked by.

'Are we there yet?' whispered the Axe.

'Ssh!' said Talula, as she threw a quick glance over her shoulder and saw that the soldier had started to follow her. 'Great,' she whispered.

With the Axe held tight to her torso, Talula squeezed through the throng. She glanced left and right, searching in vain for a courier booth with a blue and white striped awning. She saw stalls selling rugs, jewellery, clothes and an array of unfamiliar, delicious-looking food but could not find the booth Margaleet had described.

Keeping one eye on the solider behind her, Talula pushed her way through the crowds. She shoved past shoppers, who loitered at stalls, and she wove in and out of market-goers as quickly as she could. Her movement, however, was hampered by trolls, fairies and goblins who ambled in the crowded market aisles with their shopping baskets and offspring in tow. Talula couldn't go any faster and was becoming increasingly worried. The Axe was heavy and Talula was tired.

'Are we there...?' started the Axe.

'One more word and I'll sling you into the Aslantic,' growled Talula.

The soldier finally caught up and tapped Talula on the shoulder.

'You stop now,' said the uniformed fairy.

Talula froze. The crowd made room for the soldier, who came from behind and stood in front of Talula.

'Yes, sir,' said Talula, still clutching the Axe.

'What is this?' asked the guard, pointing at the bag.

'I have to deliver this to another courier, sir,' said Talula, mindful of the warning the Rataquian pixie had offered at the café in the tunnel.

'What courier?' asked the guard, folding his arms and looking down at Talula.

'I don't know the name. I was just told the courier booth was somewhere here, in the market.'

'Show me papers,' said the guard.

Talula, still gripping the Axe to her torso, began to perspire. She felt her hands begin to shake and her legs were growing weak, partly from exhaustion but also from fear.

'Yes, sir,' said Talula, slowly releasing her grip on the bag, 'Of course. They're in my pouch. I'm just going to put the bag over my shoulder to get my papers.'

Talula slowly moved the bag and carefully placed it on her shoulder. She rummaged in her pouch nervously and pulled out several small scraps of parchment.

'Show me papers now!' barked the soldier.

'I have them. I just can't seem to find them,' Talula said, trying to buy time.

'You show me what in bag,' said the soldier, reaching out to grab the black bag from Talula's shoulder.

Talula instinctively moved backwards.

'Wait…I mean. Of course,' she managed to say.

'Give me bag now!'

The fairy grabbed the strap but, before he could forcibly take the bag from Talula, there came shouts from somewhere to the right and an angry crowd was gathering around one of the stalls. The guard looked up and reached for his wand.

'Um,' said Talula, looking up at the soldier.

'You come!' commanded the soldier, as he put his hand on her shoulder and shoved her in the direction of what sounded like a fight.

'Shall I…' started the Axe.

'Sssh!' said Talula.

The soldier glanced down at Talula, who forced a smile and tried not to wince at the pain of the soldier's grip. As they approached a fruit stall it became apparent that an unsatisfied troll was on the verge of physically expressing his displeasure by taking a swing at the elfin stall holder.

'Arretirer!' bawled the soldier as he loosened his grip on Talula. 'You wait,' he barked at Talula, before marching towards the fracas.

Talula took the bag from her shoulder, clutched it once more and, ignoring both the command and the stares of the surrounding stall-holders, the young pixie slowly backed away from the fracas and into the crowd.

Talula darted through the market until she eventually came to a standstill, trapped behind a family of trolls who were haggling with a vendor over several clay pots on a stall next to her.

'Hey!' came a female voice to her left.

Talula turned to face the direction of the voice. She looked at a pretty pixie, then up at a blue and white striped awning above a courier booth.

'Finally!' Talula said, with relief.

'Talula?! Is that you?' beamed the courier.

'Rosa?! Oh my gods!'

The courier Margaleet had recommended to Talula could indeed be trusted. Rosa had also spent some time at the orphanage in Vinster. The Rataquian pixie had not, however, been an orphan but was the daughter of Mr and Mrs Fioray, both of whom had worked in the orphanage's kitchens for a few years before returning home to Rataq.

'Margaleet never told me it was you,' said Talula.

Rosa beamed at Talula and gestured for her to come into the booth away from the crowd. Talula looked left and right before entering the hut. There was no sign of the soldier.

'She always like to keep the secrets from us,' smiled Rosa. 'You remember how she always trick us? Come, sit.'

What you are doing here?' she asked.

'Oh Rosa, it's so good to see a friendly face,' said Talula, as she leaned the black courier bag against the booth's wall and slumped into one of two wooden chairs. 'Are you busy?'

'I turn away business to see you,' said Rosa, smiling. 'I have seen Margaleet more than I see you,' Rosa teased. 'She come two months ago.'

'I know, I know,' replied Talula. 'I'm a terrible friend.'

'No terrible,' said Rosa. 'Just not so good at communications, which is funny for a courier, no?'

Rosa laughed at her own joke and retrieved two small glasses from a wicker basket on the floor.

'I'm so sorry,' said Talula. 'I just seem to have been caught up in other things but I think of you often.'

'You here now,' said Rosa, handing Talula a glass of amber liquid. 'We drink to celebrate.'

Talula and Rosa clinked glasses.

'May your journeys always be safe...' said Rosa, holding her glass high.

'...And your legs always be strong!' finished Talula, downing the shot in one. 'Wa-ah!' she coughed. 'What is this stuff?'

Rosa laughed, downed the shot, and sat in the chair next to Talula.

'Good to help stay awake,' Rosa said, and looked at the bag next to Talula. 'You look tired and I think you have come for my help, yes?'

THE START OF WAR?
Talula and the Special Ops Force prepare to leave Tamor...Independently of one another.

Talula asked if she could close the booth door, to which Rosa agreed although not before lighting a dozen candles. Talula felt more relaxed away from prying eyes and proceeded to give Rosa a heavily-censored, and not entirely plausible, reason for following two dwarves to Rataq.

'You know me Rosa,' Talula concluded. 'I never get involved in anyone else's fight...'

'First rule of survival in Vinster,' confirmed Rosa.

'Exactly! But Norman's a pretty useless kind of dwarf and the Professor has just been caught up in it all,' said Talula, omitting the fact that Cashen's most senior military fairy had also been captured. 'I don't think anyone should be punished just for looking like someone else, should they?'

'You like this Norman dwarf, yes?' smiled Rosa.

'Not like that!' protested Talula. 'I just reckon that the nutter who's taken them would rather, you know,' Talula made the gesture of slicing her throat with her finger, 'than admit it was all a case of mistaken identity. Blasting doesn't sound like the type to leave any witnesses.'

'Why you care what happen to these dwarves?' frowned Rosa.

Talula was not accustomed to this level of deceit. She felt cornered by her own story and her cheeks flushed with guilt. She just needed Rosa to find out where Blasting was and point her in the right direction. She looked at Rosa and struggled to answer the question.

'Ah!' Rosa beamed. 'You are in love with this Norman! Why you not say so in first place! What you need me to do?'

Talula was suitably tongue-tied at the suggestion she could be in love with Norman but she also had the presence of mind to realise that things would move more swiftly now that Rosa had created her own 'truth'.

* * *

Professor Bauxite, the General and Norman had been moved from Dr Stobel's temporary lab to a smaller tent. Two armed fairies stood guard outside while the three captives lay on rugs in the dark, their hands and ankles bound with rope. The Professor woke from the sleeping-spell first and wiggled from his horizontal position to a more upright one. A crack of light came from the two torches outside the tent. In the shadowy dimness the Professor discerned Norman's smaller form to his left and, to the Professor's right, was the bulkier shape of the General.

'Norman?' whispered Professor Bauxite. 'Norman, wake up.'

'No...no...' mumbled Norman in his sleep.

'Norman!' shout-whispered the Professor. 'I need you to wake up now!'

'Wh-?' Norman started to come around. 'I... ow! My arms. Oh gods I ache all over... wait.. where..?'

Norman opened both eyes and stared into the dark.

'Are you alright?' asked the Professor.

'I feel like I've been hit by a brewery cart,' said Norman, hoarsely.

'You do sound dreadful but I've heard nothing from the General and I'm extremely concerned,' said the Professor.

'I'm fine,' came a whisper from the heap of fairy on the floor.

'General Macjooste, dear fellow, how are you feeling?' asked the Professor.

'Two brewery carts,' the General managed to say.

* * *

Rosa made good her word to help Talula. Not only did Rosa use her city connections to discover the whereabouts of Blasting's oasis in the province of Rijozo but she also provided Talula with some supplies.

'First, you not wear jerkin, yes?' said Rosa. 'This is Cashenen courier colour and Cashenens not so popular here right now.'

'Yeah, I know,' said Talula, removing the item and stuffing it into the bag with the Axe.

'Now, this,' said Rosa, holding up a small, thin, sealed glass tube with some clear liquid in it, 'this, is useful for emergency escape,'

'What is it?' asked Talula.

'A few drops on metal bars or chains maybe, and *poof!* You keep in this special box and be much careful. Not so good for skin,' said Rosa, handing the tube-in-a-box to Talula, who, carefully, put it in the front pocket of the bag.

'Right,' said Talula, unsure that she would ever need such an item.

'Here, I have energy food for you and this is flask of special drink,' she said, as she poured some of the amber drink she had shared with Talula into a hip flask. Rosa handed Talula the flask and Talula screwed on the lid.

'I'm not sure whether it's the ingredients or the taste that wakes you up,' said Talula. 'We certainly don't have anything like this back home.'

'I make myself,' said Rosa. 'And why you not use your own magic?'

Talula laughed and stopped when she realised Rosa hadn't joined her.

'Oh. You're serious,' she said. 'Look Rosa, I've never used magic and I'm not about…'

'Pah!' interrupted Rosa. 'I not ask you to use magic for bad things. You need speed now. You have to run many miles in short time or your dwarf love he may die. I teach you speed charm and you get to oasis in super-fast time.'

Talula had always found it hard to argue with Rosa, who was a pixie with charm and confidence in equal measures and could, if needed, sell ice to the Eskeesnos.

'What are the side effects of this speed charm?' asked Talula.

'If you use all the time, then you not be able to walk...'

'What?! I'm a courier!' said the startled Talula.

'Relax, Talula-Lula! Use your magic once and maybe you not able to walk next few days but no big damage,' Rosa smiled and put one hand on Talula's shoulder. 'Now, you listen. I teach.'

* * *

Before the royal barge left Vinster the Red Wings had fitted a handy piece of gadgetry given to them by the R&D lab. The device was a prototype and was a piece of techno-magic that, when fitted to the back of, for example, a ship, or in this instance a barge, would propel the vessel along the water far more quickly than a good wind, or indeed several horses. As a result, instead of the average travelling time of ten hours from Vinster to Tamor, the trip took just over three hours. Lord Esodo was much impressed by the speed at which the barge travelled, so much so that the Ambassador hinted to Wing Commander Adler that perhaps an exchange of technological ideas might be forthcoming in the near future, once this worrying episode had been resolved, of course.

Upon their arrival in Tamor, Lord Esodo had taken charge of the transport and the team was driven, in three unmarked carriages to the outskirts of the city and to Rataquian military headquarters. Here, the Red Wings were escorted to a large conference room where they met and discussed the rescue operation with their Rataquian counterparts, the Golden Sabres - who were already familiar with the terrain and knew the location of Blasting's oasis retreat. Refreshments were provided for the Red Wings after the briefing and the Rataquians left the conference room. Two burly Rataquian soldiers stood guard either side of the conference room door, each of them had long, curvy wands, secured in plain black, equally curvy, leather holsters.

'Friendly bunch,' murmured Wand.

Adler said nothing, focussing instead on the maps on the table in front of him. He looked up when the door opened and Lord Esodo entered.

'General Felicé he says transport is almost r…'

KABOOOOOOOOOM!

The conference room shook. Dust fell from the ceiling. Everyone, including the guards, ran to the window and looked out into the night.

KABOOOOMMMMM!

A second blast rattled the glass and briefly lit the cityscape.

'Il palazzo!' hollered Lord Esodo.

'The palace?!' exclaimed Adler.

'Il palazzo!' repeated Lord Esodo. 'His Majesties!' Lord Esodo threw his hands in the air and turned away from the window. He put his face in his hands and shook his head, as if weeping, but then pulled his hands down, looked at Adler and scowled.

'What can we do?' asked Adler.

'What you come here to do,' said Lord Esodo fiercely, striding to the table. 'This Blasting he is … is …Majya!'

'?'

'Crazy! He is crazy!' replied the Ambassador to Adler's facial enquiry.

'I hope no one has been hurt,' said Adler, earnestly.

Lord Esodo thumped his fist on the table.

'We finish this tonight!'

Flight Lieutenant Wand came over and spoke quietly to his commander.

'Shall I let HQ know, sir?'

Adler nodded once.

'Code Hidden Flowers,' Adler added. 'The royal family *must* be taken to safety.'

Wand looked gravely at his commander and went to find a quiet space.

* * *

As Norman stared into the darkness his legs, arms and

various other parts of his anatomy began to wake up. Every part of his being screamed in agony.

'Oh my gods,' Norman mumbled, as he, slowly, lifted himself into a sitting position. 'What did that Dr Stobel do to me?'

'Attempt - spell extraction,' whispered the General.

'Sorry General, sir. I can't hear you,' whispered Norman.

'Apparently she tried to extract magic from you,' said the Professor. 'Although I can't possibly imagine why she would have attempted such a thing.'

As Norman waited for his eyes to adjust, the discomfort of being tied up became unbearable, so he sat on his hands.

'Ow, ow, ow!' he said.

Norman grunted and groaned as he shuffled his body from one position to another in an effort to loop his bound hands from the back of his body to the front.

'Is everything alright?' asked the Professor.

Norman fell to his side, grunted some more and brought his bound hands to the front of his body.

'Finally,' he muttered. 'I'm fine,' whispered Norman, as he heaved himself into a sitting position again.

'Norman knows ancient Cashenian,' rasped the General to the Professor.

'Ancient Cashenian? Is this true, Norman?' replied the Professor, amazed at the possibility. 'Do you know ancient Cashenian?'

'Some... I ...mmiftupthum...' Norman started undoing the rope around his wrists with his teeth.

'Perhaps when you've finished,' said the Professor.

'Ancient spells,' added the General. 'Ask him.'

'Mrmrfmm.. ah! That's it. One mmmrrrfmfg,' Norman had loosened the rope sufficiently to be able to pull his hands free from the bonds. 'Always was tricky doing this in the dark but it's not my first time. My brothers were always tying me up. I...'

'Is the General correct, Norman? Do you know of any ancient Cashenian spells?' the Professor asked again.

Norman began to untie the ropes around his ankles.

'Not exactly. I taught myself some basic ancient Cashenian when I was still living at home but I'm far from fluent. I did find ... hold on ... over... and... I found some scrolls in the library's ancient parchments section, in the room behind the bookshelves at the end... right over left and under... I was going to ask you about them but you ...um... right and under... ah... you were kidnapped before I had the chance. They should properly signpost that section you know. Nearly broke my neck...here we go,' said Norman, as he began to unwind the rope from his ankles.

'Behind the bookshelves?' said the Professor. 'In the ancient parchments section?'

'Yes,' said Norman, as he stood up, 'Ow! My legs.' Norman fell to his knees. 'I'd have thought they'd put a proper door in by now...'

'Here, untie me,' interrupted the Professor. 'I've never heard of a room behind any bookshelves.'

'Oh,' said Norman, as he crawled on hands and knees towards the Professor. 'I just assumed...'

'You talk in your sleep,' whispered the General.

'No offence, General, sir,' said Norman, as he started undoing the rope tying the Professor's ankles together. 'You sound terrible. Maybe you should try not to talk.'

'Help me up,' said the Professor to Norman.

Norman and the Professor helped each other to stand and the pair gingerly stretched out their aching limbs before sitting down again to help the General. The two dwarves were unable to move General Macjooste from his prone position but, after untying the ropes, Norman tried to make the General more comfortable by folding the Professor's jacket and putting it under the General's head.

'Tell me about these scrolls,' whispered the General to Norman, who now sat next to the decidedly unwell fairy.

'There was a ton of stuff about the Wand Wars. It looked really interesting. I couldn't understand much but there seemed to be hundreds of small spells which, I think, are from the battle at the valley. I couldn't be sure though. Do you think these scrolls might be connected to the Torrimaya Axe?'

Had there been more light in the tent Norman might have seen Professor Bauxite and the General stare, open-mouthed, at Norman's shadowy form. Instead, there was a stunned, albeit short, silence while Norman rubbed his wrists, in an attempt to sooth the pain.

'Erm...' the Professor finally managed to utter.

'Good gods!' rasped the General. 'And you didn't tell us this earlier because..?'

'I'm sorry, sir,' Norman said, sheepishly. 'I did try, when you and Talula got me out of the library that night, Professor, but, well, events seemed to take over and then I went to your house to find you and ... well...' Norman trailed off.

'Don't worry Norman,' said the Professor, calmly. 'When, exactly, did you go to my house?

'I was worried because you hadn't replied to my messages, so I thought you might have gone home. Talula and I went to your cottage, and that's when we found the Axe.'

'The axe?' said the Professor.

'The Torrimaya Axe was in your shed,' said Norman.

'The Torrimaya Axe was in my shed?' repeated Professor Bauxite.

'Aye,' whispered the General.

'Good heavens. I wonder how it came to be in my shed?'

'You'll have to ask the Axe that,' replied Norman, 'but be prepared for a lengthy reply,' he added.

'I wonder how long it's been in the shed... wait...the Axe talks?' said an increasingly bewildered Professor.

'Not only does it talk, it said that the General, Talula

and myself are all descendants of the original Torrimaya Trio,' said Norman.

'And there's a fourth, apparently,' whispered the General.

'My wor…A fourth?!' said the Professor.

'The chronicler,' said Norman. 'But we didn't get a name. It all went a bit frog-shaped after that and, well, here we are,' said Norman.

'My, my,' mumbled the Professor. 'Never in a million years …'

'Hey!' came a voice from outside the tent. 'Quiet! Or we come shut you up - forever!'

* * *

Only minutes before the explosion Talula and the Axe had reached the southern gates of Tamor. Screams filled the air as hundreds of the city's residents took to the streets to find out what had happened to the palazzo and the royal family within. The glow did not last long which, Talula assumed, meant that magic had been used to quell the flames.

'I have a bad feeling in my…'

'Yes, yes, in your handle, I know,' said Talula, as she walked past four fairy guards, one of whom was hovering above the guard house while reporting what he saw to his colleagues.

'The Rataquians won't be happy about this,' said the Axe.

Talula stood outside the walls of the city and looked for a discreet spot to prepare for her run.

'*I'm* not happy about this,' retorted Talula, while deftly tying the straps of the bag around her torso. She looked back at the gates and saw a line of couriers preparing to take messages out of Tamor. 'I can't run on the main road or the other couriers will see me,' she said.

'If you'll allow me to use just a soupçon of my spellage,' said the Axe, 'perhaps we can reach a compromise; you run and I'll guide. I will feel the magic of the others and point you in that general direction. What do you say? Sound fair?'

Talula watched as dozens upon dozens of couriers left the city. A uniformed pixie approached the guard house and handed one of the guards a message. The guard read it and barked orders to his colleagues, who hurriedly set up a road block by the guard house.

'They'll stop and search everyone now,' said Talula.

'Fine. But not too much magic! I don't want to overdose.'

'Of course not,' said the Axe, offended by the suggestion.

'C'mon,' Talula said. 'We'd better get a move on.'

In the shadow of a palm tree Talula allowed the Axe to cast a directional charm. Talula closed her eyes, took three deep breaths and whispered the charm taught to her by Rosa.

'*Sicut venti currunt. Sicut venti currunt. Sicut venti currunt.*'

Talula opened her eyes and waited. It was a matter of moments before her feet started to tingle and her legs grew twitchy on the inside. She felt a massive surge of energy rush through her body and her sight sharpened so that, even in the dark, she could see couriers in the distance as they raced to their various locations.

'Wow,' she muttered.

Talula glanced back at the gates. She heard the rumble of carriage wheels approach and saw two guards hold up their hands to stop the vehicle so that it could be searched. She turned to face the desert and focussed her eyes miles ahead into the darkness.

'Right, let's do this,' she said.

'*Aaaaaaaaaaaaarrrrrrrgggggggghhhhh!*' said the Axe, as Talula sped off.

* * *

James Wand had experienced some difficulty in finding a private space to contact Captain Meejum. Rataquian soldiers swarmed the corridors and senior officers had commandeered every available room to formulate emergency strategies. Eventually, however, James happened upon a small broom cupboard. It wasn't an ideal location. James had shunted the cleaning paraphernalia into one corner and had overturned a mop bucket. The hulking Red Wing fairy then squeezed himself into the cupboard, sat on the improvised stool, closed the door, and had telepathically conveyed his message to Captain Meejum, in the dark.

Wand relayed Adler's request to ensure that the Cashenian royal family be taken to safety. During the transmission, however, Wand also discovered that Dr Philomena Foxglove had been arrested. Both Adler and Wand were surprised to discover that the leader of Project Green Pastures was responsible for leaking information.

'How did they find out?' asked Adler.

'One of the canine agents suggested that Dr Foxglove be brought in for questioning. She was spellbound and gave herself up during the interview,' replied Wand.

'Did she know Dr Vincenzo was working for the Rataquians?' asked Adler.

'Good guess, apparently. Dr Vincenzo and Foxglove had worked together in the past and, according to Foxglove, Vincenzo was the the most likely scientist to be working on the Rataquian project,' said Wand.

'But why would Foxglove betray her own country?' asked Adler.

'Blasting paid more than we did,' said Wand.

'All this for a few more florins?!'

'I think it was more than a few florins, sir,' said Wand.

'Greedy little…' Adler looked at Wand and stopped himself from uttering the expletive he had in mind.

'Yes, sir,' said Wand.

Adler shook his head and looked at the maps on the conference table.

'Let's run through this again,' said Adler.

The Red Wings congregated around the conference

table to discuss some of the finer points of the mission. Midway through the briefing, several young, Rataquian soldiers burst through the doors, brandishing their curvy wands.

'You Cashenens want fight! We give fight!' said a young fairy, his eyes filled with fury.

The Red Wings reached for their wands but Adler held up both hands and told his team to leave their weapons alone. Adler glanced at the young fairy's shoulder and then looked him in the eye.

'Corporal, you have every right to be angry ...'

'You! You all did this! Cashen soldiers fire from air! This is war! You our prisoners now!'

'CORPORALE!' boomed a voice from behind the young male Rataquians.

The hot-headed fairies immediately stood to attention as a fierce-looking uniformed fairy walked by them and stood almost nose-to-nose with the soldier who had led his comrades.

'Departirer!' he bellowed.

The fairies did an about turn and marched out of the room. The uniformed fairy turned to face the team. The Red Wings stood to attention and Wing Commander Adler saluted the senior military fairy before him.

'General Felicé, sir,' said Adler.

'At ease,' said the General, acknowledging the salute with a nod. 'Transport is ready.'

'Is it true, sir?' asked Adler. 'Were Cashenian soldiers seen firing on the palace from the air?'

General Felicé walked to the window and put his hands behind his back. His wings twitched as he looked out of the window. The palace fire had been extinguished but he knew all was not quiet in the city. He inhaled and turned to face Adler and the Red Wings.

'Two fairies wearing Cashenian air force uniforms were seen flying over the palazzo, yes,' said the General. 'And news of this is leaving the city by news-couriers, imps and any other means by which information can be taken across our country.'

Adler knotted his brow.

'It's Blasting,' he said.

'But no one will know this, Wing Commander. For now it looks as if your country wants to start war with Rataq.'

'But...' started Adler.

'I do not think this but what I think will not matter if Blasting is not stopped.' The conference door opened and the General turned to face the Golden Sabre who had entered. 'My team is ready for you,' said the General. 'I must stay here. The city has erupted and we must try to maintain order. But the Cashenian community it is not safe here anymore. You must hurry and find this Blasting before he starts war.'

Adler saluted, as did the rest of the team, who were then escorted from the room by the Golden Sabre. The General looked out of the conference room windows into the darkness.

'May all the gods help them in their task,' General Felicé whispered.

BLASTING'S OASIS
The gathering of the descendants.

'I've changed my mind! I can do that you know! I have rights! You'll be hearing from the guild about this!' came a small, tinny voice from a miniature cage built into Terminus's outer casing.

Theodore Blasting flicked his wand and the spell-imprisoned imp fell silent.

'When will we know if the transfusion has been a success?' Blasting asked.

Dr Stobel glanced at the half dozen thaumurtologists and engineers who were loitering near the weapon, murmuring among themselves.

'As far as we can tell, it's worked,' replied Dr Stobel, as she bent down to peer at the silent but furious imp jumping up and down in its cage. 'This is the first time the timer-imp has complained about anything, which would suggest that the magic I extracted from the General has been successfully imbued into the weapon. Imps are highly sensitive to the presence of magic.'

'Stupendous,' said Blasting. 'You will be handsomely rewarded,' said Blasting. 'And now we must prepare to take Terminus to the tunnel at Tamor for the final phase of my little plan,' he said, rubbing his hands together gleefully. 'Oh I do like it when a war is in the offing. And how do we detonate Terminus?' Blasting smiled and looked at Dr Stobel.

'Um, it's that button,' said Dr Stobel, avoiding eye contact with her employer and pointing to a silver button below the timer-imp, 'We should have a twenty minute countdown.'

'Should?' said Blasting, glaring at Dr Stobel.

'Without testing it first...' Dr Stobel noticed the menace on Blasting's face. 'I mean, I have no doubt it will work. The General's magic is very strong...' she trailed off, looked away from the General and, with the end of her sleeve, leaned over to polish a non-existent smudge on the metal casing.

'I have too much invested in this to rely on *should*, Dr Stobel,' said Blasting.

Dr Stobel stood upright and gave a weak smile. The engineers pretended not to listen.

'The engineers have assured me that the magic will detonate once the button has been pressed,' she said, glancing at the team.

'I do hope so, Dr Stobel, because everyone's final pay packet rests upon this weapon doing what it is supposed to do,' said Blasting, 'In fact, in case there is anyone who is unclear on this point, I assure you that heads will roll if the weapon does not work.' Blasting paused, 'And I'm afraid I do not mean in the metaphorical sense.' Everyone in the lab-tent stopped talking and looked over at Blasting, who signalled his sincerity with a terrifying smile. 'Right, pep-talk over with, I shall ask the transport crew to prepare for our departure,' he said, and left the tent.

* * *

'Sloooooooooooooooow dowwwwwwwnnnnnnnnnnn!' shrilled the Axe, *'nearrrrrrrrrrleeeeeeee thhththeeeerrrrrrreee!'*

* * *

'We have to get us some of these, Wing Commander, sir,' said Flying Officer Pitou.

'You not have enclosed, land-cruising, magic carpets in Cashen forces?' enquired the Golden Sabre sitting next to Pitou.

'More like moth-eaten old rugs, and we definitely don't have anything of this size or design. Who knew you could get twenty fairies on one carpet?' replied the impressed Pitou.

Some of the Golden Sabres chuckled.

'How do you power this thing? We've got to be doing close to sixty knots…' Pitou's banter was interrupted by a loud, *Whooooosssshhhhh!*

'What was that?!' asked Adler, as a pile of dust shot past them.

'Sand devils,' said Adler's counterpart, Wing Commander Abrille. 'The wind, it picks up sand which flies along ground. It will stop soon.'

Adler stared into the darkness. The thing that had rushed past may or may not have been a sand devil but, Adler thought, there was still too much magic in the air for his liking. He recalled the Rouchefort fairy triplets at Mount Dou and winced. Then the Wing Commander brought to mind his fishing cabin on the edge of Lake Maya Mora. He briefly considered the possibility of an early retirement, if he made it home alive.

'How much further, Abrille?' asked Adler.

'Maybe fifteen minutes,' replied Abrille.

'Squadron Leader,' said Adler.

'Sir?' replied Dash.

'Run through the op again.'

'Yes, sir,' said Dash, and pulled out a Finnician torch and a folded map from his inside pocket.

* * *

Norman, Professor Bauxite and the General were still in the tent. Every time the guards checked on the prisoners, Norman and the Professor scrunched up their legs and flung their hands behind their backs in an attempt to disguise the fact that they were no longer bound. The two dwarves, however, were worried about the military fairy who lay very still in the darkness.

'General? Are you still with us?' whispered Professor Bauxite.

The General's breathing had become slow and laboured and there was a distinct rattle that hadn't been there earlier in the evening. He moaned quietly.

'The General needs some water,' said Norman.

'Pssst,' came a voice from the back of the tent.

'Was that you?' Norman asked the Professor.

'No,' whispered the Professor.

'PSSST!' came the voice again.

'Are you sure?' Norman enquired, as he stood up.

'Of course I'm sure,' said the Professor.

'Oh in the name of all the gods. Norman, it's me!' came Talula's voice from the back of the tent.

'Talula?!' Norman stood up and hurried towards the direction of the pixie's voice. 'What are you doing here?'

'Just help me get underneath will you?' she replied.

* * *

'Dr Stobel,' said Blasting, as he entered the lab-tent. 'We are almost ready to leave...'

WRRRRRRRRRRRRRRRRR. KER-CHUNK. KER-CHUNK. KER-CHUNK. CLUNK... Click.

Everyone stared at Terminus.

Tick. Tick. Tick. Tick.

'What just happened?' asked Blasting.

Tick. Tick. Tick. Tick.

'Um, perhaps you should un-silence the imp,' suggested Dr Stobel, nervously.

Blasting flicked his wand at the imp, who was now standing very still.

'Now you've done it,' the imp said. 'You've got twenty minutes until this thing blows us all to kingdom come.'

The scientists and engineers looked at each other and then at Blasting.

'Who pressed the detonation button?!' bellowed Blasting.

Tick. Tick. Tick. Tick.

'We haven't touched it!' said a petrified-looking fairy.

'Nineteen minutes and fifty-five seconds,' said the timer-imp, in a resigned tone. 'I should have applied for a job with those new iBoxes. Nineteen minutes and fifty-three seconds,' it said, and sat down on the floor of the cage. 'I just wanted to retire to a nice little box in a tree somewhere warm. Nineteen minutes and fifty-two seconds.'

'Don't just stand there, turn it off!' screamed Blasting.

'I hear Toorquet is nice in the summer,' said the timer-imp, to himself.

* * *

'You'll never crawl under that,' said Norman, to Talula.

'What is to happen in here?' said one of the guards, as he opened the tent flap and peered in.

Light from the flame torches outside lit the interior of the tent and Norman fell, knees first, to the ground, thrusting his hands behind his back.

'Can we please have some water?' Norman asked.

The guard glared at the three prisoners and then closed the flap without replying to Norman's question. He mumbled something to the other guard and Norman heard the quiet scrunching of footsteps on sand as the guard left his post.

'The Rao fairy is dying,' whispered the Axe, from inside the bag. 'Get me inside.'

'Norman, take the Axe,' whispered Talula, as she squished the bag under the tent.

Norman hauled the bag inside while the Professor stood up and joined Norman at the back of the tent.

'Talula,' said the Professor. 'How on Eris..?'

'I'll explain later. How do I get in?' replied Talula.

'At the end of a rope will be a peg,' said the Professor. 'Can you see a peg?'

'In front of me,' said Talula.

'Try to remove it, or at least loosen it,' said the Professor.

Talula huffed and puffed as she struggled to loosen the peg from the sand. After some considerable effort, and the occasional whispered curse, the taut fabric of the tent loosened.

'Well done,' said the Professor, as he and Norman held open a small gap at for Talula.

Talula squeezed in and stood up.

'Let me out of this wretched thing,' whispered the Axe.

Norman opened the bag and the Axe hopped out.

'What's wrong with the General?' asked Talula.

'One of Blasting's scientists has extracted his spellage,' said Norman, quietly.

'But I thought a fairy's life-force…' Talula trailed off.

'It doesn't look good,' whispered Norman.

'Oh,' said the Axe. 'Things have advanced quite considerably during my absence. Not sure Halvar could have foreseen this.'

'What on Eris…' started the Professor.

'Ah, the chronicler's descendant,' said the Axe, bowing, in a tilt-ey sort of way, to Professor Bauxite.

'The chronicler's descendant?' said the Professor.

'Indeed!' said the Axe.

'I am the descendant of … what chronicler?' said the Professor, somewhat perplexed. 'Not Faunal Bazzite? I was just reading something about him.'

'Finally! So you'll have read my instructions as well,' sad the Axe.

'What instructions..?' asked the Professor.

'Oh, for … hasn't anyone read…?'

'What is…?' said the guard, as he stormed into the tent.

ZAP!

The guard collapsed.

'How did you do that?!' Talula asked the Axe.

'Magic,' said the Axe.

'Funny,' said Talula.

'The other one will be back in a minute,' said Norman.

'Then we'd better hurry,' said the Axe. 'The General doesn't have long…'

'Ivor?' came the other guard's voice from outside.

The second guard opened the flap and walked inside carrying a cup of water.

'What …?'

ZAP!

Norman, the Professor and Talula momentarily stared at the two huge fairy guards on the floor near the tent's entrance.

'Right,' said Talula. 'Let's help the General and see if we can't sort this nutter Blasting out, shall we?'

* * *

'What do you mean you can't turn it off?!' shouted Blasting.

'Seventeen minutes,' said the imp, sulkily.

'We've tried everything,' replied a distraught fairy thaumurtologist, 'but it doesn't work the same way as an ordinary explosive device. Something's triggered the magic.'

'Then we'll just have to get this thing to the tunnel now! Kinins, prepare the transport team,' Blasting said.

'I don't think moving a live weapon is such a good…' started Kinins.

'I don't pay you to think!' bellowed Blasting, as he stormed out of the tent. 'We have to get to the tunnel. Now!'

'Seventeen minutes and forty seconds,' grumbled the imp.

* * *

'I passed some kind of flying, over-sized, box-on-a-carpet on my way,' said Talula as she rummaged in her bag for the hip flask Rosa had given her. 'I saw a small Rataquian royal crest stuck on the back of the box, so I'm guessing it was the military. They're a way off yet. Here, give this to the General,' she said, handing the flask to Norman.

'Wait,' said the Axe. 'With all of you here, my magic is fully loaded. I know what to do. A little room, if you don't mind.'

Talula, Norman and the Professor moved away from the Axe. The Axe's head began to glow a bright, golden yellow.

'It's being doing that a lot lately,' said Talula, glaring at the Axe.

For the first time since having woken from their sleep-charms, Norman and the Professor were able to see the

General.

'Oh my word,' said the Professor.

General Macjooste looked withered and small as he lay curled up on the floor of the tent. His eyes were closed and his face was ashen. He had a white streak of hair down one side of his head. The fairy's beautiful, blue wings were now flaccid and a dull, greyish colour. His breathing was barely audible except for a gentle rattle whenever he inhaled. The General was dying.

The glowing Axe levitated a foot or so above the ground and a gentle buzz emanated from the ancient weapon.

'I hope it's not too late,' Norman mumbled.

'I think I'll take a quick look outside,' Talula said, as she turned to leave. 'See if I can find the son-of-a-troll responsible for this,' she said, under her breath.

* * *

The joint task force arrived at Blasting's oasis ahead of schedule. They had hidden the magic box-on-a-carpet behind a sand dune and the team was now hovering just above the canopy of the palm trees, unseen by Blasting's guards.

'What's going on in that little tent?' whispered Pitou, staring down at a small, glowing tent tucked behind a dense clump of palm trees.

'I do not know,' said Abrille, 'but over there is bigger light. We go.'

* * *

'Fifteen minutes,' said the imp.

Inside the lab-tent, preparations were underway to move Terminus. Despite Kinins's suggestion that his employer should get as far away as possible from both the oasis and the ticking weapon of mass destruction, Blasting stood at the back of the lab-tent, with a maniacal look in his eye, overseeing the proceedings.

'Final checks. Crew standby,' said a very stressed,

green-winged fairy.

'You see, Kinins, anything is possible,' said Blasting.

Kinins looked at the dozen, anxious-looking, fairies that surrounded Terminus, then at his employer. Blasting's aide and bodyguard closed his eyes and considered the possibility that he might never again return to his much-loved log cabin, hidden deep in a forest located somewhere on the Toorquean-Sterminian border.

* * *

The Axe continued to glow as it lowered itself to the ground.

'Oh General,' sighed Professor Bauxite, with relief, 'you're starting to get some colour back in your cheeks. In fact you look a lot more like your old self.'

'How did you do that?' whispered the General, to the Axe. 'No fairy can be rejuvenated after loss of life-force.'

'Well…' started the Axe, as its glow began to wane.

'Norman,' interrupted the Professor, 'bring in one of those torches from outside so we can see in here. You should take a few moments, General. Where's that hip flask?'

Norman handed the Professor the flask and went to retrieve a torch.

'It's impossible to rejuvenate life-force,' said the General, still lying on the ground.

'Yes, strictly speaking once a fairy has been drained of all magic, his life-force can not be replenished, this is true but, such was the power of the chieftain that he imbued me not only with every last ounce of his magic but also his own life-force.'

'And this gave you the ability to bring me back from imminent death?' asked the General, still astounded at what had happened.

'Halvar found a way to override the natural laws of life and death. What he did may have been wrong but you don't know what he was up against. The Wing Collector needed to be stopped and the future descendants of Eris had to be protected at all costs,' said the Axe, with an uncharacteristic air of humility.

'Amazing,' said Norman.

'It really is, isn't it? My magic is borne of a highly complex series of charms,' said the Axe.

'What kind of charms?' asked the General.

'The first combination was designed to cause mass destruction, to stop the war started by the Wing Collector. Halvar then imbued me with an even more complex sequence of charms, designed to counter any future threat. Halvar's piéce de resistance was ingenious because the ancestral-spell ensured my magic would only work when the relatives of the Torrimaya Quartet are present. The entire process took Halvar hours and killed him in the end. But here I am! There are bajillions of charms coursing through my sap,' said the Axe, 'and after thousands of years my magic is highly concentrated. So, as far as magical weapons go, I'm it. It doesn't get any better than me,' the Axe concluded, all traces of his former modesty having vanished.

'It seems my theory was correct, General. Halvar does indeed seem to have employed Ironstyne and Dar Wyn's theory,' said the Professor.

'Aye, $EE=mc^2$,' said the General, less than enthused by the prospect that powerful magic was now in the hands of a lunatic.

In the momentary silence that followed, the tent flap flew open and Talula rushed in.

'Something's going on in one of the big tents,' Talula said. 'There's a metal ball with at least a dozen fairies around it ...'

'It's the weapon!' said the General, as he jumped up. 'We have to stop them. Blasting wants to blow up the tunnel... Och.' The General stumbled but managed to stay upright. 'Professor. The flask if you wouldn't mind.'

The Professor handed the General the flask.

'I knew it!' said the Axe. 'I could feel the ancient magic in my sap. Let me at him!' The Axe hopped towards the tent's entrance.

'Wait!' commanded the General.

'But this is my raison d'être,' said the Axe.

'We need a plan,' said the General.

'I AM the plan!' said the Axe.

'Or,' said Talula, 'we could leave. Now.'

'Leave?!' the Axe and the General said, simultaneously.

'I heard a timer-imp counting down,' said Talula.

'Oh good gods,' whispered the General.

'That's what I thought,' said Talula. 'I'm not sure how quickly you lot can run but the timer-imp said there were twelve minutes left before detonation,' said Talula.

'But how? And why would he detonate now?' said the General, not expecting an answer.

'Ah,' said the Axe.

'Ah?' said the General, 'What do you mean, 'Ah'?'

'If, as you say, the weapon has been imbued with your spellage, General, then it's most probable that, upon the arrival of Talula and myself, the mere presence of the Torrimaya Quartet could have triggered the weapon, even without the correct incantation.'

'Incantation?' asked the General.

'The ancient detonation incantation,' said the Axe.

'Why is nothing ever easy?' said the General, to no one in particular. 'Was any of my own magic restored along with my life-force?'

'Some of your magic will most definitely have been restored but the ancient spellage from Halvar, is in the weapon I'm afraid,' said the Axe.

'So how do we stop this?' asked the Professor.

'We must go to the weapon and recite the de-fusion incantation,' said the Axe.

The General looked at the flask in his hand.

'I see,' he unscrewed the lid, 'A de-fusion incantation. Something simple I hope?' he said, still looking at the flask.

'Oh yes. It's a very simple incantation. All I have to do is draw two circles and a square, and then each of you stand in a corner of the square, touching fingertip to fingertip, while I stand in the middle, with the weapon, and you four recite the incantation.'

'So not that simple then,' said Talula.

'And what's the incantation?' asked Norman.

'Am I supposed to remember everything?! There were extremely comprehensive instructions...'

'Wait,' said Norman, 'I remember reading something about a circle, square and four in the library.'

'Finally!' said the Axe.

'Can you remember it exactly?' asked the Professor.

Norman looked down at the floor for a moment.

'Got it,' he said, with a nod of confidence.

The General took a swig from the flask.

'Wah!' he grimaced, 'What's in this?'

'Now, take me to the weapon. We don't have much time!' said the Axe.

* * *

A dozen fairies stood in a circular formation around Terminus. Blasting stood at the back of the lab-tent and Kinins waited anxiously behind his boss.

'Ten minutes until this thing blows,' mumbled the timer-imp.

'We need to move now!' shouted Kinins.

'Wands to the ready,' said the, heavily perspiring, green-winged fairy.

The transport fairies lifted their wands and pointed them at the weapon.

'Ready for instant transport in ten, nine, eight...'

ZAP! ZAP! ZAP!

From outside the lab-tent the special ops team opened fire.

WHOOOOOOSH! The silk of the tent caught alight. Blasting's transport crew, engineers and scientists abandoned their stations and ran outside.

'Come back here!' screamed Blasting.

The guards outside the lab-tent returned fire but most were paralysed by a volley of entrapment spells fired by the special ops team. As the lab-tent burned, so Blasting's entire team fled the scene only to be spelled down by the military fairies. The escapees fell where they were zapped. Dr Stobel made a dash for the foliage of the oasis but was caught by a flame-spell. She went up in a puff of smoke, to the horror of a dwarf engineer who had followed the fairy scientist.

Kinins put out the fire with an extinguishing-charm but there was very little left of the tent. Blasting's aide glared at the weapon which was now exposed to the elements. There was nothing he could do.

'Mr Blasting, sir,' said Kinins. 'We have to get you away from here.'

'We were so close,' whimpered Blasting. 'That tunnel has ruined my business, my profits, my LIFE!' he bawled. 'In a matter of minutes that irksome little corridor would have been reduced to rubble!'

'Sir, we must leave,' replied Kinins, ducking from a stray spell while trying to usher his, clearly insane, employer away from Terminus.

'Eight minutes and forty-five seconds, to be precise,' sad the timer-imp. 'Let me out!'

* * *

ZAP! PEW! PEW! ZAP! ZAP!

'That'll be special ops,' said the General, rushing out of the tent.

Talula grabbed her bag. She and the Professor tiptoed over the unconscious guards and joined the General outside.

'Quick!' said the Axe. 'Take me to the weapon.'

Norman picked up the Axe by the handle. He too manoeuvred his way past the guards' bodies and left the tent.

The foursome saw spell flashes light up the night and screams of spell-trapped fairies rang out.

'I have something that we might be able to use,' said Talula, as she rummaged in the front pocket of her bag and pulled out the tube-in-a-box.

'What is it?' asked Norman.

'Can't remember. Something to do with chains, I think,' said Talula, taking the glass tube out of its box. 'Here,' she said, handing it to Norman.

The General walked forward into a small clearing and began to flap his wings.

'General, perhaps we should all go to the weapon,' said Norman.

'Wait here,' the General commanded. 'Let me find out what's happening,' he said, as he took off and flew through the trees towards the firefight.

'Seriously. We need to get close to the weapon!' the Axe implored.

Talula and Norman looked at each other.

'The General did say we should wait,' offered the Professor, 'although I suspect this might be open to interpretation by some,' he mumbled into his beard.

'I've had enough of this,' said the Axe. 'We're running out of time.'

The Torrimaya Axe murmured something inaudible. Its head began to glow golden yellow in Norman's arms and, without warning, Norman was lifted up several feet above the ground.

'Umm....What are you doing?' said Norman, clutching both the Axe and the glass tube that had been handed to him by Talula.

Norman and the Axe sped up, making their way through the trees towards the skirmish. Talula followed on the ground.

'Norman!' shouted the Professor, as he trotted after Talula. 'We're coming!'

* * *

'This way, sir,' said Kinins, as he hurried his employer away from the weapon.

'Damn King Egbert and his damned special forces!' said Blasting, as he marched, blindly, through the palm trees.

'Hurry, sir.'

'I won't be stopped by that piffling pacifist!' shouted Blasting, as he and his aide made their way to the edge of the oasis. 'War is good for the economy. Everyone knows that! I'll make Cashen great again you see if I don't, even if I have to blow up every royal residence from here to the Glacial Regions! Everyone will want my weapons!'

Flight Lieutenant Wand flew out from behind a palm tree and hurled a flame-spell in Blasting's direction.

'Kin…!'

Blasting, like Dr Stobel, was reduced to a pile of ashes. Kinins dashed behind a tree trunk and, before Adler could point his wand again, Blasting's aide and bodyguard had vanished.

* * *

'Let me down!' said Norman, his eyes shut tight. 'I've never had any desire to fly!'

'Don't look down!' Talula shouted from below.

Norman opened his eyes and looked down.

'Oh my gods!' he said, looking at the torchlit clearing below. The Axe's head stopped glowing 'Is that the weap…aaaaaaarrgh!' Both Norman and the Axe began to fall to the ground.

'Move your legs! Move your legs as if you're running!' shouted Talula, to Norman.

Norman's legs flailed about in mid-air as he and the Axe drew closer to the ground. A spell whizzed past his ear. Norman came tumbling down amid the charred remains of the lab-tent, almost in front of the weapon. His legs did a fair approximation of running as he and the Axe reached terra firma. Norman, however, hadn't accounted for a tent peg, which he promptly tripped over as soon as he hit the ground. Norman dropped the Axe, which bounced and landed a few feet in front of him.

'Norman!' said Talula, as she watched him stumble and lurch straight towards Terminus.

'Oh no!' Norman managed to say, as he tripped over his feet and belly-flopped to the ground. 'Oomph!'

The glass tube, with the unknown substance in it, flew out of his hand and smashed to pieces on the side of the weapon's metal casing.

Hisssssssssssssss.......

A patch of the metal casing dissolved before their eyes and a minuscule drop landed on the timer-imp's cage. The door flew open and the imp jumped out.

'I'm free! I'm free!' hollered the imp. 'You've got five minutes and twenty-eight seconds,' he added, before vanishing.

'It's Fender onion soup!' Norman gasped, as he picked himself up off the ground, and stared, horrified, at the dissolved patch of metal casing.

Spells set fire to the surrounding palm trees as the special ops team and Blasting's guards battled it out in the air and on the ground.

Talula zipped over to Norman. The pair crouched down and covered their heads with their hands.

Tick. Tick. Tick. Tick.

'What now?!' shouted Talula, above the sound of spell-fire.

'I'm here!' puffed the Professor.

'Stay down!' came the General's voice to the side of Blasting's former luxury accommodation.

The Axe, stood on its tip and hopped over to Terminus.

'I just have to...' said the Axe, as it began drawing a square around Terminus with its handle.

Two of Blasting's guards began firing at Norman and Talula.

The General, who was wandless, mumbled something under his breath and one of the tables flew at the guards.

'Norman! Follow me!' shouted Talula, as she made a dash towards the weapon.

'Easy for you to say,' muttered Norman, as he crawled, on his stomach, until he reached the pixie. 'I'm really not cut out for this,' he said.

'Here,' said Talula, handing Norman one of two dismembered chair legs. 'Where do we draw?!' Talula shouted at the Axe.

'One circle inside the square and one out,' said the Axe.

While the General continued to use his recently rejuvenated magic to hurl various items of furniture from the lab-tent at Blasting's guards, Talula, Norman and the Torrimaya Axe drew two circles and a square around Terminus.

'General,' shouted the Axe. 'Come quickly and put me on top of the weapon.'

Tick. Tick. Tick. Tick.

The General bombarded a guard with cushions and then ran towards the weapon. He picked up the Axe by its handle and placed it, tip first, on top of Terminus.

'Professor, quick!' shouted Talula.

Tick. Tick. Tick. Tick.

The Professor, who had been hiding behind a large rock to the side of the lab-tent, poked his head up and looked around. A freeze-spell caught the rock and turned it to ice.

'I'll cover you,' said the General, who closed his eyes and, once again said something under his breath.

The rock came loose from the sand and hovered above the ground. As the lump of frozen stone then began to move towards the weapon, Blasting's guards fired but the Professor remained protected as he crouched down and walked, behind the moving rock, towards the weapon.

Another round of spells was aimed at the four descendants and the Axe on top of the weapon.

'General! We'll cover you!' said Wing Commander Adler, from above.

PEW! PEW! ZAPITY- ZAP-ZAP-ZAP!

The special ops team fired of a series of entrapment-spells at Blasting's guards, who fell where they stood. 'Stand in between the two circles and at each corner form a square, fingertip to fingertip,' said the Axe. 'Hurry!'

Tick. Tick. Tick. Tick.

A stray flame-spell flew from somewhere in the oasis and hit the tip of Norman's boot.

'Ow!'

'Norman!' shouted Talula.

'I'm fine,' he replied, rubbing the singed boot on the back of his leg.

The four ancestors came together and each stood in a corner of the square, fingertip to fingertip - as best as their varying heights would allow. The Axe's head began to glow white.

'Hurry!' shouted Talula, 'What's the incantation?'

With spell-fire and screams hurtling around them Talula, General Macjooste and Professor Bauxite looked at Norman and waited. Quietly at first, Norman began to recite the incantation.

The bringer of death has returned once more,
But so has the circle, the square, and the four.
No matter the evil, no matter how long,
For now and forever the force will be strong.

'I can't hear you!' shouted Talula.

'Look into my glow,' said the Axe.

Everyone looked into the Axe's glow while Norman continued to say the incantation. Moments later the others joined in and began to recite the ancient words.

The bringer of death has returned once more,
But so has the circle, the square, and the four.
No matter the evil, no matter how long,
For now and forever the force will be strong.

The ancestors of the Torrimaya Quartet, now

hypnotised by the Axe's glow, repeated the incantation, faster and louder. Spells flashed and, as quickly as the trees around them caught alight, so the special ops team extinguished the flames.

The bringer of death has returned once more,
But so has the circle, the square, and the four.
No matter the evil, no matter how long,
For now and forever the force will be strong.

The foursome repeated the incantation, more loudly and more quickly...

The bringer of death has returned once more,
But so has the circle, the square, and the four.
No matter the evil, no matter how long,
For now and forever the force will be strong.

Tick. Tick. Tick. Tick.

The Axe's white glow flashed three times and the quartet dropped their arms, thus breaking the link.

'Move away,' said the Axe, and promptly levitated fifty feet above Terminus. It then moved to one side and its head changed colour from white, to yellow, to orange and finally a deep, blood-red.

Talula, Norman, General Macjooste and Professor Bauxite stepped away from Terminus and looked up at the Axe.

With the force of a thousand trolls the Torrimaya Axe then came hurtling back down and smashed the ground.

BOOOOOOOM!

And then ...

THWAUMMMMMMMMMMMMMMMMMMMMMMMMM!

The fighting fairies fell on the spot as wave upon wave of magic undulated outwards from the Axe. The colour of the night sky changed from black to a deep, indigo blue and then to a shimmering, pale purple. A tsunami of magic rushed across the desert, across the oceans, through jungles, into forests, along rivers and up mountains. From the smallest hamlet to the biggest city, the magic from the Axe spread all over Eris.

The General shuddered. Talula, the Professor, and Norman looked skywards mouths open. The General stretched his wings and then he too looked up. The quartet waited...

Tick. Tick. Tick. Tick.

... and waited ...

Tick. Tick. Tick. Tick.

... and waited

Tick. Tick. Tick. Tick.

... until....

WAAUUUUUUUMMMMMMMMMMMMMMMMMMMMM!

Like the tide sucking in a wave, the magic returned to the Torrimaya Axe, which promptly stopped glowing and fell over.

CLUNK. WHRRRRRRRRR. CRASH! Flump... Tinkle... Ping...

Terminus, Blasting's only hope of generating more profits for his business, collapsed into a thousand pieces.

'Umm... a little help here,' said the Axe, lying on the ground.

'Why aren't we...are they dead?' asked Talula, looking at the fallen fairies as she stood up.

'I'm programmed to protect the descendants from the thaumurtological force. Everyone else will sleep until the world's magic readjusts.'

'Everyone?' said the General.

'It's a planet-wide thing,' said the Axe, nonchalantly. 'But don't worry. Everyone will be tickety-boo, very soon.'

Norman bent down and picked up the Axe by its handle.

'What did you do?' he asked.

'I've restored peace and magical equilibrium to the planet and its folk,' said the Axe. 'The descendant of the

Wing Collector not only triggered my alarm system by creating a weapon of mass destruction, he also defied the laws of magic by extracting your ancient spellage, General. He had no idea what he was dealing with and if he had managed to detonate the device... Let's just say there's every chance few would have survived.'

The General looked at the unconscious fairies on the ground, including the special ops team, and then at the defunct weapon in front of him.

'I think I should have words with the King about our own project,' the General said.

'Probably best,' said the Axe. 'Besides,' it said, cheerily, 'you have me! What better deterrent is there? If I'm needed again, of course.'

'Does that mean everything's back to normal?' asked Talula.

'Normal? Define normal. If you mean folk will carry on living in their little bubbles, blissfully unaware of the plots and machinations of some of the planet's more narcissistic minds, then yes, I suppose everything will go back to normal,' said the Axe.

'Which reminds me,' said the General, looking around the clearing, 'I'd better find Blasting,' said the General.

'I think you'll find he is no longer with us, General,' said the Axe.

'How can you be sure?' asked the General.

'I can no longer feel his magic,' said the Axe, 'although, you'll be pleased to hear that your ancient spellage has been restored,' said the Axe.

'I felt it,' said the General, as his wings twitched.

'The white streak in your hair, however, cannot be reversed I'm afraid,' said the Axe.

'A wee reminder of all this won't do me any harm,' the General said, with a small smile.

'And you have fulfilled your mission,' said the Professor, to the Axe. 'A very well done to you. And who'd have thought I was one of the descendants? With such a long history of chronicling you'd think *someone* in the family would have known,' the Professor mused.

'Well, it seems no one read the instructions and....' said the Axe

'Don't start,' said Talula.

PENULTIMATELY
Rewards and a Road Trip.

At the Trifolium Palace Honours' Ceremony fifteen members of the King's forces, and four officers from the Golden Sabres, were recognised for their gallantry with an array of military medals. Only four Vittoria Wands (the highest award, given for bravery in the face of the enemy) were awarded by King Egbert - one to General Macjooste, one to Master Norman Shale, one to Miss Talula Ewesage and the other to Professor Bauxite. The crowd cheered and gave a standing ovation to the four heroes as they accepted their medals - two gold wands in the shape of a cross.

The Torrimaya Axe, which had been sent to a restorer and now looked less like it had been buried under a pile of rusty tools in a shed and more like a masterpiece of ancient dwarf weapon-making, had been presented with an especially commissioned medal of appreciation for saving the planet - a gold medal in the shape of itself. The Axe whispered its thanks when the King wrapped the ribbon around the Axes's handle. It was then discreetly carried from the podium and escorted from the palace grounds to a special department for magical artefacts, deep in the bowels of military headquarters.

'But I want to go to the ball,' the Axe was heard to whimper, as General Macjooste followed the weapon and its escort to the gates.

After a week of celebrations, and several drunken arguments over which hero had been the bravest, the city was returning to some semblance of normality. Royal families, from all over Eris, had returned to their homelands, King Razarro and his retinue had returned to Rataq, and Lord Esodo and his family had returned to the embassy in Fortnum Park Square. General Macjooste had been ordered, by his wife as well as the King, to go on a family holiday. He was currently in a row boat, fishing on Loch Majekeye with his father.

In one wall of Vinster-on-Sterm's oldest cemetery, hidden behind a tangle of honeysuckle and ivy, was a wooden door. Norman looked around to make sure no one was watching, then lifted the latch, pushed the door inward with his shoulder and squeezed through the gap. He walked along a tree-lined avenue, past the rows of headstones, towards the path that led him to a small clearing near the River Sterm. Talula was sitting on the edge of the bank, her bare feet dangling in the water.

'Heard you coming a mile off,' said Talula, without turning around.

'These new boots need wearing in,' Norman said, sitting down to take off the recently purchased footwear.

'You can't blame the boots for stomping through the undergrowth like a legion of drunken trolls,' she retorted.

Norman took off his boots and socks, joined Talula on the edge of the bank, and dipped his feet in the cool water.

'Our carriage leaves in an hour.' he said, refusing to take the bait. 'So?'

'So, what?' Talula replied.

'Did you find your parents' grave?'

'The Professor's still looking into it for me,' replied Talula.

'I'm sure he'll find it and if he hasn't found it by the time we get back I'll give him a hand.'

'It would be nice if it's here. I like coming here,' said Talula, quietly.

The pair sat in silence for a moment. The sun glinted off the surface of the river and a gentle breeze brushed through the trees.

'So? Did you pass the AVC test?' Norman looked at Talula, who was looking at her feet as she swished them in the water. Talula tried to keep a straight face but Norman spotted the corner of her mouth twitch upwards. 'You passed,' he smiled.

'Top of the class,' Talula said, as she looked at Norman and beamed.

'I knew you would.' Norman smiled, delighted at Talula's success. 'So we can start our trip on a high note.'

'Yep,' said Talula.

'I'm really pleased for you,' said Norman.

'What about you? Any news on your application?' Talula asked.

'The University has agreed I can be Professor Bauxite's part-time assistant while I study for the Ancient Fairy and Dwarvish History degree,' said Norman.

'You got accepted!' said Talula, giving Norman a playful punch on the top of his arm.

'Ow,' Norman smiled, and rubbed his arm. 'Means I can have a look at those scrolls I found,' he said.

'Oh, yeah, the ones that would probably have been useful if we'd known about them earlier?!' Talula teased.

A fish jumped out of the water to catch a fly.

'I did try to tell you and anyway, you could say that everything happens for a reason, right? I mean, if Dr Tellurium hadn't...'

'I know, I know. If Dr Tellurium hadn't written that theory down then someone else would,' interrupted Talula.

'Well, I was going to say if he hadn't proposed his theory then we'd never have met,' said Norman. 'But you're right, someone else would have got around to proposing the theory eventually.'

'Anyway, it's all over, and we still have a planet, which is all that counts. Have you spent your reward money on finding somewhere better to live yet?'

'Still looking. You?'

'As luck would have it a perfect place has come up in Queensbridge. I spotted it when I was practising for my test. It's down a side alley. It's not big or fancy but it is clean and tidy, and there's no damp! I bought it yesterday and I'll move my stuff from Iffies when we get back.'

'So you're not moving up north then?'

Talula looked puzzled by the question.

'Why would I want to move up north?' she asked.

'To be with your family,' said Norman.

'I haven't even met them yet! We might all hate each other. Besides, it's one thing taking a trip to meet the long-lost relatives but a completely different thing moving in with them. No. I'm happy here. Vinster's my home.'

Norman's shoulders sagged, just a little, with relief.

'Will you use your family name now?' Norman asked.

Talula looked out over the water and considered this for a moment.

'I spoke to Sister Agnes this morning and asked her how I ended up at the orphanage. She said I was found wrapped in a green blanket with *Talula* embroidered in the corner. There was no last name. Apparently one of the novices was praying to St Ewesage, the patron saint of pixlings, and so they decided to make that my last name.' Talula paused.'You get used to a name don't you?'

'It does suit you,' said Norman.

'Besides, I've just paid to have some business cards printed,' Talula looked at Norman and smiled.

'And everyone in Vinster knows Talula Ewesage,' Norman said.

'This, Master Shale, is very true,' Talula said, proudly.

'Did you give one of your business cards to the General? He may well require your sleuthing services at some point in the future.'

'I'm pretty sure the General will be able to find me should he need me,' said Talula, 'and I did tell him I'd help if he's *absolutely* desperate.'

Norman looked down at the river and smiled.

'You mean a consultant, like the Professor,' he said.

Talula considered this for a moment.

'Talula Ewesage, Pixie Courier and Consultant. Has a nice ring to it,' she said.

'Oh, here, I got you something.' Norman retrieved a small box from his waistcoat pocket. Talula looked suspiciously at the box. 'Don't panic,' said Norman, in response to Talula's instant change of expression. 'It's only something small. I knew you'd pass the Know-How so I picked up something from Tiphanees.' Talula stared at the box, then at Norman. 'Go on, open it,' said Norman, holding it out to Talula.

Talula took the box. It was small, dark blue velvet, and had a flip-open lid. Tiphanees made the most expensive jewellery in Cashen and were known best for their engagement rings.

'If you don't open it, I will,' said Norman, reaching out to retrieve it.

Talula glared at Norman then opened the box to reveal a small crystal in the shape of a scroll with a gold band shaped like a ribbon wrapped around the middle.

'Oh! It's beautiful. No one's ever bought me a present like this before,' whispered Talula, as her eyes welled with tears of gratitude. 'Thanks.'

'You're welcome,' said Norman, looking, tactfully, out at the river. 'I've got a doorstop for my gran. Not quite as nice but I think she'll appreciate it.'

'A doorstop?' said Talula.

'Long story,' said Norman. After a moment he said, 'Shall we head off then? Oh, and the Professor told me we'll be going through a village called Neen on our way. There's supposed to be an ancient sword...'

'No!' said Talula, standing up and putting the present in her pouch. 'No ancient swords. No ancient anything!'

'But..' Norman started to put on his socks and boots.

'But nothing...'

Norman and Talula's conversation grew increasingly animated as they walked towards the city to retrieve their belongings, before heading off to visit their respective families.

EPILOGUE

The Battle of the Valley of the Green Pastures
Journal Extracts of Faunal Bazzite - chronicler from the Ijolite Clan
(Translated[1] by Norman Shale, BA)

~ ~ ~ ~ ~

The Summer After the Battle in the Valley.
On The Southern Route

I have been disinclined to chronicle the battle since we fled the Torrimaya range and I write only sporadically in my own diary. I have as yet been unable to transcribe the enchantments Halvar trusted me to record but hope to do so once we reach our destination.

The mood is sombre among my fellow travellers as we make our way to the Great Gathering in the south. Lady Orquidea remains in mourning for the chieftain, as do we all. Tales of devastation and death have been met with much sorrow as we stop at settlements and invite other tribes to join our group.

Her Ladyship is proving to be an honourable and compassionate leader of the Rao and is generous with her healing magic, particularly in those places where Hectorus, The Wing Collector, and his hordes, killed, maimed or captured much of the fairy population. Lady Orquidea never asks her tribe to spend their magic and yet they all do, willingly, in order to help those in need.

Wherever we go her Ladyship has asked that all Rataquian prisoners be released. This has caused much fear among other tribes and yet the Rataquians, still spellbound, acknowledge defeat with surprising humility. Many of the released have flown home. A few have asked to join us, and work twice as hard as everyone in the group, asking only for a little food and protection. They are met with much suspicion by the travellers but her Ladyship visits them each day to thank them for their

---

[1] Obsolete words have been replaced by modern vocabulary in this translation.

work - her guards protest at such an act but she is insistent. She is treated only with respect by the Rataquians. It is an interesting and humbling sight.

Lady Orquidea insists that she will not rest until she has travelled the length of the land so that she may bring together as many tribes as she can to the Great Gathering. She is ageing, however, and her fairies-in-waiting are concerned for her health. I know not if she will complete her quest.

~ ~ ~ ~ ~ ~ ~

On this day, as I sit by the side of the River Stermye, the sun shines on the water and the scene is one of tranquility, a far cry from the carnage of war. The surrounding flora and fauna have clearly been touched by magic. Although oftentimes the effect is beautiful, it is a constant reminder of the recent conflict. The butterflies are oversized and the birds sing in harmonies, which is indeed something to behold and yet this is not the way of nature. Magic has transformed the country's landscape and its folk. Some of the fairy-young were tortured and now suffer with disabilities such as malformation of the wings. The evidence of such deliberate cruelty is painful to observe.

In such a short time our world has changed, almost beyond recognition. My mind is haunted by that day, not so very long ago, when life was permanently altered for all of us, here in Cashenne. History, my mentor once said, must be recorded so that future generations may learn from the mistakes of their forebears. It is hard to write of such a thing as war. I hope our ancestors will indeed learn from this horror.[2]

~ ~ ~ ~ ~ ~ ~

---

[2] The extract ends here but the journal was found to contain loose parchments describing the events leading to the battle.

The Rataquian Invasion[3].

In the mountain community, dwarves talk of nothing but the invasion. It is said that the Rataquians consider Cashenne's fairies weak and inferior. My mentor has always said that a fairy cannot be judged by the colour of its wings.

The Wing Collector commands his legions to use every spell in the book in order to subjugate Cashenne's citizens. Hundreds have been captured, entire villages have been razed to the ground, and there is more than one account of Hectorus living up to his sobriquet by cutting off the wings of dead tribal chieftains after every battle. The barbarous leader holds the bloody wings aloft amid roars of victory from his forces.

~ ~ ~ ~ ~ ~

Chronicling instruction today involved lengthy tests on speed scribing. For hours our instructors read from ancient chronicles so that we may become better acquainted with the terminology of fairies at war. Several of my peers were unable to complete the tasks. Indeed, were my mentor not so punctilious in his teaching, I too may not have had the strength to complete the exercises.

~ ~ ~ ~ ~ ~ ~

The Battle of the Valley of the Green Pastures

It is a cloudy, grey morning, many moons after the Rataquians first landed. Chieftain Halvar's fastest scout returned this day with distressing news. Valley and Mountain folk alike were called to the tribal hall where we listened in horror to the exhausted fairy as he reported on the Wing Collector and his warriors. Not only are Hectorus' forces close, he said, but they have been committing untold atrocities against tribal friends and kin, many of whom Halvar saw at the last Great Gathering.

'Right,' Halvar said, once the scout had finished. 'We've nae choice. Summon our allies!'

---

3 Extract from loose parchments.

Messengers have now been dispatched. Fairy chieftains from the neighbouring countries of Toorquet and Stermeen, as well as the Eskeesno fairies from the Glacial Regions, have been called to arms to help vanquish the vicious Rataquian enemy.

Valley and mountain alike are swarming with activity in preparation for the battle with the Rataquians. Halvar has sworn it will be the last fight.

~ ~ ~ ~ ~ ~ ~ ~

Halvar has asked Forgemaster Sæl to produce an axe. No one knows why. My mentor has told me to wait in my quarters and so I wait. I have left open my door and the mountain's corridors team with folk. Halvar, ever the family fairy, has insisted that all the females and children of the community take shelter here. It is strange to see so many different folk seeking shelter in our mountain home.

~ ~ ~ ~ ~ ~ ~

A friend stopped by to inform me that tribal fairies from the other nations have arrived. Halvar has just marched past my quarters in the direction of Forgemaster Sæl's foundry. I grow impatient and wish to join my peers, many of whom are helping with preparations for the battle.[4]

~ ~ ~ ~ ~ ~ ~

The Summer After the Battle in the Valley.
The Southern Route

The sun is setting and we have made camp further along the river Stermye. I have re-read my journal and see that I have only partially recorded the events leading to the battle.

I was summoned to the foundry and told to bring with me blank parchments and several fine carbon sticks. I followed the forgemaster through the foundry door and was hit by a wall of heat. In the centre of the room was

---

[4] This is the last entry until after the battle.

Halvar, examining the axe that Forgemaster Sæl had made. The weapon was simple in its design, and yet beautifully crafted. The Rao insignia was on the blade.

I bowed before the fairy chieftain.

Halvar and Sæl looked me up and down. I had started to sweat in the heat but found the courage to look up at the imposing fairy before me. Halvar smiled and nodded at Forgemaster Sæl who returned the gesture and left to fetch the incanter.

I found a seat and waited in silence for Halvar to speak.

Halvar closed his eyes, took three deep breaths, and meditated on the task before him. The fairy chieftain cleared his mind and I watched as the magic force built up within his body. His wings fluttered and then he shuddered. Halvar held up the axe with both hands and cast the first enchantment.

As the minutes turned into hours, I, as promised, recorded every word spoken by the fairy chieftain. Halvar cast enchantment after enchantment[5] and the axe glowed white, yellow, orange and finally a deep red, as the chieftain imbued every last ounce of magic, as well as his own life-force, onto the weapon. The process, for both myself and Halvar, was all-consuming and the excessive use of magic aged Halvar far beyond his youthful, hundred and twenty years.

When Forgemaster Sæl returned he had with him the incanter, a pixie named Tuläher. With her dark skin, round eyes and black, plaited hair her beauty was heartbreaking. Tuläher of the Forest bowed and Halvar returned the gesture with a slow nod.

'We are Cashenne's last hope,' Halvar said. 'I'd rather cut off my own wings than use this...' Halvar lifted the axe from his side, '...but The Wing Collector must be stopped.' The chieftain directed his gaze towards Tuläher. 'When the time comes, you've to place this in the centre

---

5 See separate documents.

of the valley and recite the incantation I entrust to you,' said Halvar.

Tuläher nodded once.

Halvar scrutinised the three of us, as if committing our faces to memory. Finally, he looked back at me and he issued one final instruction. I was to deliver the enchantments I had recorded to Ladye Orquidea who would deliver them into safe hands. Then, the chieftain held up the axe and closed his eyes. He took a deep breath and his wings gave the barest of flutters. Halvar muttered something inaudible (the only enchantment I was unable to record) and when he was done he lowered the axe and took a deep breath. The chieftain opened his eyes. He bowed, handed Tuläher the axe, collapsed and died on the foundry floor.

~ ~ ~ ~ ~ ~ ~

During the final battle, Tuläher and thousands of others, were slaughtered. The Torrimaya Axe was infused with such powerful magic that when it was placed in the centre of the valley, amidst the thaumaturlogical chaos, the Axe was propelled skyward, the earth split open and great fires were unleashed from the rift. The battling fairy warriors fell screaming from the heavens, then everything went quiet.

And so it was as Halvar had promised. The Battle of the Valley of the Green Pastures was the final battle that put an end to what has recently been referred to as the Wand Wars - the war to end all wars.

Halvar's penultimate spell stated that if it is ever needed again, the Axe will return to save Eris. May that time never come.